The Man Who Looked for Death

Science Traveler Series
Book 13

The Man Who Looked for Death

Science Traveler Series
Book 13

J.L. Greger

Bug Press   Bernalillo, NM

The Man Who Looked for Death

Bug Press
An imprint of IngramSpark
Bernalillo, New Mexico 87004
http://www.jlgreger.com

ISBN (paperback): 9798989418404
ISBN (EPUB): 9798989418411
Library of Congress Catalogue Number: 2024909868

DEDICATION

For all those who don't fit in.

CHAPTER 1: A Long-Term Problem

He was thinner than the last time she'd seen him. His jet-black hair, which he still combed straight back in a ponytail, now had streaks of gray. He jumped into a red Mazda Miata as soon as it screeched to a stop in front of the two-story stucco house in an affluent neighborhood of Santa Fe.

She was disappointed. She'd waited in her car for two hours to get a glimpse of him. The house was owned by Alex Cortez, but the man looked like her husband, Alex Cortland—about six-foot tall, same head shape and narrow nose. His broad shoulders were a bit stooped now. She guessed it was to be expected. It had been fifteen years since she had seen him. She suspected he'd led a hard life, but he cleaned up well and was still a handsome devil in black jeans and T-shirt with a soft leather jacket slung over his shoulder.

The woman driving the car was what she'd expected—blonde and twenty-something. Poor thing was in for a surprise after she married Alex. She remembered when Alex had courted her twenty years before. Then, he had rented a nice house in Grants during their whirlwind courtship. Two days after their marriage by a justice of the peace, Alex had moved his belongings out of the house and into her one-bedroom apartment. Two months later, when her teaching contract with the Grant Public Schools ended, Alex had moved her to a small farm near Hanover, New Mexico.

Farm was a euphemism Alex had used to describe his ten acres. The house was a shack. It and several small, dilapidated sheds for livestock were surrounded by what once had been an orchard and gardens.

It was her own fault. She had believed Alex's promise: Once they were married, she wouldn't need to work. She'd only have to keep house and tend their gardens and orchard. She had found two years of teaching fifth grade in Grants to be unfulfilling and had gladly believed his description of his homestead near the Chino copper mine where he worked. His statements about the farm were somewhat true if you didn't expect working plumbing in the house.

She'd worked for a year to earn enough to get plumbing installed in the shack. It shouldn't have taken that long, but there was no employment in Hanover with only one-hundred-fifty people. The post office already had a postmistress. The public schools in nearby Silver City only occasionally needed a substitute teacher. Thus, she went to work in a feed store in Silver City. The best part of the job was she could get a discount on feed for Alex's two mules and for seed and fertilizer for the garden.

She couldn't say Alex was unkind. He was simply seldom around. When he finished his shift at the Chino copper mine, he roamed the area looking for gold. She went along when she wasn't working at the feed store or in the garden. Any money he earned was used to buy land or pay for mining claims on public lands. Each time he bought a parcel of land or filed a claim, Alex was sure this time he'd hit a real load. Then one day, she came home and found a note on the table.

> *My Best Pal,*
> *The cash in our saving account should pay the taxes on our land and the annual maintenance fees on the claims for several years. They're worth paying. There's copper, silver, and gold on those lands. Eventually, the extraction techniques will improve and make these properties valuable.*
>
> *In the meantime, I'll search for better claims for us in South America.*
> *Love,*
> *Alex*

She'd kept the note in her jewelry box for fifteen years now. She seldom looked in the box, except when she received an annual check from a bank in South America. There was never a note attached. The annual payment this year was replaced by a letter from a lawyer based in Santa Fe. Alex wanted a divorce and wanted to remove her name from all the mining claims.

She knew she should have gotten a divorce from Alex a long time before, but she hadn't. She couldn't explain why logically. She'd had developed her own gold mines—a restaurant and a tourist service.

However, she wasn't sentimental enough to give Alex a divorce without getting her fair share of what he had earned during the last twenty years. Judging by the house which Alex had just left, he'd struck it rich. Real estate records indicated he'd paid six hundred thousand dollars in cash a year ago for the house. He'd also staked more mining claims besides the ones they jointly owned. If he wanted a divorce, he could pay her five-hundred-thousand dollars and keep her name on the land and the mining claims they jointly owned.

She thought Alex would pay because the lawyer had admitted Alex was eager to marry again. The young woman was the only daughter of a mining engineer and now president of a gas exploration company based in Carlsbad. The young woman—Courtney Howard—had met Alex while she worked at an art gallery in Santa Fe.

Alex wouldn't want her to talk to the young woman and her family. Maybe Alex had changed, but she doubted it.

CHAPTER 2: Who Is John Doe?

A Tuesday in June

"Sara what brings you to the New Mexico Scientific Labs? Are you still wet-nursing your new partner? What's his name?" Forensic pathologist Isaac Newson pulled a green disposable cap over his short gray hair and studied FBI scientific consultant Sara Almquist.

Sara was used to Isaac's leering stare. The pathologist always seemed to look at everyone as if he could see through their clothes and see all their blemishes. *He would only see the obvious.* She was five-eight and slightly overweight. Her hair was blonde thanks to modern chemicals. In general, she looked fine for a woman of fifty. *That didn't say much.*

She suspected Isaac's stare was his way of distracting others from his own problems as a recovering alcoholic so he could control the conversation. She didn't plan to give him the satisfaction and answered his question immediately. "Jack Drum. He only fainted at one autopsy, and that body was a floater in the Rio Grande. Bodies are always ripe after a couple days in the river. You..."

Isaac winked. "I gave him the option of remaining behind the glass window. Those young dudes who look like quarterbacks on football teams are always the biggest wusses."

"You're just jealous because you're no longer young."

"No, I was never handsome or athletic like Jack." He patted his round belly under his green hospital scrubs. "I don't like jocks."

"Okay. I'm here, instead of Jack, to watch the autopsy on the John Doe found in the Gila National Wilderness. Your technician said his prints didn't match any in IAFIS, but torture or odd accidents had left one hand badly scarred."

She looked through the window as the technician anchored the stainless-steel gurney and pulled the sheet off the body. The man was relatively tall—probably six-feet—with broad shoulders for a thin man. His long black hair was streaked with gray. So was his beard. "Handsome."

Isaac looked up from his notes. "Yes, and judging by his clothes, he knew it. The tech tells me his jeans, T-shirt, and leather jacket all had

Ralph Lauren labels and were new." He shrugged. "Surprised me because his hands were those of someone who had done and was still doing manual labor—maybe farming or mining. There was embedded dirt under his nails and in the skin over his knuckles."

"Did you send the dirt for analysis? Was it consistent with the location where you found him?"

"Don't nag me. It'll be a week before we get the results. I had the tech x-ray him. John Doe is probably in his early forties. Evidence of lung damage and six healed fractures of leg and arm bones." Isaac spoke into a mike. "Gloria, hold up his hand so Sara can see the man's wrists."

The technician lifted a hand. Crusty linear sores and bruises across the man's wrists were interspersed with red gashes. The skin on the forefinger, thumb, and much of the left hand wasn't tanned like his arm but was white, shiny, and weird. Then the technician lifted an ankle. It also had bruises and sores.

"Ouch." Sara winced. "I see what you mean by past and current injuries."

Isaac turned to Sara. "It appears his wrists and ankles were bound with ropes for days before he died. However, the tour guide who found him in a shack in Golden Gully said he was lying face-down on the floor. She didn't notice whether his legs and arms were bound. The rangers' comments were more helpful. They said he appeared to be crawling away from an overturned yellow chair. They found bloody ropes and shards of a broken glass by the chair."

"Okay. He was bound in the chair. For a day?"

"At least a day. I'll be able to guess how long when I see how dehydrated he was and the depth of the wounds." Isaac pointed to his computer monitor. "Poor photos of the scene. I'm guessing the victim may have broken a glass, used the shards to cut the rope on his wrists, and then untied the ropes at his ankles. Hence, more wounds on the wrists."

"Odd that his captor left a glass near the chair. He almost escaped. What stopped him?"

Isaac shrugged. "He's got lots of contusions on his head and ribs but nothing which would kill him. At least, none that I've seen so far." He winked at Sara. "I assume you'd prefer to watch from behind the glass window. I'll leave the reports by those who found him here for you to examine." He pointed to the computer monitor.

She smiled.

He pulled his green autopsy gloves up to his elbows, turned on the audio system from the autopsy suite, and left the observation room.

Sara always found the discoveries during autopsies interesting, but she felt sorry for the victims—having all their secrets laid bare. She couldn't help but think about secrets she'd rather not have known. Thus, she sorted through the file marked John Doe 24-29 on the computer with only occasional glances at Isaac as he examined the body externally.

Isaac muttered as he worked, but his voice became clear when he reported the summary of his external observations. "Skin shows signs of too much sun—pigmentation, loss of skin tone, uneven texture, and broken capillaries. Especially on the face, neck, and lower arms. Appears the man wore short-sleeve shirts and slacks, not shorts, much of the time because skin damage is less on chest, upper arms, and legs." He examined the white, withered skin on the left hand and cut samples. "Scar tissue on forefinger, thumb, palm, and back of left hand. The second- and third-degree burns occurred years ago and healed with minimal medical treatment. Hence, the scarring."

While Isaac made the initial large Y-incision into the man's torso and abdomen, Sara reflected on how she'd been assigned to this case only hours earlier.

***

Sara had never heard of Golden Gully before Paul Carbonne, Special Agent in Charge of the Albuquerque Office of the FBI, had assigned her and her partner to the case this morning.

Her partner, Jack, had immediately described how he and one of his girlfriends had spent a weekend in Golden Gully a year ago. He had claimed the town, which had grown up in the late 1900s around gold and silver mines, was the best ghost town in New Mexico.

Carbonne had smirked. "Yeah, if you're into hokey, old-wood buildings and corny reenactments by the ten or so hucksters who live there year-round."

"You're not into New Mexico history," responded Jack.

"Oh yeah, bet they didn't tell you about the dust from the last mine there—the Little Fanny. It was so toxic that miners often worked in it less than three years before they died of black lung disease." Carbonne had pushed a sheet of paper toward Sara but addressed Jack. "The ME thinks this case may be complex and wants Sara's scientific expertise. Jack, remember Sara may seem old to you, but she understands the residents of this state better than most agents." He'd focused on Sara. "It's unfortunate, but you two will have to work this case mostly alone, and you'll be isolated. The murder site is about five hours away. We're beset with the usual summer explosion of crime. Only this year it's busier than any I've seen before."

Jack was a little green, but Sara didn't think he deserve to be chided for his enthusiasm. Sara wondered what besides a heavy case load was bothering Carbonne. She'd never seen such dark circles under his eyes or heard him be so grouchy with young staff.

Carbonne turned again to Jack. "Check with ME on when the autopsy will be done while I talk to Sara for a minute more."

As soon as the door closed behind Jack, Sara said, "'How's Barbara?"

"She can't get comfortable and doesn't sleep well. I guess it's typical during the third trimester of pregnancy."

Sara nodded. "You were a little tough on Jack."

"Barbara has been giving me a lot of talks on discipline lately. I'm not to spoil our daughter. She thinks acceding to a child's every whim isn't love." He paused. "She's also told me to make the rules clearer to agents. I don't want Jack to think he's special but..."

Sara knew Carbonne had convinced the FBI personnel office in Washington, D.C. that he needed more minority and women agents in New Mexico. Thus, Jack, who had been near the top of his class at the FBI academy, had been sent to New Mexico not to his choices in his home state of California. "More importantly, you don't want the other agents to think he's your pet."

"No worry about that. They all say you're my pet and I treat you like an older sister, not an independent science contractor."

Sara nodded again. She knew Carbonne had no illusions about law enforcement in the Southwest. After international assignments, he had worked undercover for the FBI as a homeless vagabond in New Mexico. He had seen how local police and FBI agents were often insensitive to women, the homeless, and indigenous individuals. Moreover, his wife was a Native American and administered the program for recruiting minorities into the FBI in the area. His goal as the SAC—she hated the sound of the acronym—was to increase the number of women and minorities as agents in New Mexico and to increase sensitivity of all agents to clients who were minorities or women. Jack, as an African American, was part of the process.

"You know you'll have to observe this autopsy. Jack won't recognize the important details, even if he manages not to pass out or vomit." Carbonne scanned his computer screen. "Any news from Sanders?"

"He doesn't enjoy his temporary assignment staffing the Senate Intelligence Committee. He's not used to multiple bosses who often make illogical demands. But he admitted in our call this morning that he is gaining a new perspective on foreign policy."

Carbonne's phone rang.

"I'd better go. The pathologists in the ME office like to complete autopsies for the day in the morning."

***

Sara noted Isaac was still busy dissecting the liver, so she focused on the sketchy report from the Catron County Sheriff's Office in the computer files. Two deputies had questioned two of the resident caretakers in Golden Gully—Ramona Miller and Jeanne Schultz—at four the day before, even though the body had been found around noon. One of the problems the FBI faced in the national forests of New Mexico was slow access to various areas. The death of a single John Doe in a remote area was not a high enough priority to warrant the use of helicopters.

The women doubted the dead man had been in the Last Chance Bar more than a couple of days because one of the resident caretakes walked through all the buildings in the deserted town at least once a week. Since it was June, the buildings were monitored more often. The deputies reported the women were trying to be helpful, but their statements were questionable.

The deputies had taken several poor-quality photos of the scene, collected the rope and glass shards for analyses, and sent them with the body to the medical examiner in Albuquerque, but they hadn't bothered to collect fingerprints. They had secured the murder site by putting a padlock on the door to the Last Chance Bar, keeping the key to the padlock, and posting a DO NOT ENTER sign. *Typical.* Local law enforcement officers often did the minimum when investigating murders in the national forests because the forests were under the FBI's jurisdiction.

***

Sara heard Isaac clear his throat. She looked up to see him staring at her through the window.

"The liver is swollen with fatty infiltration and fibrosis. Typical of a long-term alcoholic. The thinness of the individual suggests liver function was decreased enough to affect his appetite." Isaac made a strategic cut, removed the liver, and weighed it.

Then he began to dissect the stomach. "Evidence the subject had not eaten for at least two days. The stomach lining is irritated. Surprised there was no vomit near the body. He snipped bits of tissue and dropped them into tubes.

J. L. Greger

Sara decided she didn't need to watch Isaac crack the sternum and remove the lungs. She returned to the notes in the file.

***

Forest rangers called to the crime scene had recorded the name of the tour guide but hadn't bothered to get the names of the six tourists in her group. Their note on the tour guide was brief:

> *Etta Cortland is a well-known character in the Gila. No flight risk We advised the deputies not to question her while she was with her paying customers. She can be located most of time at her restaurant in Hanover. Good place to eat. Her chili rellenos are the best. So's her carrot cake.*

***

"Observe the lungs." Isaac plopped them on the scale. "Pneumoconiosis. Likely the individual worked in mines, probably not coal. I've seen this type of lung damage in miners working in copper and uranium mines, even open pit ones. The lack of severe fibrosis makes it doubtful that he smoked."

Sara replied for the first time. "Please send pieces of the lungs to be checked for radioactivity and trace elements. I'd like to determine the type of mine he worked in. Both copper and uranium are possible in New Mexico."

"I'd planned to. Also am sending pieces of liver for analyses."

"Better have the lab check for mercury, too. Some miners still use mercury to extract gold and silver from ore. And gold and silver are often found in tailings from copper ore."

Isaac looked up from the body. "Nice to have someone from our law enforcement services with whom I can carry on an intelligent conversation."

Sara searched again through notes in the file. She heard the whir of the saw used to remove the top of the skull. Sara didn't look up to watch as she read several more comments.

***

The ambulance crew reported the body was at ambient temperature and was just beginning to lose rigor by five in the afternoon. Presumably, the man had been dead twenty to twenty-four hours. A technician had collected samples of vitreous humor from the eyeball for potassium analysis. It would provide another estimate of the time of death.

***

Sara heard the plop of the brain onto the scale.

"Evidence of brain shrinkage. Probably due to dehydration. The bruises and contusions on the skull don't seem to have created any major hematomas on the frontal surface of the brain."

Sara looked over at Isaac. He had not identified the cause of death. She wondered whether the victim had died of a combination of non-lethal problems.

"What do we have here?" His voice had become higher as he repeated over and over, "Very interesting." Sara stood and moved closer to the window. Isaac was looking at blood clots on the underside of the brain.

Isaac straightened. "Physical damage to the pons and the medulla could have caused respiratory failure and death. Will have to examine this region of the brain and ear canal microscopically, but I don't see a bullet." He looked toward the window. "Sara, I think someone inserted a long— at least five inches—sharp object through the ear canal into the brain. Tricky to do. The murder weapon was thin. Most likely metal, like a hat pin. No, I think thicker.

CHAPTER 3: Jack Is on His Own

Sara and Jack were plotting their basic plan for the next two days when the main switchboard in the building diverted a call to Sara. She flipped the call into speaker mode.

"You big shots in Albuquerque may not have noticed, but we have a problem here in Golden Gully. The sheriff did your job and got the body removed before it began to stink, but we can't get into the Last Chance Bar to clean it up because it's padlocked."

Sara interrupted the man. "We apologize for the inconvenience. What's your name?"

"Clarence Brown, chief caretaker of Golden Gully. I don't want excuses from a secretary. I want to talk to the person in charge of the case."

Jack was surprised by Sara's attempt to sound folksy. "Y'all are talking to the boss of the shindig in Golden Gully. I'm Sara Almquist."

The man coughed. "No wonder, we're not getting any action with a little lady in charge. If you don't get here soon, we'll break the window in the bar to get in."

"Thanks for the compliment, but I'm no little lady." Sara's voice became louder and sharper as she grabbed a piece of paper and began to scribble a note. "If you enter the bar where the body was found or even touch it, I'll put you in jail for obstructing the investigation. So, listen carefully. My colleague will leave Albuquerque shortly to drive to Golden Gully. He should get there by three or four this afternoon. He'll want to talk to you and your partner right away. Where should he look for you?"

"We'll be somewhere on the main drag of Golden Gully."

"Please be more specific."

"How about...at the Golden Saloon. Only two-story building in town."

She slid the note to Jack.

You'd better checkout a van and a sleeping bag from the motor pool while I try to get Clarence in a cooperative mood. Once you're on the road, I'll convince the Catron County Sheriff to send two

"Clarence, y'all are missing a real opportunity."

Jack was struck by how Sara's voice had softened to a fake drawl again. He knew he should be on his way but stood wondering what she was trying to do.

"You know tourists love excitement. What could be more exciting than a murder? And you're an important man now. Were the tourists yesterday excited?"

"Yep, but the guide didn't give them a chance to see much in the Last Chance Bar before she rushed them away to...."

Sara waited fifteen seconds for the rest of sentence. "Did a couple of the tourists come back later? Maybe stay at one of the inns near Golden Gully?"

"How'd you know?"

"Could you give me their names and tell me where they're staying?"

Jack was amazed how Sara had extracted the names of potentially unbiased witnesses from the grumpy caller.

***

Jack looked at the van's clock. It was only nine-thirty as he pulled away from the FBI Building in Albuquerque. *That was darn good.* He and Sara had received the assignment at eight-fifteen.

Jack would have liked to have had company on the five-hour drive to Golden Gully, but he was pleased with the division of labor. Watching the autopsy, getting warrants, and negotiating with the lab director for a crew to collect samples at the site were Sara's problems now.

He knew why Sara had agreed to this division of labor. She avoided overnight trips because it was difficult to take her dog along, and she liked to have her dog—Bug—with her *all* the time.

Bug was a little, black-and-white Japanese Chin, whom Sara had trained to do pet therapy. Jack had to admit Sara and the dog were a good team. Bug seemed innately to know how to relax not only patients, but also witnesses and suspects. Then Sara could more effectively question them. On second thought, he wasn't sure who Bug relaxed more—those being questioned or Sara.

***

                                                                     J. L. Greger

His phone buzzed. Sara was faster than he expected with her first text. It was only eleven. She'd gotten the Catron County sheriff's deputies to agree to meet him at the Catwalk Resort on U.S. 180—the road from Reserve to Golden Gully—at three. They would accompany him as he toured Golden Gully and talked to Clarence Brown and his partner at four-thirty.

Darn. He'd planned to stop and have a leisurely lunch along the way. Now the schedule was too tight. Sara had convinced two tourists staying at the Catwalk Resort that they must talk to the FBI because they'd been in the group which found the body. This interview could save him hours of time trying to locate and talk to them later. He thought some more. He'd bet there weren't any good restaurants in the Gila Wilderness area anyway. Sara had also booked him a room at the Catwalk Resort for the night.

***

At two, Sara called. "The autopsy was complicated. It appears the murderer or others assaulted the victim in several ways during his last few days, but we won't be sure until tox tests are done and the ME microscopically examines parts of the brain and ear canal." She didn't pause to give Jack a chance to talk. "In the meantime, the lab techs need to look for several different types of evidence at the murder site. It will be easier in daylight than in the dark, even with floodlights."

"What are you trying to say?"

"I talked to the lab boss and Carbonne. Winslow Red Feather should be in Golden Gully ready to collect samples at nine-thirty tomorrow morning. You're on your own for tonight."

"Shouldn't be a problem."

"Not many places provide food in the area. The Catwalk Resort is probably your best option. Its dining room closes at seven."

"What else?"

"I spotted something weird in the photos the deputies took of the murder scene. The lab chief, who has two children, took one look at the picture, and informed me it was from a 'baby cam.' Probably why the murderers caught the victim after he cut the rope with the broken glass."

"Got it. You want me to find the camera and determine who got the camera feed."

Sara was silent for a moment. "You also need to secure the murder site better and get statements not only from Clarence Brown and his partner but from everyone living in Golden Gully."

"Do we know how many there are?"

"The postmistress in nearby Glenwood says there are four boxes for those living in Golden Gully at the Glenwood Post Office. She guesses she has put materials with fifteen different names in those boxes during the last few years, but she thinks only ten people, including two children, live there."

"I can't interview that many alone."

"I know. That's why I will be in the van with Winslow tomorrow. Then you and I can go on to Hanover to interview the tour director the next day. Do you want me to pick up clothes for you from your condo?"

Jack had brought only one change of underwear with him, but he didn't want to imagine Sara going through his underwear drawer. "No, I'm good."

***

Jack couldn't believe his eyes. Resort was a real euphemism for the Catwalk Resort. It was a compound of several small adobe and wooden bungalows—he guessed they were called *casitas*—around a gravel parking lot. A few trees, places for RVs to park, and small fenced pens for livestock, mainly sheep, completed the resort. Everything was neat and very dusty.

Jack didn't have time to feel sorry for himself because a pickup truck with the insignia of the Catron County Sheriff's Office was already parked in front of one of the *casitas*.

A man about Jack's age in green cargo pants and a tan shirt jumped from the truck, covered his long sandy hair with a tan Stetson, and strode toward Jack's FBI van.

"I'm Hank Eberle." He swallowed hard when Jack stepped out. "Are you Agent Jack Drum?"

Jack nodded. He wanted to say, *Surprised I'm Black?* "Thank you for agreeing to help me today. This is my first assignment outside of the Santa Fe/Albuquerque area." Jack regretted his statement immediately. It sounded too much like an apology.

Hank shrugged. "I wanted to meet Sara Almquist—the woman who talked to Sheriff Bob this morning. He thought I'd learn a lot from working with her. Seems she worked a big case in the next county. That other sheriff claimed Sara had a mind like 'a steel trap'." Hank looked back toward the truck. "My partner, Sheridan Evers, hurt his back three months ago. Sheriff Bob tries to assign him to cases that don't require much walking." Hank looked at his boots as he scraped the dirt with his foot. "You got to understand Sheridan. He's as ouchy as a horse with a burr under his saddle, but he knows everyone in the county. He won't move from the truck until we've settled the witnesses."

                                        J. L. Greger

Jack decided Hank was nervous, too. "Look Hank, we both know this is a botched case. The victim has now been dead for probably two days and was held here for one or two days prior to his death. At least one of the caretakers in Golden Gully had to have seen something, but I'm guessing they won't talk to me. Sara spent time on the phone with Clarence Brown this morning and was convinced at least half of what he told her was false. The two tourists still here may be the only people we'll talk with today with no axe to grind. Sara advised me to gush over them. Whatever that means."

Hank pushed his hat back. "We guessed Sara was pretty bossy."

***

"How did you happen to be on the tour led by Etta Cortland to Golden Gully?" Jack had strategically placed the two witnesses—Phil and Nancy Maggio, recent retirees from San Francisco—so they could view the mountains from the patio behind his *casita*. He thought the situation would be less threatening if he kept the gloomy Sheridan Evers out of their sight lines.

Nancy responded quickly. "Etta's Place gets great reviews on the web. We booked dinner for Sunday night there before we left home."

Her husband, seated beside her on a cushioned metal divan, put his arm over his wife's shoulders. "We'd planned to explore the Gila Wilderness on Monday and Tuesday. When we ate supper at Etta's Place on Sunday night, she suggested we join a tour to the ghost town of Golden Gully on Monday."

Jack smiled when Nancy leaned forward. She was like a wren—petite, gray haired, talkative with a chirping voice. "We..." She looked at her frowning husband. "...were convinced that Etta would make it exciting. She was so dramatic in her restaurant, wearing a gun holster on her hips over a blue calico dress with a red checkered scarf to tie back her hair."

Jack noted the description fit with Sara's profile of Etta Cortland. *Weird.* "Where did the tour begin?"

"We met her at the entrance to Golden Gully off U.S. 180 at nine yesterday."

"Why didn't you let her drive you in her van?"

Nancy looked at her husband.

Phil squinted. "I didn't think I could take her kitsch for over an hour in the van ride from Hanover. It..."

His wife interrupted. "We'd also prebooked a room at the Catwalk Resort for Monday and Tuesday nights so we'd have plenty of time to hike the area."

Jack made a note on his phone to explore later why Phil didn't like Etta. "What happened next?"

"Etta had us tromp through at least ten deserted buildings along the main drag of Golden Gully as she gave us her version of the history of mining in the area."

Nancy interrupted again. "Phil's a stickler on accuracy and thought Etta glamorized the Little Fanny Mine. He fancies himself a historian." She shrugged. "I was a kindergarten teacher and enjoyed her approach. It's not easy to make old buildings exciting, but she did. I also appreciated she'd packed a picnic lunch for the group. She had planned for us to eat it near the Last Chance Bar."

"Who entered the bar first?"

Phil and Nancy both frowned.

Phil said, "Etta bustled us all into the tiny shack quickly. I heard Nancy and another woman scream before I cleared the door. When I saw the body on the floor, I thought it was a staged scene. I laughed and was beginning to step around the others. I wanted poke the guy with my shoe. Before I'd taken two steps, Etta bellowed, 'Out!'"

Jack waited for more. Nothing came. "What did you do?"

"Etta is a mountain of a woman. We didn't argue. We all filed out. Nancy was the next to last one out."

"Did Etta come out immediately?"

Phil shrugged.

Nancy cocked her head. "I don't think so." She frowned. "No, she was inside when I left. She told us to sit on the grass and closed the door."

Phil seemed to suddenly to remember the scene. "I know she didn't participate in the discussion while the six of us argued. We all saw something different. One woman thought she'd almost stepped on some dried yellow stuff by the guy's knee. Several saw pieces of a broken glass and pieces of a rope. I thought I saw the body move."

Nancy shook her head. "I saw blood. Drops on the floor near his ear." Her eyes filled with tears. "He looked like Kip." She sobbed violently.

Phil stood and pulled Nancy to her feet. He enclosed her in his arms before he looked toward Jack. "Kip was a boy in her kindergarten class. His father shot him on the playground at Nancy's school last September. She still has nightmares. We both retired early a few weeks ago and took this trip looking for a place where she could forget the horror."

Jack gulped. "Sorry, I must ask. Are you sure you saw blood?" He didn't want to admit. There was no sign of blood—or for that matter vomit either—on the floor in the photos taken yesterday by the deputy.

"I never got close enough. Nancy sometimes has vivid dreams since the shooting at the school."

CHAPTER 4: Is the Show Real?

Sheridan Evers silently chewed tobacco as he drove the police cruiser to the front of the two-story Golden Saloon. He lowered the window, spat, and nodded toward the saloon's porch. "Looks like the two clowns are ready to perform. They only give honest answers when they're scared."

Sara had given similar advice, but she'd not provided much for Jack to hold over their heads.

"What do you suggest? All my partner Sara could find on them was they'd been arrested for theft in Alabama, but the charges were dropped by the circus owner after they quit."

Sheridan lifted the lid of a small round container and packed more tobacco between his lower jaw and his cheek. "They spend a lot of time sitting in their car on the back streets of Reserve playing with their computers."

Hank groaned. "Not that again. Lots of those in the wilderness sit in their vehicles in Reserve and tinker with their devices. Broadband service isn't reliable in the Gila Wilderness."

Sheridan chewed a bit. "Most don't try to hide their screens when I stop to talk." He seemed to readjust the location of his chaw with his finger.

Jack noticed Sheridan wiped the brown juice from his finger on his shirt. Jack now knew why Sheridan's tan shirt seemed to have so many brown stains.

"All, but those two, complain about the local internet service and weather when I stop them. They chatter about the darndest things like a pair of jaybirds."

Jack waited but Sheridan just chewed his cud. "What do you mean?"

"They're guilty of something. The guiltier you make them feel, the more they'll talk."

Jack studied the two men on the ramshackle porch. Neither had moved. One with frizzy red hair was leaning on the back two legs of a chair with his legs propped up on a post. His situation looked precarious because the boards of the porch's floor were splintered. The other lay on the porch with one arm supporting his head. His long stringy blond hair partially covered his face. Both wore overalls over their T-shirts. Jack thought the scene looked as hokey as the view when the curtains rose for the first act of a musical.

Jack stepped out of the truck. "Which of you is Clarence Brown?"

The front legs of the chair pounded the floor. The man with frizzy red hair jumped to a stand and bowed slightly.

"Cut the act. I'm not a tourist who will give you a tip. I'm an FBI agent who is going to get some answers." Jack hoped he'd been stern enough to scare them. He held out his hand as he climbed the porch's stairs. "Jack Drum. What's your friend's name?"

Clarence tittered. "Hear that, Green. This guy already has a stage name."

The blond somersaulted to his feet. "Jedidiah Green at your service. We prefer to be called Brown and Green, not by our first names."

Jack shook their hands. Both men were scrawny but nimble and short—under five-seven. Their hands had few callouses and were untanned and soft. These men were not miners, not even gardeners. Sara had learned they had been jugglers and clowns in a circus in Alabama. Strange they would want to live in Golden Gully. "Why did you come here after you left the circus in Alabama?"

"We were never in any circus."

"Stop the bull. The charges against you were dropped." He noted Clarence's hair was only red because of a bottle. The roots were gray. "Why do you keep up your circus act? I assume you didn't like the circus, or you would have joined another one."

Both men chuckled.

"What are you running from?" He pointed to Sheridan who spat a stream of brown juice from his open truck window. "That deputy would like to talk to you about loitering around Reserve." He pointed to Hank who was now slowly ambling from the truck. "He would, too." Jack winked at Clarence who Jack guessed he should call Brown. "I'm from California. I'm used to men like you. So, you can talk to me alone or to all three of us together."

Green and Brown stepped closer. "Let's go inside. We'll talk to you."

Jack waved at Hank. "Give me and my friends a couple of minutes."

***

Jack had expected Brown's and Green's first admissions. They were gay. He was surprised by their next. They wrote romance novels. Sales of their politely steamy books were good, and living in Golden Gully was cheap. Their jobs as caretakers at Golden Gully gave them time to write and provided interesting ideas for their varied plots. Several of their romances were set in a frontier town in the late 1800s. Others involved artisans living in a small western community in modern times.

Brown explained, "We don't need the internet to do research for our novels." He waved his hands. "We have plenty of raw material close at hand, but we go to Reserve when we want to submit manuscripts to our publisher and check our emails."

Jack decided to bluff a bit. "You mind if I check your phones. I'd like to be sure I trust you before I start asking real questions about the last few days. You easily could have been the murderers or have seen something important. 'Course, I can get a warrant for your home and confiscate all your electronic gear."

Jack watched as Brown and Green turned their backs on him and whispered.

Green nodded. Brown began to pace. "We write quickly and submit a novel about every month or two. We now have several unpublished novels on our computers and don't want you to steal them. I mean..."

Jack laughed. "I can barely write my reports for the FBI. I wouldn't know what to do with one of your stories. It's my partner Sara you need to fear. She's a fast writer, but she won't arrive until tomorrow. So, you'd better tell me everything now."

Brown muttered, "What deal can you give us?"

Jack choked. He'd been recording the conversation and transmitting it to Sara but wasn't prepared for an offer so fast. *Could these two characters be much deeper into the murder than he expected?*

Sara must have been listening to the conversation in the saloon carefully. Her email arrived immediately:

> *Read them their rights. Get their fingerprints and DNA samples. It might scare them into honesty. Tell them they probably won't be charged with abetting a murder if they admit all their actions and don't withhold evidence.*

Jack relayed Sara's sentiments and demanded their phones.

The two men huddled again. They turned, pulled phones from pockets in their overalls, and held out their hands to be fingerprinted.

J. L. Greger

Then Green pulled old chairs up to a rickety table as Brown said, "We're ready to sing."

***

"All of us caretakers have defined roles. Green and I say howdy to all the tourists. During the busy season, or when we're not around, others help."

Jack asked, "What does that mean?"

"We check every building at least once a week. If steps or floors are too rickety or walls looks unstable, we notify Joe Schultz. He's the carpenter in the group."

Jack was puzzled because the buildings all look in bad shape. "Doesn't look like Joe does much."

Brown leapt to his feet. "It's all an illusion. We don't want to be sued."

Green added, "But tourists must think they're seeing authentic old buildings. It adds to their enjoyment if they think our buildings are dilapidated."

Brown strode to the bar. "Take this bar for example." He pounded the top of the bar. "Joe worked a whole week to pit the top and embed a couple of bullets in the sides. Come around to the back." Brown slid open previously invisible panels and revealed five sturdy sawhorses supporting the twelve-foot bar. The gray battered wood, which appeared to support the bar, was really hung from a sturdy frame. Brown closed the panels. "Joe buys lumber and ages it for a year before he uses it. Everything you see here is magic." To emphasize his point, he made it appear that he was pulling a coin from Green's ear.

Jack frowned. "Do the rangers know?"

"Of course. They're the ones who insisted this place be safe. They like Joe's work so much they hire him to repair their signs throughout the wilderness. He's so busy Ray must help him at times." Brown finally sat down after pulling a feather duster from his overalls and brushing the seat of his chair.

Jack emailed Sara to verify with the rangers the truth of Brown's claims. He suspected his email was unnecessary, but he knew Sara was trying to monitor multiple details at the same time. "Brown, how long does it take you to check out the buildings each week? When do you do it?"

"We're sun people here. Green and I inspect buildings in the first hour after sunrise and the last hour before sunset. It would look bad to tourists if they saw us stamping in corners of buildings and crawling under porches to check the supports. Generally, tourists seldom get here before ten. Then from ten to four, one of us sits on the porch of the Golden Saloon and while the other one works inside. Unless it's cold, then we're both inside with a camera focused on the porch of the saloon. That way we can see when visitors arrive."

Jack was surprised by the mention of the camera. "What type of camera?"

Brown jumped up and pointed the feather duster at a camera focused on the front door of the saloon. "Just a garden variety surveillance camera, like you probably have at the entrances to your home or that you use to monitor your kids in another room. We've got cameras at the entrances of most of the buildings now. It makes our work easier."

Green added, "The rangers want us to be sure no one remains in the buildings at night."

Jack noted he'd return to questions on the cameras later. He first wanted to get the basics on the other caretakers at Golden Gully. He looked at the list of names Sara had gotten from the postmistress in nearby Glenwood. "I'd like to know more about the other caretakers. Tell me about Joe and his family."

Brown whistled. "Joe and his wife and two kids live in a mighty fine house about a quarter mile north of our main drag. The house is sturdy—insulated and cozy—but shingled with old barn wood to look like a shack. Jeanne gardens, home schools the kids, and keeps sheep. She turns the wool into fabric arts, which she sells here and at craft fairs in the summer. She and her aunt are the main ones who help us manage the Golden Saloon in the busy season."

Green put his hand on Brown's arm. "Actually, we're not sure how Ramona is related to Jeanne, but they're close."

"Wait." Jack glanced at the deputies' four-line report on their conversation with the two women yesterday on his phone and bluffed. "Those two women had a lot to say, but I'm not clear on the details about Ramona and her husband Ray."

Brown smiled. "They're an older couple and live in a mobile home about a mile from the main drag. It's kind of hidden by the sheds and pens for the Schultzes' sheep."

Green nodded. "Besides monitoring guests, Ramona is the baker for our community. Most of the time, she has breads and cookies for sale at the saloon. Does a real good business. Tourists are always hungry."

The front door of the saloon swung open. Sheridan stood in the doorway. "Thought you were in here too long. I came to see if these characters were giving you problems." Sheridan chewed his wad of tobacco.

Both Brown and Green paled and sat still for the first time. Jack hated to think how Sheridan had instilled this *respect* in the two men.

"I see Ramona a lot in the grocery store but have only seen Ray a couple times in Reserve during the last few years. Odd because Ray was a blacksmith and handyman for a rancher near Reserve twenty years ago."

Green waved his feather duster at Sheridan. "Old-timer, you know more about ancient history of this area than I do. But I heard Ray didn't want to see you."

Sheridan limped slightly as he moved toward Green. "What do you mean by that wiseass crack?"

Jack wanted to scream. He'd still not accounted for the last two caretakers of Golden Gully. Maybe, watching the autopsy would have been easier. He rose and guided Sheridan to a chair. "I know there are more caretakers. Tell me about them."

Brown smiled. "About a half-mile south of here, there's long lane leading to the cabin where Aiden Cortez lives. He's a bit strange."

Green giggled. "What do you expect? He's a hunter and trapper."

"What does he do as a caretaker?"

Brown swallowed hard. "Aiden is our protection. He'd shoot anyone who bothered our little community."

"Hell." Sheridan spat brown juice into a corner of the saloon. "That's my job."

Jack ignored Sheridan's provocative comment. He wanted to focus on Green and Brown at this point. "Does Aiden do anything else as a caretaker?"

Brown shrugged. "He traps animals threatening the sheep. You know they're important because they keep the grass and weeds neat here. Prospects a little."

"Is there a wife?"

Brown cleared his throat. "Polite people might call Eve Cooney a wife. She manages the website and Facebook page for Golden Gully and gets us publicity on other sites."

Green tugged at Brown's elbow. "She's the one who owns the cabin, I think."

"What else?"

"Never been invited inside that cabin but I think it's not much better than a prospector's shack."

Jack looked at his notes. "So, the caretakers are three households and you two."

Brown and Green nodded.

Jack's head ached as he thought about the challenges of interviewing the rest of the so-called caretakers. He wondered whether Brown's and Green's novels might give him insights into these people. He turned to Sheridan. "Now Green and Brown are going to give us a tour of the area." He grabbed both caretakers' arms. "Is there anything you want to admit to me and the deputies before we begin?"

Both Green and Brown turned pale.

"Remember my promises to you mean nothing if we learn later, you withheld information."

CHAPTER 5. The Quiet before the Storm

After Sara returned from the autopsy, she and Bug walked to a favorite spot near the FBI Building and sat under the trees. It was a typical day in late June in Albuquerque—hot and sunny. "You know Bug, we've got a long day still ahead of us. I've got to cut through some red tape—at least, it's not federal regs this time—to settle our last case. Then I've got to find details for Jack."

Bug wasn't interested. He sniffed the grass in several spots and pulled on his lead. Sara decided he was right. Bug with his flat face didn't like the heat and was eager to return to the air-conditioned building. She was hot, too.

Sara couldn't help but think a few rainy days would cool people off and lessen the velocity of new murders and mayhem in New Mexico. But she doubted it would rain again for at least a month. The so-called late summer monsoons had been disappointing during the last several years.

***

She called the forest rangers who had helped the Catron County sheriff's deputies investigate the murder in Golden Gully yesterday. The rangers in the Gila National Forest Wilderness were based at a station east of Silver City. No wonder it had taken two of the rangers almost three hours to respond to the call of the tour guide who'd found the body. Sara could see why the tour leader was so grouchy. Three hours is a long time to entertain six frightened tourists.

The rangers praised the two Catron County sheriff's deputies—Hank Eberle and Sheridan Evers—for thoroughly questioning two women caretakers. She didn't comment that she'd found the police report woefully lacking.

"But the women were clueless." The rangers noted they worked with Jeanne Schultz's husband Joe regularly and Ray Miller occasionally. "The men don't overcharge the U.S. Forest Service and deliver good work in a timely manner. Expect the women are honest, too."

"How about the others?"

There was a long pause. "Clarence Brown and Jedidiah Green are great at entertaining tourists. Joe once said, 'A ghost town needs to surprise visitors. Brown and Green do that when the rest of us are busy.'" The rangers knew there were two other residents, but the rangers had only met the woman—Eve Cooney. One noted, "She keeps to herself; except when she goes with the other two women to fairs in the summer. Unfortunately, my wife looks for Eve at the fairs because Eve's jewelry is top notch and expensive."

"Okay. Tell me about the cameras in the buildings at Golden Gully. How effectively are they placed?"

There was a long silence. "What cameras?"

"There was a baby cam in the photo sent me."

"Oh, those." After a pause, the senior ranger said, "Brown and Green should have let Joe install them. I checked the footage produced by one of the cameras once. It was such poor quality I wasn't sure if a bear or a mountain man with a fur cap and coat stood in a doorway. Then, too, they're cheap. The cameras recycle the tape every two days."

Sara thought the rangers seemed aware of the wildlife in the wilderness, the fire dangers, and the tourist count, but they didn't seem tuned into the communal life of Golden Gully.

Sanders called shortly after she finished her conversation with rangers. "I'm bored. Do you realize I'm working with staffers who have more in common with my daughter than me. Most of them finished their degree in poly sci or maybe law less than a year ago. What am I supposed to say to them over lunch?"

Sara sympathized with Sanders. Until recently he had held high level positions in the State Department in *intelligence* and then had served as the acting ambassador to Brazil for several months. He'd been removed from the latter post because of explosive and somewhat unpredictable events. American ambassadors are not supposed to get involved in armed rebellions in foreign countries. At least they aren't supposed to be caught in the action, even if they are working under orders. Sanders had prevented a drug cabal from overthrowing the government in the large state of Amazonas in Brazil but had been the fall guy. He'd lost his ambassadorship and was now cooling his heels as he worked as a staff member for the Senate Committee on Intelligence.

"I thought you had found friends or at least interesting colleagues among some of the faculty who are taking sabbatical leaves from their universities to work in the Congressional Research Service at the Library of Congress."

"I learned two of them were hoping to use me as a resource for their next books. Just what I don't need."

Sara couldn't help but chuckle. "You mean as an intelligence officer, you don't like being observed and dissected, like you did to others?"

"It's not funny. And the ones who understand my situation are alcoholics. Most of my old acquaintances in the State Department don't want to talk to me because they're afraid they'll look disloyal to their bosses or their conversation with me will trigger a Senate investigation."

Sara knew Sanders was being treated badly but she didn't think she should encourage him to wallow in self-pity. Furthermore, although she believed planning was important, she knew at times you just had to relax and let life unfold. After she retired early from being a professor of epidemiology at Michigan State, she'd planned to create a second career in fiber arts. She loved the creativity of working with fabric and yarn, but others didn't love her work—at least not enough to buy much of it. Then the flu epidemic had come along, and she was drawn into using her scientific knowledge to help law enforcement officers. She hoped Sanders would also make a serendipitous discovery. He was certainly smart and skilled. "It's hard for me to sympathize with you when we're so shorthanded here. Did something new happen since I talked to you this morning at six?"

Sara and Sanders maintained their long-distance relationship with daily early morning calls and frequent visits. Sanders generally preferred Sara and Bug to visit Washington because he didn't enjoy "roughing" it in New Mexico. Sanders liked fine dining, tasteful art shows, well-researched historical exhibits, and intelligent conversation.

"Not really, the New Mexico senator—Holms on the Intelligence Committee—suggested I might learn something about the movement of drugs, people, and ultimately intelligence into the U.S. if I visited several border crossing sites."

Sara doubted the senator would have made the suggestion if Sanders's unhappiness hadn't been palpable. "I doubt you fit the profile of the typical person meeting couriers entering the U.S. illegally."

"I agree. That's why I plan to hop on a plane to Albuquerque and talk to Carbonne. No one know more about disappearing into a crowd as a homeless man than he does."

"Oh dear, I'm leaving Albuquerque at four tomorrow morning to spend a couple days investigating a murder in a ghost town in the Gila Wilderness. There's no supporting field agent in the area. So, Jack and I are roughing it. I'm leaving Bug with a neighbor because I think it could be dangerous for him. It's not your type of area."

"Mmm."

Sara knew he was ignoring her last comment. She liked to say she was being patient as she waited for him to speak but knew it was untrue. She didn't know what to say.

"The Gila Wilderness connects to the Chihuahuan Desert which extends from the U.S. through Mexico. Maybe it's exactly what I need. Pretend you don't know me if I cross your path in the next two days. In any case, I'll call you tomorrow morning at six."

Sara had been concerned about Sanders' mental health for weeks. Now she was panicked. "You quit doing undercover work years before Carbonne did. And he says he's too long out of it now to do it again." She regretted her comment as soon as she said it. Nagging Sanders more would only steel his determination. "Promise you'll keep me and Carbonne informed of your location."

***

Sara was glad she was busy because otherwise she would have stewed about Sanders, which was a useless exercise. Sanders's pride—you could say foolish pride—was an integral part of his identity.

Jack had sent her fingerprints and the social security numbers for Brown and Green. It made them easier to trace. They had gotten jobs with two other circuses in Texas after they were fired from one in Alabama. They'd stayed with each circus for less than four months and were charged with loitering and shoplifting by the Waco police. Then they appeared to have worked in a restaurant in Silver City for six months before they migrated to Golden Gully eleven years ago.

She traced the copyright for a romance novel, *The Gal from Golden Gully* by Clarice Greenleaf, to Clarence Brown and Jedidiah Green. Next, she discovered they'd written twelve romance novels. Sara figured she'd heat up Jack's evening and emailed him an e-book copy of one of their novels: *Mogollon Maiden.*

She also emailed Jack a search warrant for Brown's and Green's RV because she doubted the two men would honor their promises to let Jack search it without legal encouragement. She would have found it hard to build the case for the warrant if the women hadn't told the rangers. "Brown and Green keep track of everything in Golden Gully with the cameras they installed in all the buildings." Luckily, the judge hadn't asked whether the cameras were effective.

Sara now focused on the other residents. As far as she could determine, Ray Miller had worked for a rancher in Reserve as a horse

                                              J. L. Greger

trainer and blacksmith until twenty years ago. Shortly after the rancher was killed, Ray and Ramona had moved into a mobile home near Golden Gully. Sara could find nothing on Joe Schultz or Aiden Cortez before they arrived in Golden Gully. Eve Cooney, Jeanne Schultz, and Ramona Miller were all originally from Silver City. Nothing in their pasts justified warrants to search their homes or force them to give DNA samples or be fingerprinted. She emailed Carbonne.

Ten minutes later he stopped by her small office. "I know this case in Golden Gully is more than you, as a scientific consultant, and Jack, as an inexperienced agent, should be asked to handle." He leaned down and tickled Bug's ears. "I guess I came down here to get my Bug 'fix.'" He looked at the papers scattered on the table Sara used as a desk and at the toys and dog bed on the floor of the office. "This office always seems like the most relaxed place in the building."

"It's because Bug and I don't play any music. We both think better in silence."

Carbonne laughed. "I don't know whether Bug thinks better in a quiet environment, but I realize he never barks unless someone steps on his paws." He tousled the dog's ears again and stood. "You didn't need to remind me Jack is isolated tonight. I know the forest rangers couldn't reach him in less than two-and-a-half hours from their station, and the Catron County Sheriff's Office in Reserve is an hour away."

"He's isolated."

"You both will be tomorrow. I talked to Winslow. Did you know he's considered one of the best game hunters in his pueblo?"

"So?"

"I authorized him to take his hunting gear along tomorrow."

"Why? All the hunting seasons are over."

"Not if a man or woman draws a gun on him."

"Great. You're telling me you expect a fire fight tomorrow."

"No, but I think you should check out a gun from our FBI armory for your trip. I know Sanders makes you practice with handguns many weekends, and you've certainly proved several times you can shoot to kill."

Sara grimaced. "It's hard to conduct a successful interview while holding a shotgun at the surrounding crowd. This is..."

"Unfair and dangerous. So, I made some calls. Turns out Deputy Sheriff Sheridan Evers lives only thirty minutes from the Catwalk Resort. He plans to drive by it tonight two or three times. The locals all know they don't want to mess with him. Some say there's no major crime in Catron County because old Sheridan has shot men twice from a distance with a rifle. Of course, it was twenty and ten years ago." Carbonne walked to the door. "Remind Jack the FBI doesn't always need to get their man. Go home and relax. You've done all the prep for your trip already."

Sara stood. "We'll be fine." She winked. "I already checked out two shotguns from the armory and arranged for Bug to stay with a neighbor for the next two or three days. The only thing that could affect my ability to shoot if attacked is fear for Bug's safety."

Carbonne gave Sara an awkward hug and rushed out. Sara thought she saw tears in his eyes.

***

She had scooped up Bug's paraphernalia and was ready to lead him out when her phone rang.

A woman's voice said, "I'm with the Catron County Ambulance Service. I've been thinking about our run to Golden Gully yesterday. I'd swear I smelled bleach—you know chlorine bleach—in the Last Chance Bar. My partner didn't notice it, but he always brags he can work emergencies because he smells nothing. It could have been my imagination, but anything is possible with the characters in Golden Gully."

CHAPTER 6: Unsatisfactory Answers

As Jack unlocked the padlock on the Last Chance Bar, Sheridan muttered, "I want to go in first and be sure it hasn't changed since yesterday when Hank took the photos." He turned to Hank, "Keep the two jaybirds from squawking while Jack and I look around."

As the rough door creaked open, Jack couldn't believe the narrowness of the Last Chance Bar. When the body and tipped chair had been on the floor, it must have been difficult to walk around them.

Sheridan noted his surprise. "Wouldn't surprise me if this was once a six-hole john or three regulars put together. I'll have to ask Joe. The jaybirds won't know."

Jack compared the room to the photo. The room was three times as long as it was wide with a counter and a small window on the long wall opposite the door. In the photo, a red gingham curtain was to one side of the window and the same fabric hung from a rod under the counter for about half its length. Boxes were under the counter. Now the dirty curtains covered the window and the area below the shelf. "Do you remember moving the curtain? Or the fabric under the counter?"

Sheridan uttered a series of curses. "Hank took a photo as soon as we entered the building yesterday. It was dark. So, a ranger pushed the curtain aside to let in some light before I could stop him. I don't remember if the rangers or Hank pulled the curtain across the window before we left. I know I didn't."

Jack realized he'd have to get fingerprints from Hank and the rangers. "Darn. How about the curtain on the rod below the counter?"

Sheridan closed his eyes. "Can't answer. Look at the first photo. The dark one."

"I don't have a photo like that."

"Hank should still have it on his phone. I'm sure it was taken before anything was touched. I'll get his phone."

Jack snapped on gloves and took shots of each wall and the floor with a camera with flash capability. He then pulled the curtain back and retook his shots.

Sheridan was sweating heavily as he trudged back into the bar. "Hank is using my phone to record the jaybirds as they talk about the history of the building and their activities during the last two days. Probably useless, like everything they say." He handed Hank's phone to Jack.

Jack peered at the dark photo. Fabric covered most of the area under the counter and the window. "Why would anyone have pulled back the fabric along the counter?"

"That's where the women, especially Etta, store modern stuff they don't want tourists to see."

Jack drew back the curtain along the shelf. Large glass pitchers and metal pans were in a box labeled: *ETTA*. Cleaning supplies, including bleach, were in another box. "Why is this stuff here?"

"Etta always serves lunch to those in her groups near here. The resident women do, too. Didn't you see the picnic benches under a tree when we came in?" He pointed to the far end of the counter. "There's a hand pump for water and a sink in this building. Only building besides the Golden Saloon where they have running water. Granted the old hand pump isn't always cooperative and you have to work to get the water."

Jack said as much for the recording as for Sheridan's benefit, "We can't be sure no one entered the building after you padlocked it yesterday, but we'll assume its security wasn't breached for now. Brown and Green said they installed a camera at the door to the building."

"More of their idle chatter."

Jack shook his head. "The rangers confirmed to Sara that Brown and Green had cameras focused on the doorways of most buildings." Jack ran his fingers along the sides and top of the doorpost. He examined several holes at the five-foot level. "No camera now, but these jagged holes suggest something was ripped from the post. Did you notice a camera yesterday?"

Sheridan chewed his wad. "Let me think." He chewed more. "Maybe—yes. Either the jaybirds or the murderer removed the camera last night. 'Course it could have been the same people."

"Agreed."

Sheridan uttered a string of expletives as he studied the floor. "This floor looks too clean. Come to think of it, I thought the same thing yesterday, too."

"Darn. That ties into Sara's last message. One EMT reported she smelled bleach when the body was removed. Someone tampered with the murder scene before and after you arrived. The lab techs will find it difficult to sort out the scene when they arrive tomorrow."

　　　　　　　　　　　　　　　　　　　　　J. L. Greger

Sheridan chewed the wad in his mouth slowly. "Guess I'd better not spit in the corner." He stepped outside.

When he returned, Jack said, "I can't decide whether someone tampered with the scene before Etta found the body or if she moved stuff around."

"The six tourists claimed she stayed inside for at least an additional five minutes after she shooed them out."

"That's consistent with Phil and Nancy's comments. Why would Etta have tampered with the body?"

"She has as many secrets as the resident caretakers."

***

Jack and Sheridan questioned Green and Brown separately in a back room of the saloon outfitted with an old card table and chairs. Both men claimed they'd been in this room editing their latest novel when Etta entered the saloon screaming. Jeanne and Ramona had immediately spread Etta's picnic over the bar at the front of the saloon for the six tourists while Etta had slammed into the back room. While Brown had negotiated with Etta, Green had called the sheriff's office and then the rangers. Both Brown and Green agreed Etta didn't want to wait for the deputies to arrive.

Brown said, "I told her if she left, it would be like being a hit-and-run driver." He looked at Jack. "I was right, wasn't I?"

Jack nodded. He thought if Brown felt secure, he was more apt to answer questions honestly. "When did you run down to the Last Chance Bar to see the body?"

"I didn't. Why would I want to see a man with his eyes vacantly staring at the ceiling and with his mouth flopped open?"

Jack tried to show no emotion. Everyone at the scene yesterday said the body was lying face down. However, the ME said lividity patterns suggested the man had lain on his back for at least twelve hours after death. Brown must have seen the body before mid-morning the day before. Jack didn't want to make Brown nervous and point out the discrepancy in his last answer. "So, what did you do after Etta appeared with the tourists?"

"Jeanne and Ramona ran down to the bar as soon as they put the food on the bar. Etta was in a state and ignored the tourists. We kept them busy by teaching them to play stud poker." Brown coughed. "Well at least, we reminded a couple of them how to play the game before we left."

"Be more specific on the time."

Brown gulped. "We couldn't leave before Jeanne and Ramona returned, but we left before the deputies and rangers arrived."

"Where did you go?"

"Around the hills."

Sheridan growled, "You were avoiding me."

Jack figured he had nothing to lose and might be able to scare Brown into making an honest comment. "I think you saw the body before Etta did. Maybe the night before."

Brown blinked. "That would mean I hid evidence from the police. Of course, not."

Jack was pretty sure Brown was lying. Green during his interview session has asked, "Where was the body? Was it hidden under the counter in the bar?" At the time, Jack had thought Green was asking a theoretical question. After talking to Brown, he suspected the lab crew might find evidence the body had been stashed there. That suggested the scene Etta and the deputies had seen was staged. *Why?* He also wondered whether Green and Brown had hidden something in the hills or talked to someone. He turned to Sheridan. "What do you think?"

"Your boss lady will get more out of these guys tomorrow."

Jack looked at his watch. It was six-thirty. The manager of the Catwalk Resort had told him dinner would not be available after seven.

He had time for only one question. He flashed the picture of the man in the morgue at Brown, who turned white and trembled. Jack knew many witnesses became flustered when they saw a victim in the morgue, but Brown's response seemed extreme. "Do you know who he is?"

"No," squeaked Brown.

Jack thought he might have worded the question wrong. "Have you ever seen this man or someone who looked like him—six-foot with long black hair?"

Brown trembled more. "Maybe. He used to roam the wilderness prospecting. Never talked."

Jack had left Brown with Sheridan and flashed the photo at Green who was chatting with Hank. Green's face had also paled but he didn't tremble as he stared at the photo.

"Have you ever seen him?"

Green nodded. "Several prospectors over the years looked like him, but there was one that scared us. He had blue—sky blue—eyes like a Siberian Husky dog."

"What made him scary?"

"We saw him kill and skin three wolves. Smiling the whole time."

***

The steak tacos and salad at the resort were wonderful. Jack would have enjoyed a couple glasses of wine but decided it would be unwise.

Sara was obsessed that it was dangerous for him to be here alone without backup. Carbonne had even cajoled Sheridan into driving past the Catwalk Resort at eight. It had been embarrassing when Sheridan arrived and insisted on escorting Jack to his *casita*.

At least, Sara had provided him with entertainment—a novel by the Brown and Green team. He quickly skimmed the novel *Mogollon Maiden*. It was a real bodice-ripper. The daughter of a ranch foreman was seduced by the rancher's son and then killed by the rancher. The book wasn't explicit, but it painted scenes which his mind completed vividly. He expected it had sold well.

He was watching the news on the TV when he heard a noise near his window. He flicked on the front porch light and thought he saw a man rapidly retreating. He thought he heard a rifle shot and grabbed his gun before he cautiously exited the *casita* and scanned the parking lot. There was no movement. Three other vehicles were parked in front of other *casitas*. In the distance, he heard the roar of a souped-up vehicle on the road.

He checked the FBI van. No one had tried to enter it because the alarm was still on. Instead of tossing his jacket on a chair when he returned to the *casita*, he checked the closet and hung his jacket on the lone wood hangar. Sara had really spooked him.

He tried to sleep but couldn't. He woke around five-thirty in a fully lit room. He thought he heard a door of a vehicle slamming in the parking lot. He opened the door and saw the manager carrying a grocery bag toward the main *casita*. Last night he'd been told breakfast would be served from seven to nine.

***

Wednesday

With a copy of the search warrant Sara had obtained in his pocket, Jack approached Brown's and Green's RV from the back. Although it wasn't quite six, the sun was up. From a distance, the RV appeared to be attached to a rickety shack. Up close, he saw the shack along with the RV were on a concrete platform. He tapped on the old wood walls. The old boards appeared to be affixed to a sturdy frame. He ignored the door on the shed with a *WELCOME* sign and tapped instead on the front door of the RV. Almost immediately, he felt the RV bump a bit on it supports.

Less than a moment later, Brown rolled down the window on the front door of the RV. "We were getting ready to do our morning inspection of Golden Gully. Come on in."

Jack was showing Brown the search warrant when he saw the far end of the RV. He couldn't keep his jaw from dropping. It looked like a tent with fabric draped from the ceiling around a thick pile of mattresses and comforters. All in shades of purple. Most of the fabric looked like velvet or satin.

Brown must have noticed Jack's amazement. "We match our decor to the type of prose we're writing. We're in the middle of a book with lots of luscious purple prose now."

Green pointed to a built-in bench behind the driver's seat. "I suppose it's silly, but we find we can write more quickly when we set the mood. Writing quickly means more profits." He opened the lid of the bench. "When we're writing a sunny romance, we decorate the RV with yellow gingham."

Jack peered into the bin and saw yards of yellow gingham and old-fashioned quilts mainly in yellow and gold. He knew by the broad smiles on Brown's and Green's faces they expected him to be embarrassed. He counted to five and spoke calmly. "You're like my partner, Sara. She has a ritual in her office. She can't write until her dog Bug is settled on his bed near her desk."

Jack opened the doors to a large stainless-steel refrigerator/freezer. The freezer was packed with a variety of packaged dinners. The refrigerator's drawers were filled with fruits, vegetables, cheeses, and eggs. It looked like his mother's refrigerator and freezer—packed with healthy food. He noted a microwave oven, a small sink, and a two-burner cooker were on the counter. He opened the doors underneath. Canned goods and plastic canisters of pasta, rice, and crackers filled the shelves.

"Disappointed? Green and I try to eat healthy, but we aren't great cooks."

Jack nodded. He opened the next door. There was a lavatory and shower. "Bet it gets stinky in here sometimes."

"Not after the first year. We put all our profits from our first book into building an attached bath and party room." Brown opened a door and led the way down two steps and then pushed open a second door. "Joe built this addition for us."

The wood-paneled room, which appeared to be about half of the shed Jack had circled on the outside earlier, contained a ping pong table, a table, folding chairs, and exercise equipment. There was an external entrance and three interior doors. "We wanted a place where members of the community could meet with us without seeing our private side. We wouldn't have answered the knock on our van door if it wasn't you with a warrant."

Brown opened a door to a bathroom with a tub and shower. "We also wanted a warm, vented bathroom attached to an underground septic tank. We don't use the toilet in the RV except in emergencies."

Green opened another door. It was a giant walk-in closet filled with books of all types, jigsaw puzzles, and board games. "It gets boring here in winter. We host the other couples for game and puzzle nights a couple of times each month."

"Do they all come?"

"Always the Millers and the Schultzes, sometimes Eve Cooney, never Aiden Cortez."

"Where do you monitor the feeds from all the cameras you installed in the other buildings?"

Brown opened a door to a laundry facility with one monitor on a large table and a file cabinet. Green pushed buttons and displayed on the monitor the current views from the cameras attached to the entrances of ten buildings in Golden Gully. As expected, there was no feed from the camera that had been in the Last Chance Bar. "When did you lose the feed from the Last Chance Bar?"

Brown shrugged. Green said, "About a week ago. I guess we should have been alarmed, but we're not into electronics. I didn't see anything unusual in the bar when I looked in the window Monday morning."

Jack didn't mention the curtain had been pulled shut last Monday morning according to everyone else.

CHAPTER 7: Warnings

Sara felt all her muscles relax when she walked into the dining area at the Catwalk Resort and saw Jack enjoying an omelet. Winslow rushed up to Jack. "We left at three. Sara played the recordings of your interviews as we drove. We even listened to the rambling conversation—I don't think it could be called an interview—Hank did with Brown and Green. We're up to speed."

She saw the worry lines on Jack's face disappear as Winslow spoke. Jack would never admit it, but he was relieved to have company.

***

Jack had glared at Sara when she insisted both vans should be driven to the Last Chance Bar. She knew her comment, "I have my reasons," had annoyed him.

Now as she opened one of the two long cardboard boxes that he'd transferred from the lab van to the van he'd driven, Jack smiled. "Winslow was right. You came prepared."

"I think we should leave one in the back but have one in front."

"What about Winslow?"

"He brought along hunting supplies, but I suspect the killer won't realize Winslow could reveal a lot of his or her secrets today. They'll think of us as the bad guys."

Jack nodded. "Nothing here is what it appears. We could spend days searching this place and find nothing they didn't want us to find. Like the camera someone ripped off the door jamb of the bar sometime after the deputies took pictures on Monday and I arrived yesterday."

Winslow signed. "Means the murder scene wasn't secured."

"That's an understatement. I made a list of inconsistencies last night and lengthened it this morning." He turned to Sara. "We should focus our attention today on the other eight residents of Golden Gully. I think—well I hope—Green and Brown will give straight answers if confronted with facts."

Sara sensed Jack was withholding something. He still seemed tense. "What else?"

"There's something strange almost creepy about Sheridan Evers. Brown and Green didn't say anything, but they behave differently around Sheridan. Almost like they're afraid of him." He waited a second. "And Hank Eberle is odd, too. No one can be that green. He doesn't do anything by standard protocols. He apologizes when I correct him, but he's clueless even though he's been a deputy for three years."

***

Jeanne had just begun lessons with her children when Sara and Jack arrived at her door at nine. Despite her surprise, Jeanne answered all their questions calmly until Sara showed her a picture of the man in the morgue.

Jeanne turned pale and her hands trembled. "I...I've seen him before. His hair had less gray then. He stopped by one winter afternoon when Joe was out. He demanded to see Joe. I gave him coffee while he waited. Suddenly, he jumped up and left."

"When was this?"

"Twelve...no thirteen...years ago. The girls weren't born yet."

Sara thought it strange Jeanne would remember a man after meeting him only once. "Why do you remember him?"

"He had the strangest blue—light blue—eyes. Like a husky's. No, more like a wolf's. His voice was low when he growled. "Joe better be here the next time I come by."

Jack had questioned Joe while Sara talked to Jeanne. Now they switched interviewees. Sara asked Joe only a few questions before she showed him the photo of the man in the morgue. Joe examined it carefully and frowned. "No, I've never seen this man. But mountain men are usually all bundled up, and there's not much to recognize."

Sara knew Joe was lying. *How did he know this man was a mountain man?* The man in the morgue photo wasn't bundled up. Sara tried not to change her expression and quickly ended the interview.

***

Jack and Sara separated the next couple also before they asked any questions. As soon as Sara had settled Ramona at the kitchen table, she said, "Ramona, I understand you're the baker in this community. I still find adjustments for altitude are hard especially for cakes. What's your secret?"

Ramona had responded enthusiastically and then had explained she had been raised in Silver City, but Ray had been raised in Catron County. When they were first married, Ray had been a blacksmith and horse trainer on a ranch, and she'd been the schoolmarm in a one-room school. After their daughter was born, she'd started baking for the rancher and his hands. "We were happy."

"What changed?"

"Children grow up. Our daughter fell in love with the rancher's son. His father had other ideas for his son's future. After she died, we moved here almost twenty years ago. Five years later, my niece Jeanne came to stay with us. Soon Joe was fixture here, too."

Sara wanted to ask how the daughter died, but she wanted an honest response to the photo more. Besides, she could learn the story from old records. "So, you've seen everyone who passed through here. Do you remember this man?"

Ramona fingered the photo. "Is he the man in the morgue? I remember when we had to identify our daughter in the morgue." She paused. "People look different after they die, especially good people. I bet that's not the problem with this one." She paused. "I've not seen him before."

How did Ramona know the victim was not a good man? Sara asked a few more questions and traded with Jack. While Ramona had smiled confidently at Sara during their conversation, Ray avoided looking at Sara even when she said, "Ray, how do you stay so thin with a wife who's such a good cook?"

Ray had mumbled he was active. Sara had responded, "Must not be easy. How did you get the limp?"

Ray had finally looked at her. "You must be the lead agent. The kid didn't have the guts to ask such a direct question. 'Course, he's not as green as Hank."

Sara saw this as an opportunity. "Tell me about Hank Eberle. Isn't Eberle an old family name in this area?"

Ray smiled. "You did your homework. John Eberle was the first miner to build a cabin on the creek back in the late 1800s. Hank's his great grandson or great, great grandson." He looked down. "Product of too much inbreeding."

"What about Sheridan Evers?"

"Evers is smart but past his prime."

Sara stared at him waiting for an explanation.

Ray sighed. "Might as well tell you. You'll dig it out anyway. Sheridan shot me in the leg twenty years ago. He did it to keep me from killing Boss Crawford. Boss owned the biggest spread in the area. I was his blacksmith and horse wrangler." Ray heaved several sighs.

"What did Boss do?"

"He shot my daughter when he found her in bed with his son."

                                    J. L. Greger

"What did the son do?"

"Ran away. We never saw him again."

"What happened to Boss Crawford?"

"Boss Crawford pulled a gun on me when I hunted him down. Sheridan shot me so I couldn't be charged with murder and then shot Boss Crawford." He shook his head. "Sheridan was crack shot in his day. He claimed self-defense. The jury agreed."

Sara thought it was time to be honest because Ray had been. "The reports in the old newspapers made Sheridan look like a hero."

"Papers lie. Sheridan barely kept his job as a deputy."

"Is that why you seldom go to Reserve—to avoid Sheridan."

"Yeah, he's always lurking there."

"What about this man?" She shoved the photo forward. "Ever seen him?"

"Hard to say. Lots of prospectors and hunters in the Gila Wilderness. At least two looked a lot like the photo. One roamed through here for years, scaring the womenfolk."

"And?"

"It could be Aiden Cortez on a bad day. But the last I saw Aiden, there was no gray in his hair."

***

As soon as they reached the van, Sara said, "They're all lying, except maybe Ray."

Jack nodded. "You're going to say I'm crazy. But five minutes after I started talking to Ramona, I had a weird feeling. Her mannerisms, looks, and speech pattern were like those of the mother in the novel *Mogollon Maiden* I read last night. I'm afraid the novel is not much more fictitious than most of what we heard this morning. They're all hiding something."

"I think the characters in that novel were probably based on the Millers. Ray told me the story—at least part of it."

"Silent Ray?"

"Did the lawman in the book remind you of Sheridan?"

Jack started the van. "You're scaring me. The lawman in *Mogollon Maiden* killed the murderer in a duel and tracked the son to a cave which he stoned in and left the son to die."

Sara thought for a moment. "Start driving to the Cooney/Cortez shack but take your time. We may have stirred up a hornet's nest. Sheridan could become dangerous if he knew we'd learned of the old story. However, I doubt he'd guess Ray would have been the one to talk. He'd be more apt to go after Brown and Green, especially if they're blackmailers."

"Agreed. The vibes between the duo and Sheridan yesterday were bad."

"But Sheridan could have made Brown and Green disappear years ago if their story bothered him. I'm more worried about the last part of Ray's story. He said the man in the morgue could be Aiden Cortez. If so, Eve Cooney might not like talking to us."

Jack drove in silence for several minutes. "I thought you were being silly this morning when you made me and Winslow put on vests." He paused. "We have a more immediate problem. They all said the path to the Cortez/Cooney shack was badly rutted and easy to miss when it turns off U.S. 180."

***

They had just turned onto the path when they heard a harsh sound and felt a thud on the back of the van. Then another crashing sound. And another. The latter two seemed to hit the side of the van.

"Jack, turn..."

Sara didn't finish her sentences because Jack was wheeling the van back onto the highway. He raced to the Catwalk Resort.

***

Sara grabbed the shotgun and looked in all directions as Jack leapt from the van to examine the back and passenger side.

"Two bullet holes in the side of our van. One in the rear door. I think this was just a warning. If they had wanted to kill us, they would have gone for our tires or the gas tank."

Sara whispered, "Winslow is a sitting duck alone at the bar."

CHAPTER 8: Winslow's Perspective

Winslow looked around the Last Chance Bar after Sara and Jack departed. Jack had done a good job of describing and photographing details that were unclear in the original shots by the deputies. Somehow, the scene seemed less exciting than Winslow expected. Maybe it was because he was tired. The drive had not been as much fun as previous field trips with Sara. She had been concerned about Jack's safety and talked little as they listened to Jack's recordings of his interviews. Usually by the third day after a murder, Sara had accumulated lots of clues and talked about the clues and asked for advice. But today, she had little evidence to discuss besides the autopsy.

Even the autopsy had provided less than satisfying results. He guessed the fact that the potassium levels in the vitreous humor in the eyeball were interesting. Sara thought so. It indicated the victim had been dead about thirty hours when the tech at the morgue had drawn the sample at ten on Monday night. It suggested the victim was killed during the late afternoon or early evening on Sunday. This made Sara happy because it reconfirmed the estimate made by the ambulance crew based on body temperature.

The lab used rapid DNA tests to confirm that the shards from the glass and the bloody pieces of rope at the murder scene contained the victim's DNA. However, the DNA didn't match DNA of anyone in public data sets. All it proved was the victim had not been in the military, worked for a government agency, or had a criminal record. Winslow had ordered the lab to do the slower but more accurate standard DNA analyses because they might detect DNA from the killer which could be present in amounts undetectable by the rapid DNA tests. His order had made Sara smile, but she had not been hopeful.

Winslow guessed one reason he liked Sara and Jack was they were like him. They were single and outsiders at the FBI—they weren't white males.

Sara seldom said much about her big-time spy boyfriend—Sanders. She mainly talked about Bug, her constant companion. On this trip, she had said nothing about Sanders, except to sadly note she wouldn't see him this weekend. That was too bad. She deserved a boyfriend who would take her away from the drudgery of working at the FBI. Everyone in the building knew Carbonne depended on her to work the most impossible cases. It made the "jock" agents jealous. He was glad Carbonne had at least given her Jack as a partner.

Under her and Carbonne's tutelage, Jack was not developing like a typical agent. Although he looked like a jock, Jack listened—usually—to what staff told him. Most of the agents in the building seemed to ignore Jack. Maybe because they were older and married. Jack wanted to be married. He bragged about past girlfriends, but his last girlfriend had dumped him a few weeks earlier.

Winslow guessed he was the saddest case. He'd tried—boy had he tired—but he'd never had a steady girlfriend since he went off to college. Now he had little in common with his old friends on the Zuni Rez. And this case was depressing. No one seemed to have noted the victim was missing. The residents of Golden Gully were only annoyed his murder might ruin their tourist business.

Winslow decided moping was a waste of time. He needed to get down to business.

He quickly noticed there was no collectible DNA or fingerprints in about a four by six-foot oval on the floor or on the top surface of the counter. Those surfaces had been washed with bleach. However, he found blood in all the cracks and crevices of the wood floor under the far side of the long counter. There was blood on the fabric that hung from the rod, too. A few specks of blood and yellow gunk—probably vomit—were on the floor outside the cleaned oval. He couldn't assess how long the blood had been there, but he knew a new technique in the lab would be able to distinguish stains from the last week from ones that were several months old.

He guessed the victim had been hidden below the counter with curtain pulled to conceal him before or shortly after he was killed. All he could do now was collect samples and carefully identify the location where each was collected.

He checked the lid and side of the bleach bottle and the soap dispenser stored under the counter. The few fingerprints on them were at least partially covered by prints produced by gloved hands. There were clear prints on the box labeled: *ETTA*. He loaded the box and its contents into the van along with the window and counter curtains.

Finally, he examined the chair. The old wood chair had been painted yellow a long time before. The paint was peeling to reveal blue paint underneath. The caning on the seat was damaged. He studied the

                                      J. L. Greger

caning material carefully. The medical examiner had said the murder weapon had been a rod about an eighth of an inch thick. The size of the caning was right, but he doubted the strength of the old material. He felt the wood on the legs of the chair. He thought wood splinters from the chair wouldn't be strong enough to be the murder weapon. Maybe a nail from the chair could have been the murder weapon. No nails appeared to be missing from the chair, the counter or flooring. Besides, old nails tended to be thicker than modern ones. There were dozens of fingerprints on the chair, but all had been smudged by hands wearing gloves.

It was only ten, but he'd completed his tasks He was beginning to disassemble the security system that Jack had fashioned yesterday when a blonde woman in a pink shirt and khaki shorts strolled into the bar. "Oh dear, I hoped to get here in time to take photos of the murder scene."

Winslow stared at her. "Why?"

She flashed a perfect smile. "They'd make a real splash on our website and Facebook page."

"What type of weird website do you host?"

"The one for Golden Gully." She paused. "I guess I should introduce myself. I'm Eve Cooney. Brown and Green called me yesterday and suggested publicity on the murder might bring tourists to Golden Gully. I agreed, but I was busy yesterday and found the bar locked up last night. I could take a picture of you inspecting the scene. Are you an FBI agent?"

He studied her face and realized she was wearing a lot of makeup. *Was she hiding something?* "No, I'm a member of the FBI lab." He decided to use Sara's technique and see whether he could learn more about Eve. After all, Eve was on Sara's interview list for today. He turned his phone recorder on and tried to sound like Sara. "As I remember, Sergeant James Cooney was the man who discovered gold in this area in the 1870s. Are you related to him?"

Eve batted her eyelashes. "You're a clever man. No one has ever asked me that question before. Yes, my family has lived in New Mexico for over a hundred years."

"Around Golden Gully?"

"Not exactly."

"Why do you stick around here? Do you have a secret source of gold or silver near here?" She looked offended. He guessed it was harder to keep people talking than it looked when he watched Sara do interviews.

"My, you're inquisitive. I was raised in Silver City and trained with Native American silversmiths not far from here."

Winslow was from the Zuni Pueblo at the edge of the Gila Wilderness. His uncle was a silversmith He didn't remember seeing a pretty white woman training with his uncle or any of his friends on the pueblo. Course, she could have trained with Navajo silversmiths. "Funny I never saw you around the Zuni Rez."

She bit her lip. "I left the area to work in Rau Jewelry in New Orleans about fifteen years ago. I expect you were a preteen then."

He hoped he wasn't blushing. She had turned the tables on him and guessed his age correctly. He looked at her more closely. Maybe, she was around forty. It was hard to tell with all the makeup. He figured he had blown the interview but might as well ask one more question. "I thought all the caretakers for Golden Gully were couples. Who's your partner?"

"Aiden Cortez. He's been away for a week or so hunting."

Winslow knew she was lying. No professional hunter wanted pelts gotten in the summer, and the hunting seasons for elk and deer were all over. "Summer isn't a good time for hunting."

"He's also a prospector...and a lousy partner and lover. He's talked to me less during the last month than you just did." She stomped out. Winslow watched her ride away on an old Indian motorcycle.

Winslow wondered how much of what the woman had said was true. He quickly finished packing up the security gear and removed the yellow tape from around the building. He texted Sara and sent her the recording of his conversation with Eve. Suddenly he didn't feel like hiking the Catwalk. He felt like talking to his uncle and a young woman who had just moved to the Rez to teach in the middle school.

CHAPTER 9: Carbonne Worries at a Distance

Carbonne wasn't surprised when he got Sara's "mayday" message, but he was worried. He'd known more than two people were needed to handle the case in Golden Gully, especially since the supporting local law enforcement staff were known to be weak.

His worries increased as she explained that she and Jack had uncovered several secrets while talking to the caretakers of Golden Gully. The most disturbing was that one Catron County sheriff's deputy might have a reason for wanting to stop Jack and Sara's investigation. The fact that Winslow's location was unknown increased his concerns.

As Sara had summarized the details, Carbonne did four things. He ordered Sara and Jack to retreat to their *casita* but maintain their call with him. He thought the *casita* was safer than being inside a regular van with no armor. He ordered the SWAT team for the FBI in Albuquerque to report to his office immediately. He asked his secretary to put out an all-points bulletin on Winslow. He called the Sheriff of Catron County.

Ten minutes later, the SWAT leader told Carbonne what he already knew. The nearest airport to Golden Gully was in Reserve. There was no way for FBI agents to get to Golden Gully in less than four and a half hours without a helicopter. They could reach it by helicopter in less than two hours. The closest law enforcement officers were an hour away in Reserve.

By the time the SWAT team had reported, Carbonne had talked to Catron County Sheriff Bob Eberle. The sheriff admitted he'd heard rumors about Deputy Sheridan Evers but reiterated that he trusted the man. However, he was unable to locate either Sheridan Evers or Hank Eberle. Hank had called in sick today. The radio in the squad car Sheridan was using had been turned off. Sheriff Eberle agreed he and another deputy would immediately leave Reserve and would be at the Catwalk Resort in an hour.

The SWAT leader—Scott Carpenter—sent six of the SWAT team to Kirtland Air Force Base to depart on a helicopter to the Golden Gully area. He had determined the parking lot at the Catwalk Resort was large enough for a helicopter to land. Details of their rendezvous would be determined while they were in the air.

***

Sara's voice broadcast from the speaker phone on Carbonne's desk. "Jack just spotted a sheriff's car enter the parking lot at the resort. One man appears to be in the car."

All conversation in Carbonne's office ceased.

"A man just ran from the car." Silence. "Jack can't believe it's Sheridan Evers. He doesn't usually move that fast. The man doesn't appear to be carrying a shotgun or rifle, but Jack assumes he's got some sort of handgun."

Scott said, "Don't do anything. Stand back from windows as much as you can. Which of you has the best rapport with the man?"

"Sheridan is a man's man."

Jack spoke in the background. "He called Sara the boss lady even though he'd not met her."

Scott looked at Carbonne, who nodded. "Sara will be the spokesman because Sheridan appears to believe she has more authority. Do not open the door. Put me on the speaker phone after he makes his intentions clear. Introduce me as Scott. Don't say I'm the SWAT leader. Until then, tell me what he does. Every detail." Scott didn't pause. "Barricade the glass door to the patio of your *casita*. My men have already called the resort manager and told him to stay inside his *casita*. He was instructed to call all the occupants and tell them to remain inside their *casitas*, too. The last thing we want is hostages."

Sara replaced Jack at the front window as Jack began to cover the back window with a mattress.

Sara voice now echoed a bit as she stood at the window. "Sheridan is almost running toward us." Pause. "No, he's going to the van. We left it at least thirty feet from the entrance of the *casita*. We figured if someone shot the gas tank, the resulting fire would be less apt to engulf the *casita*." Pause. "He's walking slowly around the van. He's spotted the two bullet holes in the side of the van." Pause. "I can't see him because he's behind the van. There's another bullet hole there. The van is shaking. He must be trying to open the back door."

During the pause, groaning noises were broadcast.

Scott said, "Who's groaning?"

"It's Jack. He's pushed a heavy desk behind the mattress to keep it upright by the patio door. Now he's trying to move an old recliner." Without a pause, "Sheridan is running from the van toward his squad car." Pause. "Wait, he's pulled out a bar—I think a tire iron—from the trunk.

                                             J. L. Greger

Don't you think I should call to him. He could do a lot of damage with the tire iron."

"Stay quiet. Better if he vents his anger on the van than you. He may not know you're in the *casita*." Scott emailed messages. The one to Carbonne said:

> *Pull all files on Sheridan—work, military, medical. Search warrant should not be necessary due to emergency.*

Carbonne smiled. Sara had gotten a warrant for Sheridan Evers's medical and military files yesterday. She'd also asked an FBI analyst to rush the review of the files when they arrived this morning from the VA and to forward the review to Carbonne as well as to herself. "Got them." He skimmed the analyst's report and read key words: "Army sharpshooter in Operation Desert Fox in 1998. Never wounded." He turned the page. "Was shot in 2004 while apprehending a suspect. Suspect killed and Raymond Miller wounded." Carbonne looked up from page. "Confirms the story Sara got today from Miller." He looked back down. "VA psychiatrist reports Sheridan suffers from depression. Supposedly he is only dangerous to himself. Dated May of this year." He closed the file. "That's it."

Scott pointed to a member of his team. "Talk to that psychiatrist. That doc's covering up something."

Sara voice broadcast at a higher pitch than before. "I hear banging noises. I think Sheridan is slamming the back door of the van repeatedly."

There was the sound of glass breaking.

"Oh. The glass windows in the doors must have broken."

"What's he doing now?"

"Can't see him. Bags and boxes from the van are being scattered on the gravel. Fast." Pause. "He just threw something at the open area beyond the parking lot."

A loud explosion echoed in the room.

Carbonne yelled, "Sara, you okay?"

Sara's heavy breathing could be heard clearly on the speaker. "It was a bomb or grenade. How did Sheridan know it was in our van?" Pause. "I don't think he would have looked for it and thrown it if he'd planted it."

Scott said, "Could be a change of heart. Or a ruse to gain your confidence. What's he doing now?"

"Can't see, but I think he's rummaging in the van more." Pause. "Wait, he's walking slowly to his car." Pause. "Putting the tire iron back in the trunk." Pause. "He's sitting in the car."

One of Carbonne's phones buzzed. It was the Catron County Sheriff. Carbonne pushed a button so the call could be heard by everyone from the speaker on his desk. "Sheridan just broke silence. He said we should put out an APB for Hank Eberle. It seems Sheridan swung by the Catwalk Resort around ten last night. He saw a man walking toward Jack's *casita*. He turned off his lights and watched until the man touched the door of the van, then Sheridan shot his gun into the air. The man fled in a pickup."

"Why didn't he notify Jack?" Scott nodded in response to Carbonne's question.

"Sheridan does things his own way. This morning after Hank Eberle called in sick, Sheridan decided to watch Hank and quickly realized Hank was trailing Jack."

"Where?"

"You don't understand Sheridan. He'd never gives me details. All he said was Hank parked in a thicket of scrub pinions near the Schultzes and the Millers for a while before he crawled into the FBI van. Then he left."

Carbonne didn't wait for Scott to speak. "Why didn't he report to you?"

The sheriff coughed. "Officially I run this office, but Sheridan only reports in as he sees fit. Anyway, Sheridan didn't get too worried until he found a wad of paper under the passenger seat in his squad car instead of his master key set."

Carbonne wished the sheriff talked faster. "What was on the paper?"

"Sheridan didn't say. He told me he raced down U.S. 180 toward Eve Cooney's place, but thought he was too late when he heard three shots. Then he saw the FBI van racing toward the resort. I understand your people saw what he just did."

Scott spoke, "Irregular but effective."

"Sheridan called me because he wants to come into the *casita* and show your people what he found. He thinks Hank probably fired the shots and you must act immediately—before I can arrive."

Jack yelled in the background, "No one could be as naive as Hank pretended to be. Sheridan is strange, but we've caught him in no lies."

Sara agreed. "We have no choice but to trust Sheridan."

                                                      J. L. Greger

CHAPTER 10: The SWAT Leader Takes Control

Sara opened the door and yelled, "Sheridan, bring your evidence and stop ten feet in front of our *casita*'s door. Then drop your holster, any other weapons, and the evidence. Step back three paces. Jack will frisk you while I keep a shotgun aimed at your chest."

Scott switched off the speaker so only those in Carbonne's office could hear him. "Can she pull the trigger if necessary? Around the building, she acts like a motherly sort."

Carbonne snorted. "She's shot men and women who were attacking her or others on at least three occasions. She just doesn't like to give the tough image of a gun-toter. Her significant other is Eric Sanders."

"The spymaster who served as the acting ambassador to Brazil long enough to clean out a drug cabal?"

Despite the urgency of the situation, Carbonne couldn't resist poking the pompous leader of the SWAT. "Didn't you see her wearing a sling about a month ago. She was shot while helping Sanders in Brazil. I don't want her hurt today. Treat her as a valued FBI asset, which she is."

Scott switched on the speaker phone. "Sara, turn up the speaker's volume so Sheridan can hear me."

He waited a few seconds. "Sheridan, I'm Scott Carpenter, the SWAT leader. My team will be in Golden Gully soon. You will not escape if you don't cooperate. Listen carefully."

Sheridan yelled. "I'll listen to the local crew until your guys arrive. Simpler that way."

Scott flipped a switch. His voice didn't reverberate as it did when he had been broadcasting to Sheridan outside the room. "Sara, tell me what's happening."

"Sheridan is walking to the spot I directed. He's dropping his holster, pulling a handgun from his boot, and putting it on top of a folded sheet of paper."

Jack yelled in the background. "Sheridan, I'm going to frisk you now. Sara has a shotgun focused on you. She's a good shot."

Sara spoke softly. "Looks like he's clean. Jack is bringing the paper, the holster, and a loose gun back to the *casita*."

A door slammed. There was a pause.

"Oh my. Looks like Hank is operating at the level of an early teen. Jack's going to take over the shotgun while I photograph and send the page."

***

Scott stared at the page. Hank had printed and written "Eve" repeatedly at the top of the page. Many of the Eves were encircled by hearts. He saw the name Eve Cortez twice. Both times it was crossed out. Then he saw big hearts with Eve and Hank written in the middle. What alarmed him was at the bottom of the page. It was a list headed by the title "Threats." The list included the names: Aiden Cortez, Jack Drum, and Sheridan Evers. The name Aiden Cortex had been crossed out.

Scott thought all the writing and printing were done with the same blue pen and looked like the same person could have produced all of it. Carbonne sent a copy of the page to a handwriting expert in the lab anyway and marked it "urgent," while he ordered a psychologist to report to his office immediately.

A member of the SWAT team whispered to Scott, who immediately smiled. "Sara, let Sheridan inside. A VA psychologist has confirmed Sheridan isn't dangerous. Seems Sheridan had voiced concerns during his appointment with the psychiatrist about an unnamed partner who was delusional three weeks ago."

***

Sara yelled, "Sheridan, come on in."

A door slammed shut.

Carbonne said, "I'm getting all records on Hank. Won't be much. He's not been in the military."

Sheridan's bass voice mumbled, "Ma'am don't shoot while I pull a couple pages from my jacket." He said more loudly, "Forget the useless records kept by the Sheriff Bob. Go to Hank's high school records."

"Hell." Carbonne muttered, "Are we going to be dealing with sealed juvenile records?"

"Yup," said Sheridan. "Eberles are an old family in the area. When Hank had problems in eighth grade, police were never involved. His parents shipped him off to New Mexico Military Institute. After only a few months, he mysteriously transferred to an all-male military school out east. He seemed to do well and took the class to become a deputy after two years of working at a local garage. I warned Sheriff Bob that Hank was a real turnip seed. Sheriff Bob didn't listen and assigned Hank to ride with me, even though he knows I don't like partners."

Scott wished Sheridan would speed up his story.

　　　　　　　　　　　　　　　　　　　J. L. Greger

"When Hank started talking about Eve Cooney all the time, I knew we had problems. She's forty, if she's a day. I had a friend at New Mexico Military Institute copy a few pages from Hank's file. In the first month at the academy, Hank pestered secretaries and women in the cleaning staff. Interesting, he only bothered blondes."

Scott pushed himself to be in front of Carbonne's computer so he could look at the pages. "You think he'll kill Eve Cooney?"

Sheridan sighed. "Don't know. He obviously didn't want Jack and Sara to get to Eve. The bullet holes in the van suggest he was waiting for them in the scrub pines by the trail to her cabin. He'll might go crazy if Eve rejects him or if he thinks he's surrounded by the FBI. Dumb kid talked about the FBI siege of the Branch Davidians in Waco several times."

Scott looked up from the computer. "Why didn't you warn your sheriff?"

"I did, but Bob thought the kid's questions were logical. Waco happened before Hank was born. I gave him a few facts. But..."

Scott looked away from the computer. screen "With your and the sheriff's help, the six SWAT team members on the helicopter can take him. Is there a back way to the Cooney cabin?"

"I've seen Eve on a motorcycle in Golden Gully when I knew she hadn't used U.S. 180. Means there is a back way, but only by motorcycle, horse, or on foot."

Scott pounded the keys of the computer. "Any horses in the area?"

"Ray Miller keeps a few. Doubt he'd let your men use them. He wouldn't want them shot."

He paused. "Sara is a blonde. Of course, Hank saw her with Jack." He paused. "If she made a comment that she was escaping Jack, she could probably get Hank to talk to her. Maybe come into view so your sharpshooters could see him."

Carbonne cleared his throat loudly.

Scott said, "Might be a problem. The SAC says she's off limits to be used as bait."

"Besides I'm not pretty like Eve."

Sheridan said, "Eve's not pretty. She was made-up for those photos. A man in shorts with good legs and a blonde wig could do it for Hank when he's randy." Jack must have done something because Sheridan added, "Jack's legs are good enough, but he couldn't pass as a blonde."

Carbonne said, "It'll be an hour at least before the SWAT team lands. How will we keep Hank calm until then? Are we even certain he's near or in Eve's cabin? He could have watched the whole scene at the resort."

The sheriff's voice blared from a speaker, "I should arrive at the resort in ten minutes, tops. I might be able to calm Hank."

Scott said, "Sheriff, try to reach Hank. Tell him Sheridan is hurt. You need his help and will pick him up. See what he...."

Sheridan interrupted, "Won't Hank want to meet Sheriff Bob at my location?"

"Not if he wants to keep an eye on Eve."

Sara spoke, "Should we move Sheridan's car to the back of the lot to prevent anyone in the *casitas* being hurt?"

Carbonne reiterated, "Remember he could be watching the lot now."

Scott stiffened with annoyance. There were too many bosses in the room. "This is what we will do." Scott's voice was strong. "The sheriff will make the call to Hank. Jack will call the manager to ascertain the location of all guests. Sheridan will move his car to a far end of the parking lot, lift the hood, and return to the *casita*. Sara will advise me as we listen to the sheriff's conversation."

***

The sheriff tried to reach Hank on his phone both with a call and a text. When he got no response, Scott said, "Try your police walkie-talkie. He may not be in the cabin with Eve, but in his truck."

"He shouldn't have access to our walkie-talkie system from his truck," squeaked the sheriff.

Sheridan growled, "Bob, did you forget? You let him install the scanner in his truck two months ago."

"Calling Deputy Hank Eberle. Urgent. I need help." The sheriff repeated his call three times.'

After the third time, Hank spoke. "What do you need?"

"Sheridan hurt his leg trying to crawl under his car after it died. I can't get him into my squad car alone. Can you help me pick him up? He's moaning like crazy."

"No can do."

Scott sighed. He texted the sheriff:

Beg. Say Sheridan's leg is bleeding,

J. L. Greger

"Sheridan's leg is bleeding bad. Where are you? I can pick you up."

There was a long pause. "I'll be standing at the foot of the hill to the Cooney cabin on U.S. 180 in five minutes."

"I might not get there in five minutes but certainly in ten. Roger." After a moment's silence, the sheriff said, "I've switched off the police radio. Now what?"

Scott replied. "Stop at the resort. Your deputy will get into a waiting vehicle with my crew."

"Is that necessary?"

"You told Hank you were alone. We'll keep you covered. The crew will drive down U.S. 180 and see if Hank is at the specified location. Once they're out of Hank's sight, they'll turn around and park. Jack and your deputy will hike back toward you."

"Where will Sheridan be?"

"He'll remain in the vehicle with Sara. They're still debating which of them will be driving."

"Have Sheridan drive. He can U-turn a car and slam to a stop faster on gravel than any other deputy."

CHAPTER 11: Shoot Out

The sheriff's car had barely nosed into the parking lot when Sara drove the resort manager's red Jeep Wrangler forward. She glanced at the front seat well on the passenger side of the Jeep when she heard a string of curses. Sheridan had insisted he should not be visible when they drove past Hank because Hank might recognize him. But getting Sheridan into a position from which he could unwind quickly had been impossible with the front passenger seat in place. So, Jack had removed the front passenger seat.

A uniformed deputy jumped from the sheriff's vehicle into the back seat behind Sheridan. "I'm Tim Eberle. Why didn't you drive Sheridan's police car?"

"Remember, your boss told Hank it was broken." Sara wondered whether Jack, who was kneeling in the back seat behind her, realized Tim appeared to be as dumb as Hank. She thought so when she heard Jack groan.

Sara drove at thirty miles per hour northward on U.S. 180 because she always drove slowly on unknown roads. Everyone—especially Sanders—complained about her driving skills, but she wasn't going to speed up today. She scanned the right side of the road. Nothing moved.

Wait! Movement behind a bush not far from the edge of the road. She forced herself to keep driving at the same speed. "There's something behind a bush about twenty feet before the turnoff to Eve's. Has on a green jacket."

Sheridan moved at her feet. "Hank has a green camouflage jacket. Often wears it over his bulletproof vest."

Sara repeated Sheridan's comment. "Will turn in a little over a quarter of a mile. Sheridan says there's a low spot in the road there where we won't be seen from Hank's viewpoint."

She pulled the car to the side of the road and stopped. Jack and the deputy jumped out of the back seat and ran back toward the spot where Hank was waiting. Both Sheridan and Sara climbed out. She knelt in the back seat on the passenger's side and Sheridan assumed the driver's position. She looked at the loaded shotgun, handgun, and stun gun arranged on the back seat.

This plan would fail if other cars got in the way. So, Jack had convinced the resort manager to stop all north-bound traffic on U.S. 180, while Sheridan had ordered Ray to stop all south-bound traffic at the intersection where the road from Golden Gully entered U.S. 180. The problem was Ray hadn't notified Sheridan yet whether he was in position.

"Jack and the other deputy are running back to the site." Sara spoke normally assuming the mike she was now wearing was transmitting. "There aren't many shrubs by the side of the road for them to use as camouflage. It will take them several minutes. Sheridan and I are in position. We're not sure about Ray." Sheridan lowered all the windows. She rested the shotgun on the back windowsill. She and Sheridan had agreed the extra support of the windowsill might prevent her from jerking up when she fired the gun, which she prayed she wouldn't need to use.

"I'm approaching the site." Sara thought she head a nervous trill in the sheriff's voice.

Sheridan's phone buzzed.

Ray said, "I've already stopped one vehicle."

Scott said, "Stay calm, sheriff. Hank thinks he's going to help you rescue Sheridan. Nothing about your car should make him nervous. Just keep him occupied and get him in the back seat of the car. The other four will do the rest." Pause. "You do have a box in the passenger side front seat? As we discussed, it's safer if Hank is in the back seat not in front beside you."

The sheriff's voice trembled. "I'm not sure this will work."

Jack reported, "I'm twenty feet from Hank but across the road in the gully. The deputy is behind a shrub thirty feet away on the same side of the road as Hank."

When the sheriff said, "I see him," Sheridan moved the Jeep forward slowly.

The sheriff's voice was jerky and unnatural. "Hank, jump in. We... need to get back... to Sheridan fast. Couldn't stop the bleeding."

Sheridan drove the Jeep over a small rise in the road. The Jeep would now be visible to the sheriff and Hank. Sara raised her head. The sheriff hadn't followed Scott's directions. He'd opened the door to the front seat on the passenger's side. Hank was leaning into the front seat.

Sara aimed.

"Is the box for me?" asked Hank in a normal tone of voice.

"No, something I'm delivering to someone else. Hank, get in." Then the sheriff's voice was muffled.

Hank screamed, "What's going on?"

Sara heard a shot. She wasn't sure from whose gun. Hank suddenly slammed the car door and stepped forward.

Sheridan said, "Jack's shot is blocked." She pulled the trigger. Hank didn't move. She'd either missed Hank or his bulletproof vest had worked. She shot lower. Hank crumpled to the ground.

"Good shot. It's up to Jack now." Sheridan glided the car to a stop twenty feet behind the sheriff's car.

Scott's voice rang from the radio. "Talk to me."

Sheridan said, "Hank had on his bulletproof vest. Sara's second shot was good. Get the ambulance here fast."

Sara didn't wait to hear the response as she tore out of the Jeep. Jack was bending over Hank, who was groaning loudly. As Sara ran forward, Jack looked up. "You hit the pelvis. He's bleeding..."

The siren of an ambulance overpowered Jack's words. Sara figured Ray had let the ambulance through when Sheridan told Scott the shooting was over. She knew her first aid skills were insufficient to help Hank.

She glanced at the sheriff's car. Tim was leaning into the front seat of the car from the passenger's side. Sara raced to the driver's side of the car and opened the door. Blood dripped from the sheriff's hand onto the ground.

Sara scanned the car's interior. She saw a blanket in the back seat. She pulled a folding knife from the pocket of her slacks. With a few swipes, she'd created several strips. She twisted two together and wrapped them around the sheriff's lower right arm. "Give me a pen or pencil."

The deputy's ashen face was blank.

"To tighten the tourniquet."

The deputy fumbled in his pocket and turned away as Sara wrapped the fabric strap around the pen and then turned the pen to tighten the fabric strap around the sheriff's arm. The blood dripping from his hand became a trickle.

Sara heard a gurney being rolled toward the car. "We've got the blood loss from the wound in the sheriff's hand under control for now. Take care of Hank first."

The sheriff moaned. "Stupid to reach for the packet."

Sara thought it unkind to agree. "Hank was onto us. He had on a bulletproof vest and must have had a handgun ready to shoot." She looked up and saw Jack retreat as an EMTs bent over Hank. "How's Hank?"

"Bad. I'm going to fill Scott in."

Sara prayed silently for Hank. "We need the help of a spare EMT over here," she called to no one in particular. It seemed like five minutes passed—but it was probably only a minute—before an EMT took over the sheriff's care.

The EMT had no sooner gotten the sheriff on a second stretcher than the deputy—Tim—complained he was feeling faint. Sara grabbed the man's arm and pushed him onto the back seat of the sheriff's car.

She noticed Sheridan was behind her when he growled. "Tim, be a man. Don't bother the EMTs."

Jack yelled from the Jeep, "Think we'd better check Eve's cabin before the ambulance leaves."

***

An old Indian motorcycle was propped against the porch of a small ramshackle cabin. An SUV was parked at the side. Sheridan said, "Eve's inside. These are her two vehicles. I'm less apt to frighten her because she knows me." He opened a back door of the Jeep.

Sara gulped. She picked up the shotgun. There were two bad possibilities. One was Eve was Hank's partner and was waiting for them armed. Or Eve was hurt or dead inside.

Jack jumped out of front passenger space. "Leave all the doors open as partial shields. I'll run and try to look in that small side window as you..." He pointed to Sheridan. "...walk slowly to the front door. Call Eve's name when I signal. Sara, try to distract her by tooting the horn as soon as I clear the vehicle."

Scott's heavy breathing preceded his announcement. "Hurry. The ambulance must leave in five minutes."

Sara honked the horn. "Eve, are you okay?"

No answer.

Sara honked again. "Eve, yell, if you're okay."

Jack peered in the window and rushed to the door. "She's tied to a chair."

Sara conveyed the message to Scott and entered the cabin as Jack pulled a rag from Eve's mouth.

"Stupid punk hit me when I resisted his advances. He caught me before I could escape."

"Hank?"

"Yes. I bit him when he tried to tie me in this chair. Made him madder. He slugged me. I screamed. He stuffed the rag in my mouth and stomped out to his truck. He had the nerve to drive away and leave me. I could have died."

Sheridan shook his head and trudged to the back room of the cabin. "Want to make sure no one else is here."

Sara notified Scott that the ambulance crew could leave with Hank and the sheriff but requested a second ambulance be sent for Eve and Sheridan. She'd listen to Sheridan's panting for the last hour and thought he was in the bad shape but doubted he'd admit it.

She picked up the rag and cut the rope with gloved hands and stuffed them into evidence bags. She thought the scene in the cabin looked contrived.

CHAPTER 12: Control

"We're worse off than we were when we started." Jack was looking under clothes and trash strewn across the floor of Eve's cabin with gloved hands. "I don't see anything useful. This is Winslow's domain." He nodded toward Eve who was sitting backwards in a straight chair with her head resting on the back. "She won't even speak. And we've got a useless deputy moaning as he lies on the back seat of the sheriff's car. Darn."

"Winslow should get here in an hour. He told the Arizona State Police when they stopped him that he'd turned off his phone and zoned into his 'indigenous self' once he left here."

Jack snickered. "He was thinking about the new junior high science teacher on the Zuni pueblo. He's mentioned her several times to me. He knew her as a child but lost contact when they both went away to college."

"Good. Winslow is lonely. I hope he can convince this woman to transfer to a school closer to Albuquerque. I'd hate to lose him at the FBI."

Sheridan came out of the back room. "Come look at this."

***

The bedroom didn't resemble the main room of the cabin The large four-poster bed covered with pink bedding and a rose coverlet almost filled the room. "Did you touch anything?"

"Hmmf." Sheridan held up his gloved hands. "I know our sheriff's office looks pretty incompetent, considering crazy Hank and the crybaby Tim." He placed a wad of tobacco in his cheek. "Sheriff Bob didn't exactly shine either. But I'm not incompetent. I only moved the covers enough to see whether there was anything interesting in the bed." He pointed to a phone now lying on a chest of drawers. "Only thing I found."

Sara gazed at the starkly neat bedroom with only two pieces of furniture: a bed and a chest. It exuded a vibe different from the careless, sloppy feeling of the main room. Maybe Eve had given mixed signals to

Hank, too. "Jack, what if Hank is naive and not crazy? Eve could have led him on."

"Doesn't matter. If she said no this morning, he raped her."

"Yes, but I doubt most of what she said. The scene's so hokey. Even Hank wouldn't have tied her up so loosely." She glanced at the bed. "The lab needs to check for semen, not just DNA on the bedding, and someone needs to listen to the recordings on this phone."

Jack stared at Sara. "Winslow will take care of those details when he arrives. You're ignoring the eight-ton elephant. A SWAT team should arrive in a helicopter in fifteen minutes. We need to put them to work and utilize the helicopter."

"I know, but SWAT team members don't do interviews willingly. I'd also like to get Eve out of here so we can really search this property."

Sheridan gave a broad grin. "I'll handle Eve. It will be easy for me to convince her that no one will believe her story if she doesn't submit to a rape test. I'll remind her how gossipy the staff in the in the clinic in Reserve are. When I'm done, she'll beg to be sent to University Hospital in Albuquerque."

Sara decided it was best not to think about what Sheridan would say. "Other ideas?"

"You've got a semi-load of details to handle in Reserve." Sheridan panted a bit and dropped on the bed. "Hank has an apartment on the second floor of a house owned by a retired schoolteacher named Ophelia Murphy in Reserve. As I remember, she taught Hank in eighth grade. She might be able to give insight into Hank's personality. You also need to get all Hank's employment and school records, and the reduced staff in the sheriff's office won't be able to help you."

Jack pointed at the crowded main room of the cabin. "We haven't even looked at the shed out back and Eve's SUV. Winslow will need help to collect and transport samples."

Sara's phone rang, and Scott's voice blasted from it. "Change in plans. EMTs have stabilized Hank. Taking him to a doc in Reserve is a waste of time. I've ordered the ambulance to go to the Catwalk Resort and wait for the helicopter with the SWAT team to land."

Sara walked to the front porch as Jack and Sheridan went to talk to Eve. "I'd like to put Eve on the helicopter. She needs a rape test. We believe she knows important details, but we can't get her to talk." She hesitated. "Could two or three of the SWAT team stay here with Jack and me? We're swamped."

J. L. Greger

Scott laughed. "Great minds think alike. I've reassigned three members of the SWAT team to remain with you. Otherwise, the helicopter will be overweight with the team and all the medical evacuees."

Sara lowered her voice and explained that she thought Sheridan was close to a heart attack. She ended by saying, "I can get Eve and Sheridan to the helicopter landing site at the resort in ten minutes."

***

Jack drove Eve to the pickup point in the FBI van because Sara wanted to talk to Sheridan alone. As soon as Sara started the Jeep she said, "Sheridan, I've arranged for you to have a physical at the University Hospital. I don't like your continual panting."

Sheridan shrugged. "They'll tell me what I already know. My heart is failing."

"They may be able to fine tune your medication," She looked in her mirror at Sheridan gasping in the back seat. "And get you started on a weight loss program." She winked. "I don't want anything to happen to you until you answer all my questions."

He chuckled. "I figured you were black-hearted. What do you want to know? I bet you read *Mogollon Maiden* by Green and Brown."

"If you saved Ray's life by shooting the rancher after he killed Ray's daughter, why does Ray avoid you?"

"You know the answer. It's hard to face someone when you owe the person too much."

Sheridan had given a logical but incomplete answer. "Okay. What happened to the rancher's son?"

"Brown and Green got it wrong in their novel. The son drank too much and was often in jail after bar fights." Sheridan seemed to choke a bit. "You can confirm those points in the records of the Catron County Sheriff's Office. When he stole money from his mother the second time, she told him to leave, but she kept sending him checks monthly. After two years, the checks weren't cashed. She asked me to find her son."

"Why ask you? You killed her husband."

"Nothing she hadn't thought of doing. He beat her and the son regularly."

"And?"

"The son died in a DWI accident in Colorado."

"Who will get the ranch when the widow dies?"

Sheridan cleared his throat. "The widow died fifteen years ago. Her two daughters run the ranch now."

"Will anyone confirm your story?"

"Gravestones."

Sara figured she might as well change the topic. He wasn't going to say any more about the long ago shooting. "Why did Eve come to Golden Gully?"

"Don't know. Expect it was because of Aiden. He—like other prospectors before him—used the old cabin on and off. 'Course she and her relatives in nearby Alma owned the cabin and the land." He shrugged. "Eve's a good goldsmith and should have stayed in New Orleans when she left here about sixteen years ago."

Sara spotted the ambulance at the resort and the helicopter circling overhead. There were so many questions she wanted to ask Sheridan and so little time. "You make this area sound like it's a western version of Peyton Place."

"What do you expect in a county with only three thousand people?" Sheridan coughed violently. "I should tell you one other detail. You'll probably find out anyway. The rancher's widow and I kept company for a short while before she died. We kept it quiet to avoid nasty rumors."

He climbed out of the Jeep as soon as Sara pulled up next to the ambulance. "You're smart to get me out of here. I've got too much baggage in this case, but I gave you honest leads. Hank's landlady—Ophelia Murphy—can answer the rest of your questions."

***

The helicopter landed. When the blades stopped churning up dust from the parking lot, two SWAT team members jumped out and helped the EMTs slide stretchers with Hank and the sheriff on board. Two others talked to Jack and escorted Eve on board. Two more greeted Sara and shook Sheridan's hand. "We've been told you're a legend in western New Mexico."

Sheridan looked at Sara. "Are you the two she's going to boss around for the next two days?"

Both SWAT members looked surprised. They pointed to one of the team members talking to Jack. "He's also staying."

"Don't let her fool you into thinking she's soft. She's black-hearted."

Sara gave him a hug and pushed him toward the helicopter. "Take care of yourself."

Just before he climbed into the helicopter, Sheridan said, "Trust only Ray and Ophelia. The rest are lying to protect each other."

***

Sara felt tired as she looked at the three agents in their SWAT garb. They looked rested and ready to attack. "I know this assignment will

                                           J. L. Greger

seem boring when you're fired up for action on a SWAT team, but we need help with the grunt work."

One stepped forward. "I'm Beau." He pointed to the other SWAT team members. "They're Mace and Garth. Scott said you would take the lead, but we can reduce the sheer volume of work to be done. We're yours until Scott sends a plane back to pick us up at the Reserve Airport late tomorrow afternoon."

Sara felt her jaw drop. Beau had never bothered to speak to her previously when they passed each other in the hallways of the FBI Building in Albuquerque. He was being polite and helpful now.

Beau continued, "On Scott's orders, I've already determined the resort is booked up for tonight. The three of us can't fit into one room with Jack. I arranged for a car rental and a hotel room for Mace and Garth in Reserve. It appears there's a lot of groundwork to be done there. You can brief us on the characters in this case while we drive to Reserve in Sheridan's car."

"What about Jack? He needs help. Tim's useless."

"Later. Let's go."

Sara felt the case was being ripped from her hands. She was surprised how good it felt to be relieved of responsibility. Besides, arguments over turf were always a mistake. Before she could move Sheridan's police cruiser, the resort owner insisted the three SWAT team members—now reduced to being just FBI agents—re-bolt the front seat into the Jeep.

As she drove to Reserve, Beau summarized his plans. "The lab tech, Winslow, when he gets to Golden Gulley can check out the sheriff's car and send Tim back to Reserve in it. Then Winslow can help Jack. Back to our concerns. We think everyone in the Catron County Sheriff's Office should be interviewed. The sheriff's actions were suspect today."

"He was nervous, but neither Hank nor Sheridan appears to trust him. I think I trust Sheridan, but the skeletons in his closet make..."

"Us nervous. We were glad you found a way to remove Sheridan from the scene. We suspect the rest in the sheriff's office will talk more if he's not around." Beau continued, "These two agents will remain in Reserve and interview the deputies and staff."

"Find out why the sheriff hired Hank. Sheridan was convinced it was an obvious mistake."

Beau ignored Sara's comment. "We were pleased you negotiated with the sheriff for use of Sheridan's vehicle for the next couple of days. Mace and Garth will use that car. The locals are apt to be more cooperative if they perceive the FBI is working with the local police.

Anyway, it works that way on the pueblos." He smiled. "You and I will return to Golden Gully in the rental car."

Sara noticed Beau used "we" as if it was the royal we. She decided he meant he and Scott, which she assumed equated in his mind to the royal we. "I think before Mace and Garth talk to the sheriff's crew, someone should secure Hank's apartment, search it, and interview Hank's landlady who lives on the first floor of the house. Sheridan seemed to think she could provide details to help us psychologically profile Hank."

"Why? He's a paranoid schizophrenic."

"Jack and I think he's just dumb and naive. I suspect Eve manipulated him."

***

When they reached the car rental, Sara said, "I have one more job for you. Since I can't get to a psychologist, you need to assess whether I—having shot Hank—am emotionally able to continue working on this case."

Beau laughed. "Scott already took care of that. Carbonne and a psychologist assessed your actions since the shooting and judged you psychologically sound. The paperwork has already been filed."

CHAPTER 13: John Doe Has a Name

Jack was frustrated. Tim wouldn't stop wailing although he had refused an EMT's help. To escape Tim's groans, Jack had fiddled with the keypads on the doors to the shed behind Eve's cabin for twenty minutes after Sara and the three agents left.

Finally, Winslow arrived and checked out the blood and prints on the front seat of the sheriff's car. Jack sighed with relief as he watched Tim drive away in the car. When he returned to the cabin, he found Winslow had played with Eve's phone for less than two minutes before he found the code to unlock the shed's doors.

***

Jack couldn't believe his eyes when Winslow opened the shed behind Eve's tiny cabin. First, it wasn't a shed. It was a modern lab filled with equipment. The only pieces he could identify were a computer and a 3-D printer.

Winslow oohed and aahed over the equipment and explained that Eve had the capability of creating three-dimensional wax models of jewelry, casting molds from the wax models, and then pouring liquid metal into the molds. Winslow thought her set of grinding tools was more complete than those in his uncle's silversmith shop. Eve also had several large ceramic jar mills. Winslow guessed Eve used the mills to pulverize ore so it would be easier to extract metals. The cabinets below the mills were filled with barrels of what appeared to be gravel, which Winslow hypothesized was some type of ore.

One curious aspect of the building was the two suites of rooms at the front and the south side. The suite on the south consisted of a large bathroom with makeup and beauty products filling all the cabinets and a small bedroom with a large closet filled with women's clothes. The rooms were painted pink and were as messy as the cabin.

The largest room in the second suite at the front of the building contained a modern kitchen and laundry with a huge double-door refrigerator/freezer and an ample wooden table. The shelves were packed with canned and dried foods. The second room was a modest bedroom with a bed, dresser, and two chairs. All the clothes in the bedroom's small closet and the chest were for a man. The third room was a spartan bathroom with a shower. All the rooms in the second suite were painted light blue and neat as a pin. However, two six-packs of beer were wedged under the bed.

Jack guessed that Eve and Aiden lived separate private lives and spent more time in the shed than in the cabin. He wondered whether the cabin's main function was to distract visitors from entering the shed.

As Winslow studied the equipment, Jack studied the building's construction. It's floor and lower walls were coated with some sort of epoxy. Winslow said he'd seen the same type of epoxy in animal care facilities. Expensive, durable, and waterproof. Jack noted old boards were merely hung on the outside like Joe' Schultz's house. He suspected Joe had built this shed, too.

One thing was missing. Eve had to store gold and finished jewelry somewhere. Jack tapped the floor and walls to detect hiding spaces but found nothing.

Jack decided Joe must know a lot more about Eve than he'd admitted this morning. Besides, Winslow would be busy for hours as he retrieved data from the computers and took samples for DNA and fingerprint analyses.

***

Joe Schultz was annoyed when Jack arrived at his home at suppertime. He became more talkative when Jack explained Joe either could cooperate now or he would be sent to the FBI building in Albuquerque tomorrow for questioning.

Joe insisted on talking to Jack outside his home in the FBI van. He admitted Eve Cooney had him "shore up" the cabin about fifteen years ago. "It was my first project here. Fourteen years ago, she handed me the plans for the lab and said it was the first stage of her plan to build a jewelry business." He sighed. "Only she didn't want me to tell anyone about the lab." He swallowed hard. "I haven't been in it since I helped uncrate a couple large pieces of equipment."

"Where did she get the money?"

Joe shrugged. "I've learned it's best to not ask too many questions here. I was grateful for the work. The money I earned made it possible for me to build the workshop behind my house."

Jack guessed Joe knew more than he admitted, but someone— probably Sara—needed to find the weak spot to make him talk.

***

As soon as Jack entered the cabin, Winslow announced. "I identified the guy in the morgue."

"That's progress." Jack asked no questions during Winslow's long spiel because they would only lengthen it. *Winslow was a great tech but talked too much.*

Winslow concluded his dialog by saying, "The man in the morgue has the same DNA as I found on a toothbrush and a comb in the blue bathroom in the shed. Our John Doe is Aiden Cortez. Of course, I used rapid DNA tests, and the lab will have to use standardized procedures to meet legal requirements." He didn't take a breath. "It would help if you could get DNA and prints from Eve. Most of what I found today is probably hers, but I found DNA from several individuals on mugs and in the bedding. I've already told the agents in Reserve to try to get samples."

CHAPTER 14: A Surprising Teacher

Garth and Mace high-fived each other and jumped into Sheridan's police cruiser as soon as Beau and Sara left the rental lot in Reserve. The day had been a waste of time. Mace had known it would be as soon as Scott announced to them, "We've got to save the SAC's newest rookie and non-agent Sara Almquist. They're being attacked by a rogue sheriff's deputy in Catron County." Mace had thought Sara had probably driven the poor deputy crazy with useless details.

Once they were in the air, Scott had cursed a lot as the action in Golden Gully had spun out of his control. Mace had been glad when Scott decided to let the helicopter continue to its destination. The cleanup sounded easy. Everyone but Sara could see Hank was a schizoid who had killed the John Doe in the morgue and was ready to kill others. He had to give Sara credit. She had managed to stop the crazed deputy even though he wore a bulletproof vest. She'd probably been lucky.

Garth yelled, "Forget about Sara. If we're smart, we can knock off in an hour. All we have to do is secure Hank's apartment and talk to his landlady. We'll assign the lab tech to do the details. Then we can pick up beer and catch at least the last half of the Dodgers vs. the Rockies game."

***

Mace rang the doorbell. A skinny, old broad with her gray hair in a short bob answered the door. "Ophelia Murphy?"

The woman nodded.

"We need to ask you questions about your renter—Hank Eberle. We have a search warrant to collect samples from his apartment, his car, and wherever he parked it. It won't take long."

"Why isn't Sheridan with you?"'

"Ma'am. Deputy Sheridan Evers was feeling poorly. He's on his way to University Hospital to undergo tests. We're with FBI." Garth and Mace showed her their badges.

"Oh dear, the rumors must be true. I'd heard there was a shootout somewhere near Golden Gully."

"Rumors are often exaggerations. Hank refused to talk to the sheriff. They were both injured."

"Hmmf. They were both shot. I'm surprised either of them could hit each other. The shooting must have been at close range." Miss Murphy walked away. "Well, come on in and sit down." She pointed to an old sofa where a golden retriever lounged. "I expect you have questions." She pointed to the dog as she sat down in a straight-backed chair. "Come here." The dog slowly walked to Miss Murphy and lay down at her feet.

Mace wished there was some place to sit other than the sofa, which was coated with dog hair. "We'll be recording our conversation."

Mace tried but he could never get a short answer to his questions. After an hour, Mace knew the records in the sheriff's office couldn't provide as much information as Ophelia Murphy. Everyone in the sheriff's office, except for Sheridan, had been Ophelia's student in her seventh and eighth grade English and social sciences classes in the Reserve school.

Her description of the sheriff could be summed up in one word— mediocre. "There no doubt Sheridan should be sheriff, but he doesn't want to run for office." She petted her dog. "And there are still rumors..." She didn't complete the sentence. "Sheriff Bob takes care of the paperwork and glad handing, but Sheridan has made all the decisions for years, except one. He would never have hired Hank."

She took her time but affirmed all the information Sheridan had supplied on Hank and then added her opinion. "The boy is obsessed with sex. Several of his essays in eighth grade were descriptions of having sexual contact with blonde women. I convinced his parents to send him to the New Mexico Military Institute for high school."

Mace had almost exploded with laughter as Ophelia Murphy described Hank's essays. "Perhaps Hank was trying to annoy you." Mace imagined all her students had thought Miss Murphy was a prude. Even on this warm June day, she wore a long-sleeve white blouse buttoned to the neck.

"Yes, Hank wanted to embarrass me." She clucked. "But I wasn't always an old maid." She paused. "That's another story." She paused again. "After Sheriff Bob hired Hank, I marched into his office with copies of several of Hank's old essays and made him promise to have Hank ride with Sheridan."

"Why did the sheriff listen to you?"

"I taught Sheriff Bob. Really, all the Eberles."

"Wait. Is Sheriff Bob Eberle related to Hank?"

"His father is a cousin to Hank's grandfather."

Mace must have showed his surprise.

"Don't apply your big city prudish ideas here." She waved her hands. "Everyone here is related—well except the Green and Brown duo, Sheridan, the Millers, the Schultzes, and me. What do you expect in a county of three thousand people?" She stood, opened an old oak filing cabinet, and began to hand pages to Garth.

Mace looked over at Garth who was photographing the pages. "What are these?"

"Family trees of course. I'm a genealogist." Almost as an aside, "I had to do something interesting here in my spare time. The trees helped me understand my students' problems better."

Mace remembered Sara and Beau wanted to learn about Eve Cooney. "I know Eve Cooney is from Silver City, but do you know anything about her?"

"I didn't have her in class. She's a niece of Sheridan's old girlfriend."

Mace didn't attempt to hide his surprise. "The widow of the rancher he shot twenty years ago. I thought that was a secret."

"That's the biggest non-secret in Catron County. She and Sheridan were an item even before she became a widow." She raised her eyebrows. "Do you understand what I'm saying?" She pointed to one of the family trees Mace was studying. "She's a Cooney from Silver City."

"Wasn't it suspicious?"

Ophelia frowned. "Don't be provincial. They were two sensible people who had shared experiences. The rancher was part of the Eberle clan. I guess he's probably a second cousin once removed to Hank and to Sheriff Bob. I suspect that's why he shot his blacksmith's daughter. He thought he was above the law. All the Eberles do."

Mace felt confused by all the names swirling in his head. He needed to question Ophelia more, but he thought he'd be more focused if he gathered information from other sources first and studied the genealogical trees. "We'd like to collect samples in Hank's apartment yet tonight. But I have one last question for you. Weren't you scared to house Hank upstairs?"

"It's not easy to find a renter who is quiet and a good handyman, and I never was blonde. Hank is only fixated on blondes. Besides, Hank was afraid of me. I rapped his knuckles more than once with a ruler. It's painful if you do it right." She stood and led him to a door on the side of the house and unlocked it. "Hank could enter here without bothering me. He parked his truck in the nearby shed with all my garden equipment."

***

The small living room and kitchen were neat. They looked like they were ready to be inspected by visitors. So was the small bedroom, but the door to another room was locked.

"Looks like it's a standard lock like you'd find in any hardware store." Garth pulled out a master set of keys from his satchel. "Yep, just enough to keep the old gal from spying."

Garth and Mace gasped when they entered the previously locked room. Photos of women were taped all over two of the walls. Many of the pictures were of Eve. She was scantily clad at best in most. Mace gasped. "Sure, looks like Hank didn't force his attentions on Eve, like she claimed today."

"These might be old shots, and the relationship might be over." Garth put on gloves and opened the door to the closet. A row of shirts and jackets hung above an old oaken chest of drawers. "Bonanza!"

An iPad and a phone were in the top drawer of the chest. In the second drawer were hundreds of loose photos. In the third drawer were underwear and T-shirts. In the fourth drawer jeans. "We're going to need the help of the lab guy, Winslow." He thumbed through the photos. "The old broad was right. Hank likes blondes."

"I think we'd better document the general layout before we remove any photos from the walls." Mace studied the photos on the wall. The subjects looked willing. Not Peeping Tom shots through an open window. "Wait. Some of the girls look young—prepubescent."

Mace was composing an email to Sara and Beau when he received one from her.

I expect you're bored in Reserve. Before you leave tomorrow, check with the Catron County Clerk in Reserve. I'm interested in all mining claims made by Aiden Cortez, Etta Cortland, and Eve Cooney during the last twenty years.

I'd also like to learn about old (before 2000) mining claims made by everyone with the last name of Cooney. Catron County split from Socorro County in 1921. So, the old mining claims from the 1880s to 1920s might be in Socorro even though the claims are now in Catron County.

Surgeons at UNM Hospital are still working on Hank. The sheriff is okay.

Mace groaned. Sara and her details. She and Miss Ophelia would hit it off. Two broads who never stopped talking. He wrote:

> *Ophelia Murphy had a lot to say. Hank's apartment suggests we can hold him as potential pedophile. He was intimate with Eve Cooney. We need Winslow's help ASAP.*
>
> *Sheridan had an affair with the rancher's wife before he shot the rancher.*
>
> *We'll go to the sheriff's and county clerk's offices tomorrow, and then return to interview Ophelia more. Attached are copies of genealogical trees she made of Catron County residents. The man, who Sheridan shot, was a member of the Eberle clan.*

He heard steps on the stairs, pulled his gun, and stepped into the main room. Ophelia was inspecting the refrigerator.

She turned. "You can tell a lot about a person by looking in his refrigerator. This one says a bachelor lives here and eats elsewhere most of the time."

"Please, don't touch anything. Do you often…"

"I don't come up here uninvited, but I was thinking. You need to understand something about Eve Cooney. She doesn't care about anything but money now, but she wasn't always that way. I remember her when she came to the prom with Bob Eberle when they were in high school. Sweet but too smart for Bob."

CHAPTER 15: Another Complication

Sara and Beau jumped from their rental car and ran into the dining area of the resort at five to seven. The manager cleared his throat loudly. "Your friends said you'd be late when they requested their dinners packed to go at six. I assume you'll want the same."

Sara didn't even look at Beau. "We'll eat here."

The manager led them to the patio adjoining the main dining area. Sara noticed a man at one table when he said, "Vaiter, I vant anozer glass of vine."

Sara managed not to falter as she walked past him because she remembered Sanders last words on the phone. "If you see me in the next few days, pretend you don't know me."

As soon as they were seated, Sara whispered in Beau's ear. "I don't think we should talk shop in public." She leaned back. "Why don't you tell me about your family while we wait for our meals."

While Beau talked, Sara watched the man with the German accent. It was Sanders. Carbonne and Sanders must have talked, and Carbonne must have suggested her assignment was dangerous. It was nice that Sanders wanted to protect her, but mainly she was annoyed. Sanders could befuddle an already confusing situation.

His German accent seemed silly. If Sanders wanted to engender conversation, a Texas accent would have been better. She thought a second. Sanders was smart enough to know he couldn't fake a Texas accent or talk about Texas topics. Like her, he found football boring. He had no knowledge of agriculture or ranching but knew a lot about the oil industry. However, his perspective was that of a scion of a family, which had been leaders in the development of the oil industry in the Middle East over the last hundred years, not of a wildcatter in the American Southwest.

Maybe his choice of accent was logical. He spoke fluent German and Portuguese and passable Spanish and Arabic. That's what didn't make sense. The German accent he was using seemed wrong. She had limited linguistic skills. Her German teacher in high school had sadly noted after he had worked with her for hours to improve her pronunciation of German words, "Maybe with your accent you could pass as a Berliner."

She thought about Sanders's fake accent. He substituted the vee-sound for *w*'s, trilled his *r*'s, and substituted a zee-sound for *th* in words. All logical. She noted he cut and ate his meat European style—always keeping his fork in his left hand. She decided no one here would know his German accent was flawed.

However, she couldn't stop wondering: *What was Sanders trying to do?* Poor dear. He may have been an administrator too long and had lost his ability to blend in anywhere that wasn't sophisticated and urbane. Maybe he was trying to send her a message. *But what?* Or had Sanders experienced some sort of nervous breakdown? He'd been depressed since his experiences in Brazil. Until now, she hadn't thought he was dangerously depressed.

"Sara, have you heard a word I've said? You seem to be a million miles away."

She'd been rude to Beau in a way she accused many of the agents of being—interested only in their own world. "I'm tired and was mentally making a list for tomorrow's activities." She'd listened enough to Beau to know the agent had a teenage son and daughter. "Do you find it harder to relate to your son or your daughter? I always thought the guys were easier to manage when I taught at Michigan State after I proved I wasn't afraid of them. The girls never stopped arguing their case."

Beau nodded. "That's why my wife is the boss at home. She can outargue my daughter. I can't."

Sara plastered a non-committal smile on her face as Beau talked more about his family. She had not given Sanders's secret away. She decided to relax, let Sanders make his objective clearer, and enjoy her dinner. The food served was Southern-style cooking with a nod to New Mexican cuisine. The crispy chicken and smashed potatoes were served with a green chili gravy and a side of boiled pinto beans.

Sanders called to the waiter, "How var to make it to Alma and Silver City?"

Sanders was certainly trying to sound German, but he'd also given her a clue. She hadn't planned to stop in Alma.

Sara saw Beau's plate was empty. "Tomorrow Jack and I will help you and Winslow search Eve's place before we interview Etta Cortland in Hanover. I'd also like to stop by Alma." She stood.

"Why Alma?"

"Cooney's Tomb is there. Sheridan emphasized gravestones as he was leaving." She shrugged. "Seems right. You know there are rumors of a lost gold mine near here discovered by Sergeant Cooney. I wonder whether Eve stayed in the cabin because she was looking for it."

     J. L. Greger

Beau lowered his voice. "Maybe she found it. She is a goldsmith. Do we know her source of gold?"

Sara decided she'd underestimated Beau as another macho agent. "I'll try to get a subpoena for all of Eve's financial records to see whether she purchased gold for her jewelry making. I've already asked Mace and Garth to check with Catron County Clerk in Reserve for all mining claims in the names of Cooney and Cortland. We can discuss details tomorrow at six."

"At breakfast."

"No. It would be smarter if I came to your room. It will be more private." As she hurried away, she wished Sanders would visit her tonight. She was unsure which of them needed help the most. But she was sure he didn't want her to blow his identity.

CHAPTER 16: A SWAT Leader Serves as a Regular Agent

"What's the delay?"

Scott was determined to keep Eve under observation until Sara could get a search warrant for all of Eve's property. So, he faked his most concerned voice. "The University Hospital is overcrowded as usual. Let me see if I can speed up the process. They often don't get procedures done until two in the morning." He'd ducked into one of the curtained areas of the ICU.

A few minutes later, a nurse performed the rape test. Afterward, Scott led Eve to a conference room. He didn't mention that the nurse reported Eve had no bruises or evidence of recent sexual intercourse. Of course, it didn't disprove Eve's signed statement "I have a few questions before you can leave."

"I thought Sheridan had asked all the necessary questions."

"This is an FBI case." He leaned forward and asked suggestively, "Would you trust Sheridan?"

Eve coughed. "No one trusts Sheridan. Always sneaking around."

Scott thought a lie might trick Eve into telling the truth. "He seemed to think Hank was trying to learn where you kept your gold."

"Hank has only one thing on his mind, and it's not gold."

"Oh?"

"He's been insanely jealous and jumpy the last few days."

"I'd think Hank was less jealous once his competitor for you was out of the way. Funny, he didn't recognize the body."

Eve's face scrunched in surprise. "What? Oh, you mean Aiden."

Scott continued to stare at Eve.

"Hank's just as sneaky as Sheridan when he wants to be."

He sent an email to Jack but smiled at Eve. "I'm sorry but I'm not clear on the events of today. When did Hank tie you up?"

"After Sheriff Bob called. Hank said he didn't want me to leave without answering his questions."

"What questions?"

Eve twirled a curl of her light ash blonde hair around her finger. "The same old one—had I shacked up again with Aiden?"

"What difference would it make with Aiden dead?"

Eve kept playing with her hair. "You don't understand Hank. He's always so emotional. Look how he put a bomb in the FBI van and shot Sheriff Bob for no real reason."

Scott's phone pinged. He read the text from Jack:

Hank made stupid mistakes repeatedly. Like touching evidence without gloves. Never seemed nervous or temperamental to me, but he did place a bomb in the FBI van for no apparent reason. Sheridan said Hank was "slow and steady."

Scott frowned. Sara had told him she'd warned Sheridan not to tell Eve about the attempted bombing. Of course, it didn't mean Sheridan had listened. *How did Eve know about the attempted bombing?* "We've got a problem. I was just informed I can't get you back to your home tonight. A plane will leave Albuquerque around noon tomorrow to pick up the three agents from Reserve. You could jump on the flight to Reserve."

"Good."

"I can get the hospital to let you stay overnight. There usually is an empty bed in some double room with a dying patient. Or I could let you stay in an FBI safe house. The latter will be free."

"Where will I get a soft bed the fastest?"

"I can drive you to the safe house now."

***

Sheridan was in the kitchen regaling an agent with a story when Scott and Eve arrived at the safe house. Sheridan ended the story abruptly and started his planned spiel. "You're looking at the best goldsmith in New Mexico. Too bad she lost the prospector who supplied all her gold for in kind services."

Scott wondered whether Sheridan was putting it on too thick.

"I bet she hides it in her root cellar out back. Neighbors see her entering the cellar all the time."

"Old man, you talk too much." She turned to Scott. "Anything to drink here to help me ignore him?"

Scott opened the refrigerator door. "Soda and water." He pointed to the coffee pot on the range. "Probably stale."

"Wonder how much she paid poor dumb Hank to bump off Aiden. Guess we'll never know." Sheridan leaned back in his chair. "Poor boy died for nothing."

Scott watched Eve's face to see how she reacted when Sheridan said Hank had died. He was shocked. The muscles of her jaw relaxed and the lines on her forehead lessened. Her lips quivered. "That means I went through a rape test for no reason."

Scott studied her. "Sheridan's wrong. Hank's surgery was successful."

***

Scott emailed Sara:

We couldn't get Eve to admit anything.

Hank claims Eve gave him the gun he took when he used on the sheriff. A good lawyer will make an insanity plea for Hank. Even so, a judge may give you a warrant for Eve's property now.

Sheridan is a character. I _think_ I trust him.

Carbonne insisted I leave my most recalcitrant agents with you. Beau and Mace are good agents but can't accept women in authority. Garth just doesn't like women. Carbonne said not to worry. You'd train them like dogs and break them of their bad habits.

J. L. Greger

CHAPTER 17: Gold!

Thursday

Jack thought the bags under Sara's eyes were lighter than the night before, but she still looked tired when she showed up at the men's room at six in the morning. Last night when Jack stopped by her room, she'd been nervous and kept glancing at the half-closed door to the bathroom. If she had been a suspect, he would have insisted on checking.

This morning, she was all business.

"Beau, I want to make the best use of your time before you return to Albuquerque. When do you plan to leave?"

"Scott's sending a small plane to the Reserve airport to pick up Garth, Mace, and me. It should arrive around five. I figured I'd turn in rental car then."

"Good. You'll have plenty of time to help Winslow finish collecting samples at Eve's cabin and then go to Alma."

"Why?"

"The family trees Garth sent indicated two families of Cooneys lived in Alma. I wondered if they were annoyed that Eve took over the Cooney property near Golden Gully. Might also be a way to crosscheck Ophelia Murphy's comments."

"Not worth the time."

Sara looked annoyed by his defiance but stayed in control. "You might get clues about where Eve stores her gold."

"Oh, that." Beau rolled his eyes.

Jack had listened to Beau's comments on the phone with Garth the night before. He knew the three SWAT members didn't like taking orders from a "nit-picking" woman who wasn't even an agent. He tried to smooth the awkward situation. "Beau was telling me about a root cellar on his grandparents' farm on the Oklahoma panhandle last night. I thought we all could look for a root cellar on Eve's property this morning before you and I leave for Hanover to talk to Etta Cortland."

***

Jack and Beau hacked through the bushes on the hill that led from U.S. 180 to Eve's cabin for thirty minutes while Sara and Winslow walked along the hillside behind Eve's shed before Sara yelled, "Found it."

Jack and Beau found Sara standing by a low, sod-covered incline extending from the hill. Trees had been planted in front of a wooden door surrounded by old logs. The structure looked ancient—not like one of Joe's manufactured old shacks. Jack was surprised it had taken Sara and Winslow so long to find the entrance. He guessed it hadn't. Winslow had already sawed off the padlock holding the wooden door shut and was kneeling on the cement studying a gray metal door three feet into the hill.

"I studied the codes on Eve's phone last night. Two of the four codes I found opened the doors on the shed. I figure one of the other two will open the lock on this metal door." Winslow tried one. He fiddled with the dial on the door. Nothing happened. Winslow tried the other code. There was a click. He pushed the metal door open.

The space wasn't large. Three wooden shelves stood in front of him. Boxes—plain cardboard boxes—were stacked on the middle tier of shelves. On the top shelf were three old bushel baskets. Three wooden barrels stood on the lowest shelf.

"Looks like all hat—no cattle." Beau felt around the doorway for a light switch. He found a small shelf with a box of candles and a box of matches. He lit a candle.

Sara lit another candle and crawled farther into the cellar feeling the floor and walls. "Except at the doorway, the floor and walls are dirt. Probably the original cellar."

Winslow lit a third candle and pulled at the shelf. "Appears to be solid. Not a door to an inner passage." He felt the ceiling. "I've studied Eve's messages on her phone and computer. She's a—I don't know how to say it..."

"Calculating woman," said Sara.

Winslow nodded. "She wouldn't install a metal door inside this old root cellar for no reason. There must be something valuable here." He pulled out a box from the second shelf and looked inside. A few potatoes lay on the bottom. He returned the box and pulled out a second one. It contained a cannister of what looked like flour. He felt around in the flour. There were no hidden objects. The three other canisters in the box contained corn meal, coffee beans, and beans. All had no hidden objects.

Sara had stopped crawling on the floor as soon as Winslow opened the first box. She'd catalogued what he found in each box and its location. "Considering the well-stocked kitchen, this root cellar doesn't make sense as a food storage unit." She pointed to the rough cement around the gate. "This doesn't look like Joe's work, or else he was in a hurry."

Winslow pulled another box from the second shelf. It was heavier than the last box even though it contained four canisters like the previous one. All contained powders. One powder was reddish, one was gray, and two had a sheen. Winslow pulled his gloved hand through the material in one cannister. "Don't know about this stuff. I don't feel anything hidden at the bottom."

"We need to send samples back to the lab. I wonder whether these are pulverized ores from various sites." She pointed to numbers written on the sides of the canisters.

Jack pulled the last box from the second shelf. It also contained four labeled canisters of powder. "This stuff must have value. Do you think this powder is what Eve and Aiden produced when they processed ore in the ceramic mills in the shed?"

While Winslow collected samples from each canister, Jack attacked the large barrels on the lowest shelf. One was filled with salt pellets, one with furs, and one was empty.

Beau had stood back and watched the search until now. "I think we have a big problem. Searching the cabin was legal—it was the site of an alleged crime of rape—but this root cellar and even the shed aren't the crime scene."

Jack smiled. "You' haven't worked with Sara before. She started writing up the search warrant for all of Eve's property before the ambulance pulled away with Hank and the sheriff."

"Fixing to get a warrant isn't the same as getting one."

Sara didn't even look up from her notetaking. "The warrant came through last night after I convinced the judge that Eve seemed to have inordinate control over Hank, and Hank might not be able to explain his side of their relationship unless we had more information on her."

"No judge would give me a warrant on such a weak request."

"I also included copies of photos from Hank's bedroom wall that Mace sent and Eve's signed statement that Hank raped her and then tied her in a chair. The pictures don't prove the situation yesterday wasn't a rape, but they created doubt in the judge's mind. I also noted Winslow couldn't find any of Hank's DNA—only Eve's—on the rope used to tie her up."

Jack pulled a bushel basket from the top shelf. It was light. The basket seemed to contain nothing but corn husks.

Beau blinked. "You convinced a judge that Eve framed Hank with so little?"

Sara nodded. "It helped that Sheridan remembered a rumor. Seems Eve framed a guy in Silver City for rape when she was a teenager using a similar set up. I found the old police file."

Jack ran his hand through the corn husks. His fingers touched something hard. He pulled out a vial.

Everyone gasped. The gold flakes glowed in the candlelight of the otherwise dark root cellar.

"All your so-called evidence doesn't prove Eve is guilty of anything."

"True, but the judge thought I'd built a valid argument for wanting to learn more about her, especially since she had a lot to gain when her business partner, Aiden, died. Seems Eve had a life insurance policy for $100,000 on Aiden."

They found twenty more vials with what appeared to be gold flakes in the bushel baskets on the top shelf.

CHAPTER 18: A Surprising Source of DNA

Jack was quiet during the first hour of the drive to Hanover while Sara dozed. "You embarrassed Beau. It wasn't necessary. You could have told him."

Sara was still not completely awake. "What are you talking about?"

"Beau had no idea how thoroughly you and Sheridan had discussed Eve."

"He didn't ask. I just followed the evidence."

"I'm used to how you think. Beau isn't. I knew you were setting Eve up as you questioned her about her partnership with Aiden even though I didn't know where you were going. When you wanted to talk to Sheridan, I figured there was a reason. Then too, you had Winslow take more samples than even your usual overkill."

"I just accumulated data until I had enough to make a judge suspicious. Granted I encourage Sheridan to reminisce with Eve on the flight to Albuquerque and text me what he learned."

"Beau won't forget."

"Good. Do you think he'll value Winslow more?" She smiled. "The DNA on the rope was convincing."

"No. He won't want to work with you or me on another project. The guy is used to winning kudos for his efforts."

"Then we don't have a problem. I already emailed Carbonne and Scott that Beau's sense of logistics had multiplied our efforts by several fold. Besides, he'll look golden when he marches into the FBI building with samples of gold."

"Sheridan was right. You are black-hearted."

"You've overlooked one point. Scott knew of my attempts to get a search warrant for all of Eve's property. Don't you think it odd he didn't inform Beau? The camaraderie of the SWAT members may be only surface deep."

"Black-hearted." Jack snickered.

Sara sighed. "I did what had to be done. It was a slow process. I was up much of the night working with a data analyst and was too tired to sit down and explain my actions to Beau before we went to Eve's property this morning." She paused for only a second. "The analyst profiled Etta for me. Her restaurant—Etta's Place—is considered the best in southwestern New Mexico. I think we should go directly to Hanover, so we don't miss the lunch hour. We can return to Silver City later, if necessary."

"Whatever."

"The most famous item on her menu is New Mexico Twinkies—jalapeno peppers stuffed with cheese and fried. Her pork posole with blue corn muffins gets five stars."

"Darn, I didn't know we're going on a restaurant tour."

"I'm trying to sound positive. Not much else is in Etta's story. She took a teaching assignment in Grants after graduating from Penn State. Married a man name Alexander Cortland after two years. Had a daughter two years later. She started the restaurant six months later."

"Sounds boring but normal."

"Not to a woman. You don't start a restaurant with a six-month-old baby unless you're desperate. Looks like Alex Cortland was the problem." She scrolled through files on her laptop. "Appears that an Alex Cortland worked at the Chino copper mine near Hanover for five years about twenty years ago, but his employers, Freeport McMoRan, have few records on him. He evidently took off from work for large stretches of time. They finally fired him eighteen years ago—about the time his daughter was born. The analyst could find no records of Alex Cortland before his stint in Chino. U.S. Passport records indicate Alexander Cortland entered Brazil fifteen years ago and was never heard of again."

"So, he was a wanderer who assumed a fake identity and probably died in Brazil."

"Not if Sheridan is right. Remember the women and Ray talked about a strange blue-eyed mountain man who roamed this area for the last twenty years Sheridan thought the mountain man might be..."

"Aiden Cortez. Winslow proved it."

"Sheridan also thought the mountain man could be Etta's husband."

"Sheridan is the king of conspiracy theories."

"Maybe, but the analyst found some interesting items. The photo in Alexander Cortland's passport record looked a lot like our John Doe—black hair, six-foot, blue eyes."

"So, you had Etta's bank records searched?"

"Couldn't. I had no basis for a search warrant."

                                                        J. L. Greger

"Aha. That's what you want today. An excuse to get a search warrant for Etta's property. Did it ever occur to you that she might freely admit she knew our John Doe as Alex Cortland."

"She didn't when she found the body at the Last Chance Bar. At least neither Hank nor Sheridan mentioned it."

"Darn, we're back to having to trust Sheridan and Hank again. They might not have told us everything."

"Talked to the forest rangers by phone. Their story was consistent with Sheridan's and Hank's comments. They didn't think Etta knew the victim and was only upset because finding a body ruined her tour."

"But you also said. Let me see if I can remember your words. 'The rangers were more 'attuned to trees than people.'"

Sara sighed. "We're on a fishing trip." She scanned her laptop again. "Here' are a few bits on the daughter, which may be helpful. Etta appears to be protective of Jennifer Cortland. She home-schooled her for six years and then sent her to a boarding school in Pennsylvania for junior high and high school."

"Where did she get the money?"

"Good question. The analyst said the restaurant appeared to have been successful for the last ten years." She closed her laptop. "The daughter just graduated in June. If we're lucky, she may be at Etta's Place today."

***

Although it was only eleven, cars filled the parking lot around Etta's Place. Sara noted most of the license plates were from New Mexico, suggesting the restaurant was a favorite with locals. She and Jack walked to the back of the restaurant and saw a van and a car with license plates registered to Etta.

"She should be here. But she'll resist talking because the restaurant is so busy."

Jack laughed. "I'm more optimistic. I was thinking because both the car and van are here, it means the daughter might be here, too. I bet she'd like to learn about her father. I know when I was her age, I asked everyone about my dad. He'd walked out on us when I was five. It's terrible to barely remember what your father looks like."

Sara stopped walking. "What a great angle. You should focus on the daughter. I'm sorry I forgot to show you the pictures of Jenny that the analyst found in the private school's yearbook." She frowned. "Average looks, black hair, pale skin, tall, and slightly overweight."

They climbed the steps to the porch and were greeted at the front door by a hostess. She was young, about five-eight, and dark-haired, but wore a name tag with the name *EDIE*. Jack flirted with her while Sara checked out a poster entitled *TOUR A GHOST TOWN WITH ETTA* and then studied the tables. Many were vacant. She heard noisy laughter from a side room. She wandered to it. A large group of mainly middle-aged men were congregated there. A blue banner with a gold embroidered wheel proclaiming NM Mountain Rotary hung from the podium at the front table.

Jack touched Sara's arm and pulled her toward the hostess. "She's ready to seat us. It seems that there's a new waitress here named Jenny, but she's a blonde." Jack strategically seated Sara so she could view the entrance to the kitchen. "I figure all waitresses will have to enter the kitchen occasionally."

Sara didn't waste time studying the menu. She'd decided hours ago to take the analyst's advice. Instead, she opened her laptop and checked it every time a waitress emerged from the kitchen. When a thin blonde emerged, she shoved her laptop toward Jack. "Imagine the girl in the picture if she lost twenty pounds and bleached her hair blonde."

He stared at the screen and then glanced at the young woman. "Would help if I could see her eyes." As she passed by the next table, he knocked over a water glass onto Sara's lap. "Oh miss, can you help us? My friend has had an accident."

Sara didn't appreciate Jack's joke, but she had to admit he was developing rapidly into a skillful agent who could extract info from anyone.

The young woman handed Sara several cloth napkins and leaned over the table as she replaced Sara's place setting.

When she walked away, Jack smiled. "Blue—light blue—eyes. The name tag said *JENNY*."

"Looks like Etta's little girl has changed a lot since the photos were taken last fall."

***

Sara broke pieces of her muffin onto her bowl of posole as Jack moaned. "You eat posole like my grandma ate her beans and cornbread. All broken up and stirred together. Yuk."

She had savored only two mouthfuls of the mixture when she spotted Etta at the doorway to the kitchen. Sara hated to leave her tasty meal, but Etta held car keys in her hand. She might be planning on leaving.

Sara rose quickly and rushed to the kitchen. "Etta Cortland. I'm with the FBI. I must talk to you."

Etta continued walking through the kitchen. Sara risked knocking over a waitress to get between Etta and the back door. "I won't bother

J. L. Greger

you long, but the FBI must investigate the murder of the man you found in the Last Chance Bar." Sara shoved her ID toward Etta's face and studied the woman. Etta was taller than Sara—maybe five-ten—but was about forty pounds heavier. Her graying brown hair piled on top of her head made her appear even taller. Etta was an imposing woman in her blue denim loose dress.

"You took your time getting here."

"We were relying on the local sheriff."

"Hmmf. I'm surprised it took you so long time to decide that Hank's a fool and Sheridan's an old git."

Sara guessed Etta had heard about the shooting the day before but didn't want to be distracted from her planned set of questions. She held up her laptop and flashed a picture of the John Doe in the morgue. "Had you seen this man before?"

"No."

"Look carefully at the picture. It might have been twenty years ago."

Etta glanced at the screen, turned away, and then turned back and stared at it silently.

Sara decided subtlety wasn't appropriate. "I think this man is your husband. Seems strange you didn't recognize him."

Sara was surprised when she heard a young woman say, "You told me Dad died fifteen years ago. Let me see the photo."

Sara noted the young woman was the blonde waitress whom she and Jack had identified. Jack was standing near her elbow. "Etta, is this the first picture you want Jenny to see of her dad?"

Etta seemed to shrink. "Jenny dear, I need to talk to this agent. Go back to work. I'll explain everything later."

Jack led Jenny out of the kitchen. Etta led Sara to her tiny office by the back door of the kitchen. She waved her hand at an old metal folding chair as she collapsed on a similar chair behind a small card table next to two file cabinets. It didn't look like the office of a successful businesswoman.

"I imagine you were in shock to see him after all these years. Passport records indicate he entered Brazil fifteen years ago."

"Don't need to play games with me. I got a letter from Alex's lawyer two months ago. Alex wanted a divorce. I knew he was alive and back in New Mexico."

"I'd like to see the letter."

Etta rose and pulled open a file. "Here."

Sara photographed the letter. "Did you reply?"

Etta shrugged.

"Did you see Alex?"

"Not until I saw his body in the bar."

Sara decided this was chance to test Hank's and Sheridan's accounts of the murder scene. "How did you find him in the bar?"

Etta hesitated for a moment. "Stretched out on the floor face down."

"How did you know he was dead?"

"He didn't move when I stumbled on him. The bar was dark."

"Did you recognize him?"

"Don't get smug with me. You wouldn't recognize your husband lying on his face if you hadn't seen him for fifteen years."

"When did you figure out it was your husband?"

"As soon as I turned him over and saw those blue eyes staring at me."

"The tourists said you were in the bar quite a while."

"Hmmf. I went there to get the supplies I needed to serve lunch. I still needed the supplies."

"Were they under the counter? Did you have to move the fabric hiding that area?"

"You're a nosy one. Ramona and I always close the curtain under the counter, so tourist don't see our secrets."

"Did you find it that way?"

"Guess so." Etta stood. "Are we about done? I'm fixing to go to Silver City to pick up a few supplies before dinner."

"Only a few more questions. Did you turn the body back over before you left?"

"Stupid question." Pause. "Yes, no need for others to see those eyes."

Etta's answers were consistent with those of the foresters, Hank, and Sheridan. Although Sara suspected Etta knew more, she had no reason to hold Etta for more questioning. "Can you prove the victim was Alexander Cortland? Do you have any old items he handled. We might be able to lift samples for DNA analysis."

"You kidding? Why would I want to keep anything from the jerk who left me destitute?"

"How about the original paper mining claims or the deed to your land?"

"Get out of here before I call a lawyer."

Sara heard a ping and checked her laptop screen. "Go ahead and call. Your daughter gave my partner a cheek sample for DNA analyses. She's eager to know whether the victim was her father."

"We'll see about that."

"She's eighteen and legally of age. By the way, the posole and muffins were great.

CHAPTER 19: Enough Bossy Women

As Sara and Jack drove away, Beau muttered, "Bless her little pea-picking heart. That broad would drive any man crazy."

Winslow smiled. "You got to get used to her. She's solved several cases by putting lots of little details together."

"More likely she badgered witnesses until they confessed to shut her up."

Winslow shrugged. "I've got to collect samples from several more jars and lock up the root cellar and lab before we go to Alma. If Sara and Jack don't need me to collect samples in Hanover, I want to deliver the powdered ore and gold flakes to the New Mexico Bureau of Mines and Mineral Resources in Socorro directly. It will save days of delays because then the state lab won't have to send those samples to Socorro for analyses."

"I've got a better idea. You do your work here and then drive to Socorro in the lab van. I'll take the rental car to Alma and then go to Reserve. That way we may both get home at a decent hour."

***

The Cooneys in Alma were of two camps. The men thought Eve was a conniving hellcat. The women said a mountain man had broken Eve's heart years ago and she'd never recovered. All agreed Eve was the sole owner of the property by the stream. She had bought them out about eighteen years before. The women said Eve wanted the cabin because it was where she rendezvoused with her lover. The men suspected she'd discovered Sergeant Cooney's long-lost gold mine, but they admitted they'd accepted her offer for the land because they were strapped for cash.

As Beau drove to Reserve, he listened to the recording of Mace's and Garth's interview with Ophelia Murphy. It made him sick to realize he should sit in on their next interview with her. This case was filled with more bossy, conniving women—Sara, Eve, and now Ophelia—than he could shake a stick at.

***

J. L. Greger

He met Garth and Mace at the Main Street Grill in Reserve. The building was a modern structure sided with rough wood inside and out, but the food was good and hearty.

Garth had spent his morning interviewing everyone at the sheriff's office. Garth sneered. "They all appear to be Eberles. Don't think the FBI will be recruiting any of them."

Mace's morning with the county clerk had been more interesting. He'd found twenty mining claims—originally posted sixteen to twenty years ago—in Alexander and Etta Cortland's names, five claims—posted three to fourteen years ago—in Aiden Cortez's and J. Schultz's names, and two more claims—posted in the last three years—in Alex Cortez's and Courtney Howard's names. Etta had paid the annual fees on the claims she shared with Alex. Aiden Cortez had paid the annual fees on the other claims.

"The clerk was real nice," said. Mace. "I made her show me the map. All are officially on federal land, but the five with Joe Schultz are next to Eve Cooney's property."

Beau sipped his coffee. "Wonder if Eve knew."

"Yes. The clerk remembered Eve came in six months ago to look at mining claims." Mace looked at the ceiling. "She remembered because Eve was madder than a wet hen. Kept screaming, 'I can't trust that man as far as I can throw him.'"

"Did the clerk remember what claims Eve looked at?"

"Cortez's claims." Mace smiled. "I texted everything to Sara already."

The agents decided to endure another interview with Ophelia Murphy together.

***

Beau tried not to laugh as he looked at Ophelia Murphy. She was dressed in a light blue shirtwaist dress that looked like those his mother wore in old pictures. "Did Hank ever bring Eve Cooney or any woman to his apartment?"

"Not that I know of. I told him at the start I didn't want him running a bawdy house upstairs."

Beau showed pictures of several women. Ophelia quickly identified Eve. "Men wouldn't notice her if she didn't wear such tight clothes and keep her hair such a light shade of blonde." She studied a second picture for a long time. "Haven't seen Etta in years. She's not aged well." She stared even longer at the two remaining photos. "I saw the blonde...last summer. She was sitting in a pickup truck with Eve in front of my house. I remember because it was the only time, I had to remind Hank or my rules."

"Of what?" Beau didn't try to hide his annoyance.

"That's not the way to speak to a lady who is trying to be helpful. I reminded him of my rules about female visitors."

"Her name, Ma'am?"

"I don't know it."

"How about these pictures?"

Ophelia glanced at them. "Oh, my. Now I understand your real target." She pointed to the morgue picture. "You're trying to identify the man found dead in Golden Gully a couple of days ago." She tapped the old passport picture of Alexander Cortland. "I bet you've got the run-around. He called himself Aiden Cortez when I met him at a church social with Eve a couple of years ago. Charming man, but Sheridan called him 'greasy.'"

Garth smiled as he asked the last question. "Gossip in the sheriff's office is you have a crush on Sheridan Evers. Is it true?"

"Hardly a crush. I've seen him twice a week for ten years now."

***

The phone line was silent for a long time—at least for a conversation with the know-it-all Sara—after he updated Sara. Finally, Sara sighed. "I don't know if Aiden Cortez, aka Alex Cortland, was a Don Juan, but he certainly left a trail of angry women. I expect Courtney Howard, when I track her down, will be angry, too. Thanks."

Beau hated to admit Sara had been gracious. She could have pointed out that she'd been right to go all out to get a warrant for Eve's property. Eve now looked like a prime suspect.

He also felt sorry for Jack and Sara. They might never get straight answers in clannish southwestern New Mexico. Again, Sara had been right to depend on Sheridan—an outsider—for getting the dirt on the Eberles and the Cooneys. He smiled internally. Sara would also have to get information from another outsider—Ophelia Murphy. Ophelia would be good medicine for Sara.

J. L. Greger

CHAPTER 20: Jack Sees Too Much

Sara closed the door to the FBI van. "How do you want to refer to him—Alex or Aiden?" Before Jack could answer, she was studying her phone.

"Still as John Doe. I suspect we'll find a few more names for him before we're through."

Sara didn't look up. "Suspect most who knew—certainly the women—used a word that begins with 'b' when they referred to him."

"Where do you want to go next? Back to Golden Gully and question Joe Schultz or go on to Silver City as planned?"

"Silver City. Promised Sanders that I'd meet him at a homeless shelter."

"What? When did you make that promise?"

"Last night." She sighed. "It's a long sad story. I don't want to go into details, but I've got to find him. I suspect you'll have to do the interviews in Silver City alone, and I'm going to have to take several days off." She wiped her eyes. "Hate to bother you, but I may need your help. The place is on Gold Street in Silver City."

Jack started the van. "I'll get us to Silver City. Program the GPS to find this homeless shelter. Then tell me what your super spy is doing this time."

She was silent for several minutes before she began to speak. "He's not a super spy now. That's the problem. The situation in Brazil was stressful. I counseled him to relax for a while before he took another position. I meant two or three months. He thought a month was enough. The staff position with the Senate Intelligence Committee was the wrong position." She wiped her eyes. "He's made decisions and managed others for years, but as a Senate aide, he has to ask permission to take a lunch break."

Jack broke the silence after a minute. "You'd said he was unhappy but was learning a lot about international relations from a political perspective."

"I was being optimistic. He's depressed. His call two days ago—on the day you came to Golden Gully—worried me. He was obsessed with going undercover. He talked about Carbonne's undercover stints as a homeless man in Albuquerque. I thought...

After a long pause, "What? I've not been your partner long enough to read your mind."

"Thought Carbonne would talk him out of his foolish idea to assume a disguise." She straightened. "The GPS is programmed now. It will direct us to the homeless shelter, homes of several of the Cooneys, and a car rental agency. I'll need a car to handle Sanders's problems. I've asked a field agent in Roswell to investigate Courtney Howard's background. He's the closest FBI agent to Carlsbad."

"I'm still clueless."

"Sorry. I'll tell you more later. I don't understand the situation myself."

Jack was thankful the drive took only twenty minutes. He'd never seen Sara so quiet and nervous. She was chomping her gum. He'd noticed she only chewed gum after spicy meals or when she was nervous. She was always a noisy chewer, but today she snapped her gum in a way that would put most teenagers to shame.

***

The lunch hour was over at the homeless shelter. Only two men with gray hair hunched over their food trays at a table near the kitchen. Three young men entered the large gray room and strutted around the perimeter. They stopped five feet from the table with the two old men. "Those apples sure look good." One of the young men grabbed an apple.

The old man with the longest hair said, "Don't," but didn't look up.

Sara, who had been talking to the supervisor of the facility, jumped. She turned toward the man. Her mouth flew open when she saw the teenager grab a second apple.

The same old man said, "Put it back."

The teen laughed and bit into the apple, chewed, and then spit bits of apple onto one of the trays. "Is this what you want? It's the right texture for you now."

The supervisor pushed a button on his phone and whispered, "Need an officer fast."

Sara pulled out a Taser.

The teen picked up one of the trays and threw it on the floor.

One old man shivered. The one who had spoken stood. "Go away."

The teen reached back to slug the old man.

Jack yelled, "FBI stop." He was too late. The old man brought his booted foot up and swept it around to the young man's heel. The young man fell on his back.

A second teen raced forward. The old man brought his leg up between the teen's legs and kicked. The teen fell forward onto his friend.

Before Jack could act, Sara said, "Let the man do it his way, but get out your handcuffs."

The third teen backed off but reached into his pocket. Jack didn't see anything in the teen's hand, but Sara screamed, "Knife."

The old man leaped forward kicking at the teen's hand. An object clattered to the tile floor. The old man used another kick to flatten the young man.

Sara pointed her Taser at the young man. "FBI. You all are going to sit quietly while my partner handcuffs you. If you don't, I'll use this Taser."

One young man started to stand. The old man tripped him. Sara said, "Those kicks are nothing compared to my Taser."

As Jack handcuffed the second teen, a police officer waving his gun raced in. "What happened?" The officer stared at the facility supervisor.

The manager shrugged. "FBI agents were on the scene."

"Who do we arrest?"

The old man said, "No one. These teens learned they weren't as tough as they thought. A few years in the military might improve their skills."

Sara said, "I'm with the FBI. We didn't try to stop this because it was apparent the man..." She pointed to the old man. "...had everything under control. I think his suggestion is a good one. Please drop these boys at a local recruiting station." She picked up an open pocketknife from the floor. "This belongs to one of them."

Jack decided so many rules had been broken that he didn't want to go on the record as saying anything.

The police officer nodded. "Good idea. I've arrested these boys several times for roughing up homeless men and migrants." He looked at the manager. "Okay with you?"

The manager nodded. He walked over to the old man. "I never saw you here before. I don't want to see you again because the word will get out. You'll attract those looking for a fight like rotten meat attracts flies."

Sara turned to the manager. "We wanted to question this man about something he saw. We'll take him away." She grabbed the old man's arm and pushed him to the door. Jack figured Sara seemed in control and raced to the police car to retrieve his handcuffs before the officer drove away with the three thugs.

***

"Get that silly wig and make up off." Sara had placed the old man in the back seat. She was twisting around from the front seat and staring at the man.

The man pulled the long gray hair off and wiped a bit of putty from his face. "When did you know it was me?"

"As soon as you spoke."

"Why didn't you stop me? Or them?"

Jack though they were good questions. He questioned Sara's actions too.

"Figured I was seeing the actions of a man afraid of getting old. Knew you had to get it out of your system."

Jack felt sorry for Sanders. Sara was not giving him sympathy.

Sara gave one of her annoying smiles. "I had my Taser out, but I knew you could handle those wanna-be men." She laughed. "You proved your daily workout has maintained your physical skills."

"Jack," Sanders said. "Remember never to become involved with a tough woman. They don't yell at you. They just let you make a fool of yourself."

"You didn't make a fool of yourself. Well, not if no one realized who you really were." She turned to Jack. "Better drive to the car rental place. Sanders and I...."

"Jack, drive a couple of blocks away and park." Sanders spoke slowly. "You two need to listen."

***

"There is a lot of talk on the streets in Silver City about the dead man found in Golden Gully. The word is he had a big row with a blonde in a bar a week or so ago. They said the fight appeared to be over money."

"Who's they? Where did you hear this tale? I thought I told you last night to stay out of my case and just concentrate on getting your head screwed back on right."

"You're using bad interrogation techniques when you don't give me a chance to answer. The answer to your first question is I don't know. Two bums—I suppose I should call them homeless men—were talking behind a bar called Cheers. I doubt I could identify them. Furthermore, I'm certain they'd deny everything when you showed them your badges.

　　　　　　　　　　　　　　　　　　J. L. Greger

You'll have to talk to the employees, who are apt to be resistant. The odor emitted by their trash was the worst on the street."

Jack was struck by how Sanders's voice had the same Eastern patrician sound as when he'd lectured to classes at Quantico. As an FBI agent in training, Jack had been impressed. Now as an agent, he agreed with Sara. Sanders was not suited for undercover work, except perhaps as an eastern snob.

Sanders continued, "The men remembered because the blonde woman was young."

Jack sighed. "Probably Eve Cooney."

"Don't know."

"Okay, you've had your fling at playing detective. Thanks for the help. But you also proved my point. When you were at the peak of your game, you'd never have lost your temper over a stupid apple. You blew your cover for nothing."

Jack watched Sanders in his rearview mirror. Sanders seemed to shrink with Sara's comment.

"It all started last week when two of the other aides started calling me the 'old soldier.' Then two days ago, my daughter called me 'stuffy,' and a young senator on the committee asked me for 'fatherly' advice."

Sara got out of the van and slid into the back seat next to Sanders. "Honey, the other aides are jealous." She massaged his hands. "And your daughter called me, too. You drive her crazy. She's clerking for a district federal judge in Manhattan. She's not a little girl, but you treat her like one." She kissed his cheek. "I really think you should take the advice I gave last night."

"I would feel uncomfortable seeing the psychologist you work with in Albuquerque."

"You'd feel more uncomfortable seeing a psychologist in Washington. My friend doesn't know anyone important in Washington."

"I will have plenty of time to ponder it while you and Jack interview the Cooneys in Silver City."

Sara patted his hand. "Jack can keep this van and do the interviews while we return the old clunker you rented and rent a decent car to drive back to Albuquerque."

Sanders placed Sara's hand back on her own lap. "No, I insist. I will wait in this van while you two do the interviews. I might even call the psychologist you suggested."

Jack wished he'd missed the scene as he started the van and drove to the home of the first interviewee. He felt uncomfortable seeing the inner workings of Sara's and Carbonne's relationship. He pitied Sanders and suspected Carbonne had decided starting a family with young wife was a way to avoid Sanders's situation.

CHAPTER 21: Progress?

A gray-haired woman with a cane answered the door. She was delighted when Sara and Jack showed their FBI badges. "Harv, we've got visitors. Maybe they can explain what is going on in Golden Gully."

She led them to a man in a wheelchair. "We're so worried about our daughter. We hadn't heard from her in days, but our relatives in Alma called to tell us about the murder in Golden Gully. Awful, just awful."

"Now, Mother, calm down." The old gentleman patted his wife's hand. "Let's tell the story right. Our daughter, Eve, called this morning and said she'd spent the night at UNM Hospital." He pulled Sara aside. "I wish Eve hadn't called. It upset her mother, and Eve wouldn't even say whether her partner had hurt her."

This was a good time to question the man while Jack was comforting the woman. Sara pulled the man in the wheelchair a few more feet away from Jack and turned the chair. "What's her friend's name?"

"Aiden Cortez. He extracts gold from special copper tailings he gets from the Chino mine." The man shook his head. "He claims there's a seam of gold there that the mine owners missed. Occasionally he also finds gold ore in stream beds. She makes the gold into jewelry."

"Where does he live?"

"Eve doesn't say."

Sara sensed the old man was uncomfortable because he had lowered his voice for the last answer. She heard Jack ask the woman, "Did your daughter ever mention a friend named Hank?"

"No. Mainly she talks about her work."

Sara pushed the wheelchair next to the sofa where the old woman sat. "Eve's workshop is great. She must be successful to have such a fine work area."

"Oh, my yes, she sells her jewelry in Santa Fe and New Orleans at Rau Jewelers. That's where she trained for a year after her accident."

The man added, "We loaned her money to build the workshop after she returned from New Orleans fifteen years ago. She repaid us in three years."

"Eve looks so healthy. What type of accident did she have?"

"She fell and had internal injuries."

Sara noticed the woman's voice had lost its lilt but decided to push forward anyway. "Must have been a bad fall. Where did it happen?"

The woman began to bawl. Jack scowled at Sara.

The man turned to Sara. "She was hiking with her boyfriend even though she was five-months pregnant. She fell into a stream bed and the boyfriend ran off."

The woman continued to sob, as the man continued. "When Eve finally crawled home, it was too late. The baby was dead. We took her to doctors in Albuquerque, but it was hopeless. She couldn't have children. We encouraged her to go to New Orleans. She'd already worked with local silversmiths and had applied for a position at Rau Jewelers in New Orleans because she wanted to learn to work with gold."

"What about the boyfriend?"

"The bum disappeared. She never saw him again."

Sara doubted the father's answer. "What did the boyfriend look like?"

"We never met him or saw a picture of him. Eve wouldn't even tell us his name?"

"Strange. A young woman—Wasn't Eve in her early twenties then?—usually likes to talk about her boyfriend."

The woman began to sob again. The man said, "We assumed he was a Native American. She'd spent a lot of time working with Native craftsmen in the area. Most were married. She's always refused to answer our questions and...."

The mother interrupted. "I suspected she fell when they were arguing."

"About what?"

The woman stopped crying and looked up. "Whether to get married."

Sara decided further questions on this topic would yield little. "Let's talk about her business partner now. Have you met him?"

The woman smiled. "Once when we surprised Eve and took a Sunday ride up to Golden Gully. He was handsome with such unusual light blue eyes."

"Anything else you remember about him?"

"He was working behind the workshop. Eve yelled at him and shooed us away when I smelled almonds."

The man shook his head. "Eve was a headstrong child, but after her accident, she developed a real temper. I felt sorry for the guy that day."

Sara looked at Jack. He nodded. "I'm sorry to tell you but I think the man murdered in Golden Gully was your daughter's business partner."

"Mother, I think we said too much."

"Not really." Sara smiled and lied. "We have a number of suspects and are trying to develop timelines at this point."

***

Sara looked around her motel room. It was nice to not to have to blockade the door and cover the patio window with a mattress. She hoped to get a good night's rest. Sanders busied himself arranging food from a Chinese takeout while she and Jack assessed their progress.

"I talked to four people in three Cooney households after we spoke with Eve's parents. They were eager to talk but had little info."

Sara scanned her laptop screen and opened a file. "My phone call to the owner of Rau Jewelers in New Orleans confirmed her parents' comments. Eve Cooney worked with the owner's father for a year, but his father died five years ago."

"Darn, secondhand evidence."

"Not totally. Rau Jewelers still sells Eve's work. The owner felt her work was more refined and delicate than most pieces produced in the Southwest and so appealed to a wider audience. He claimed she's not as productive as she used to be. He estimated he could sell at least twice as much of her work in rose gold. Evidently, it's her specialty."

"Did you locate who sold her work in Santa Fe?"

"Yes, and that's when things got interesting. Eve's gold and silver jewelry is sold by a shop on Canyon Road. Guess who's the manager of the shop?"

"I hate guessing games."

"Courtney Howard."

"Darn, you're lucky. You always pick the most interesting parts of cases."

Sanders snickered. "It's not luck. She has a nose for good leads."

Sara acted as if she hadn't heard the last comments. "Let me tell you about the Howards."

"This is all from the agent in Roswell?"

"Correct. Courtney's father—Tex—is an old-timer in the oil industry. He's now the president of a gas and oil exploration company and is known for his violent temper. He apparently has sued most of his business partners over the last twenty years. Appears he bought the shop in Santa Fe where Courtney works. Courtney's mother is a Dallas socialite."

"Do you think Courtney has met Eve?"

"Probably, but the Roswell agent didn't talk to anyone in Santa Fe."

"Enough shop talk," Sander announced. "It's time to eat."

Jack held up his hand. "One more piece of business. Did you learn anything about Joe Schultz before he came to Golden Gully?"

"Still working on it. I think we shouldn't try to interview him tomorrow. We don't have anything to force his hand."

"Alleluia. We can drive straight home tomorrow because you already returned Sanders's rental car."

"We could talk to Ophelia."

"I read Mace's report. My mother didn't raise a fool."

Sara was glad Jack had made the decision because Sanders had an appointment with a psychologist in Albuquerque at one the next afternoon. She hoped Sanders's delusions and fear were transitory and would respond to cognitive behavioral therapy and wouldn't require antipsychotic and antidepression drugs. What she'd read in the literature online was not encouraging. She blamed herself for not noticing his symptoms sooner. No, that wasn't right. She was guilty of not having the guts to force Sanders to face his symptoms and seek help sooner.

Her inclination was to protect Sanders in his weakened psychological state but suspected it was more important to respect his choices. Even so, she had sent an email to his supervisor on the Senate Intelligence Committee saying he had the flu.

She regretted lying but recognized she might be wrong about his delusions. Through his undercover work, he had found the best clue of the day. When she and Jack had questioned the employees in the dive called Cheers, they'd been shocked. A waitress and a barkeeper had not only recognized the victim but also one of the women in his life. They described argument as a 'real lulu.'"

CHAPTER 22: Decompression

Friday

Sara studied her messages—or lack of them. The medical examiner had not sent his final report on the victim. Winslow had been sent to collect evidence at another murder scene. Many of the samples collected in Golden Gully had not been tested for DNA, even by the quick-and-dirty method, but the ore samples had been delivered to the proper lab in Socorro. On his own initiative, Winslow had also delivered samples collected from along the quarter acre behind Eve's root cellar, which was covered with a fine gray gravel and a few "interesting" soil and rock samples from along the stream. Beau, Garth, and Mace had not filed their reports on their activities in Catron County, either.

Jack was catching up on the paperwork from another case and monitoring all the suspects at University Hospital. Sheridan was undergoing more tests. Eve had made it clear before she left for the airport, she'd only answer more questions in the presence of a lawyer. Doctors advised Hank was still mildly sedated. He'd responded to all of Jack's questions the same way, "Had to protect Eve."

Sara couldn't believe it. She didn't need to do anything more this afternoon. She couldn't decide whether she was relieved or disappointed.

She'd like to pick up Bug from the neighbors and go home, but Sanders wouldn't be back with her car for another hour. Sara rechecked her "to-do" list and called the four tourists, besides Phil and Nancy Maggio, who had been on Etta's tour of Golden Gulley. They were all eager to hear about developments in the case but provided no additional information. Sara wasn't in the mood to chat.

She was surprised Sanders still had not returned from the psychologists by two-thirty but was not alarmed. She started tracing Joe Schultz's background. She was glad she'd asked all the residents of Golden Gully for their birth dates and birthplaces when she and Jack collected their cheek swabs for DNA. Although people often lied about their past, they usually seemed to report their birthdates—at least the month and day—honestly. She quickly determined Joe had given the same date when he renewed his driver's license. She then checked records on his vehicles, particularly an old Ford truck. It had been purchased in Silver City fifteen years before. Using records of various insurance exchange and credit card companies, she found evidence suggesting he'd moved from Wisconsin about twenty years ago. It made sense: Joe had reported he was born in Milwaukee, Wisconsin.

She checked Wisconsin obituaries for anyone with last name of Schultz during the past thirty years. She hoped she'd find an obituary in which a Joe or Joseph Schultz was mentioned as a relative. Dozens of obits met the criteria. One surprised her. A young man named Paul Schultz had died in a deer hunting accident twenty-one years earlier near Mineral Point, Wisconsin. The obituary noted he had three brothers: Aaron, Joseph, and John. All appeared to live in Mineral Point at the time. She found no records of an Aaron or a Joseph Schultz—in the appropriate age range—still living in Wisconsin but located a John Schultz who still lived in Mineral Point. She called.

A woman answered and claimed John was baling hay and couldn't be reached until after seven. She claimed his brothers—Aaron and Joseph—had left Wisconsin about twenty years before after the death of another brother. They had never written home to their mother or her husband, John.

Sara suddenly realized it was late in the afternoon. She called the psychologist's office. A secretary said Sanders had left the office two hours earlier. Sara tried to control her panic. She texted and emailed Sanders. She ran down to Carbonne's office.

Sanders and Carbonne were talking.

Carbonne waved Sara in. "We couldn't decide whether you were serious about not treating him like a wounded bird or whether you got absorbed in a case. We expected you to come looking for him at least an hour ago. I called Barbara. She suggested we meet at Tamaya for supper at six-thirty."

Sanders pulled out a chair for Sara. "It's Friday night. The psychologist said I had a normal amount of depression about the turns in my career and should relax more." He leaned close to Sara and whispered, "No apparent delusions."

"Why are we are sitting here? Let's pick up Bug and go to Tamaya."

***

Barbara waddled into the outside section of the cafe at Tamaya. The summer heat and nine months of pregnancy had taken their toll on the vivacious woman. She was flushed and looked uncomfortable. "I think this was my last week at work before our daughter is born." She lowered herself onto the chair that Carbonne held for her and then grabbed his hand. "I can manage work at my desk, but it's too hard— looking presentable and acting enthused—as I talk to audiences."

Sara studied Barbara's face. "I know some women brag about working until the day the baby is born, but that's silly. You must have tons of last-minute things to do. You're not only having a baby, but you're a new homeowner."

Carbonne waived to the waiter. "On the way over, Barbara gave me a list of things to do this weekend." He turned to Sanders. "No one ever warned me about the endless work around a house. I guess it's why I lost contact with so many friends after they bought a home. But you never mentioned being stressed by little errands and repairs. What's your secret?"

Sara wondered whether Sanders would be honest. She patted Bug who sat in his stroller between her and Sanders and watched the waiter take Carbonne's and Barbara's drink orders.

"I have employed a trusted housekeeper for many years. She's the daughter of my parents' housekeeper. She maintains my condo in Washington whether I'm there or not—like for the months I was in Brazil. She employs workmen to do repairs as needed, pays household bills, and shops for my groceries—I leave her a list of what I want to eat, of course. She also performs the same services for another nearby household on Capitol Hill in D.C."

Carbonne's jaw dropped. He just stared at Sanders. Barbara pursed her lips.

Sara doubted Carbonne and Barbara had ever appreciated how privileged Sanders's lifestyle was. She had found it hard at first to adjust to Sanders's expectations. He thought a well-run home was always meticulously clean and the refrigerator and freezer were always full of whatever ingredients he wanted.

Sanders had adjusted to her farm-style cooking and less than perfect housekeeping. He had not only learned to accept the clutter associated with Bug but seemed to enjoy the dog's company almost as much as Sara. Sara had even trained Sanders to do his own laundry when he stayed at her house and to make his own coffee in the morning. The latter had been easy. He was used to making his own coffee at his own condo.

She decided the pause after Sanders's admission was too long. "Well, Sanders hasn't seen our 'to do' list for this weekend yet. He's doing laundry while Bug and I visit Hank and Sheridan at University Hospital on Saturday. Then we're grocery shopping."

"Paul has a bit more strenuous weekend ahead," said Barbara. "The walls in the baby's room need a second coat of paint, and the crib needs to be assembled."

Sara tried not to smile. Barbara had disliked how Carbonne had imitated Sanders and used only his last name. She'd insisted before she married Carbonne that he accept she would call him by his first name: Paul. It was one of the reasons that Sanders had claimed "poor Carbonne is henpecked." Sara looked at the beaming Carbonne and knew he was happy with his choices. She studied Sanders and doubted the same could be said for Sanders.

CHAPTER 23: The Twilight Zone

Saturday

Bug strutted down the long, window-lined hallway from the campus entrance of University Hospital. Jack was waiting near the entrance to the food court. He'd not seen Bug in action before at the hospital and snorted. "That dog thinks he owns the place."

Sara looked down to see Bug was sitting properly at her feet. "Of course. He's an official pet therapy dog. Let's visit Sheridan first."

As they walked along the hallways and rode the elevator, Bug stayed close to Sara's side except when a patient or staff person greeted him by name, which occurred several times.

The door to Sheridan's room on the third floor of the old wing of the hospital was open. A ramrod straight, older woman stood at the door complaining. "They said they'd release you at ten. It's five minutes after ten now, and no one has come with your release papers yet. Don't they realize we have a five-hour drive to get home?"

Jack slowed and stepped behind Sara. "Must be Ophelia Murphy. Sheridan said she was going to drive him home."

"Coward."

***

Bug sat when Sara extended her hand to show her badge. "Miss Murphy. We've come to talk to Sheridan a bit before he leaves."

"Better hurry. They'll be releasing him any moment."

Sara saw no reason to say that she'd seldom seen a patient leave the hospital less than two hours after their expected release time. She saw Sheridan sitting on a nearby chair. Bug walked up to him, waved his luxurious black and white tail, and settled at Sheridan's feet.

Sheridan petted Bug. "You didn't tell me you had such a well-behaved dog. Should have known. You've trained Jack and Winslow the same way." Sheridan looked up and saw Jack standing behind Sara. "Sorry, but it's true."

"Sheridan, we understand that Sheriff Bob..." It seemed strange to refer to the Catron County Sheriff like a cartoon character. "...has recommended you act as sheriff until he recovers."

Ophelia Murphy retreated from the door apparently so she could participate in the conversation. "Hmmf. That mama's boy wants to turn a little wound to his hand into a three-month vacation."

Sheridan smiled at Ophelia. "Now dear, why don't you check on my paperwork at the nurse's station?"

As soon as Ophelia stomped off, Sheridan pulled his snuff box from his pocket and packed his cheek. "Ophelia doesn't like my habit. I have to sneak a pinch when she's not around."

"What's your take on Hank?"

"Eve's lying. Hank wouldn't have tied Eve up or hurt her. I'm going to have find out why, or I'll have to add another charge against Hank." He frowned. "Or will the FBI prosecute him? I'd rather you didn't. Federal prosecutors are less sympathetic than local authorities. Hank's not a bad boy, just easily confused by women and not too bright."

"You didn't see the walls in his bedroom. He likes them young."

"Oh, dear. The locals might understand him shooting Sheriff Bob but not messing with their little girls."

Sara heard Jack behind her humming the theme song to Rod Serling's *The Twilight Zone.*

"I think jurisdiction on this case depends a lot on what Hank says when we question him. The murder in the Last Chance Bar occurred on federal property—the Gila National Forest. That's FBI business. He shot the sheriff on the state easement along the road." Sara nodded toward Jack. "He and I don't want to extend our authority to something under the sheriff's jurisdiction unless the two crimes are tied together in an important way. Do you want to be present when we question Hank? We're going to talk to him after we leave you."

"Not me nor Bob. Ophelia wants to get home. She doesn't like to drive after dark, and this trip gives us a chance to eat in a better restaurant than we have in Reserve. We thought we might go to the Olive Garden. I talked to Sheriff Bob last night. He hates the hassle of interviewing suspects. Hank's your problem while he's in University Hospital."

Jack had crowded close to hear Sheridan. He snorted. "Man, what's with Sheriff Bob?"

Sheridan spat into a cup but otherwise ignored Jack's comment. "I'll talk to the local district attorney to arrange the arraignment of Hank for next week on assault of a law enforcement officer. The other matter will upset Ophelia—bad image for her house—but I think the district attorney will be angry if I don't share the photos with him." He's shook his head. "Poor Hank. Suppose I've got to start the paperwork to remove

J. L. Greger

him from the sheriff's office permanently. Doesn't look like we'll be able to call the shooting of Sheriff Bob an accident like I'd hoped."

Jack hummed the theme to *The Twilight Zone* again. Sara suppressed a cough. "How could you pass it off that way?"

"The local DA and any locals recruited for a jury would know Sheriff Bob is high strung." He looked around the room. "Ophelia's not back. So, I can admit that Bob winged a deputy a few years back when he was arresting a drunk driver. We in the office covered for him."

Jack pulled Sara toward the door as he hummed *The Twilight Zone* theme. Sara braced her legs. "One more question. Did Joe Schultz ever talk about his family or past?"

Sheridan looked down. "I wondered when you'd get suspicious about him. Never heard him say one word about his childhood—anything before he came to Golden Gulley. Unusual." He sighed. "Did you look at him? Looks a lot like your victim—nose, eyebrows, chin—but hair and eye color are different. And of course, Joe's thirty pound heavier."

***

The conversation with Sheriff Bob was short. He handed Jack a short, typed note:

> *Deputy Sheridan Evers will serve as Sheriff of Catron County until I've recovered from my injury.*

The signature was unreadable. Sheriff Bob said, "I'm fixing to sit this case out. Don't want my family to have to choose between me and Hank."

"Darn chicken excrement," Jack said as he led Sara to Hank's new room outside the ICU. "Try to look pretty and wink at him. I don't think Hank knows you shot him."

***

Hank was sitting up in bed when Sara entered the room. She winked at him.

"You're too pretty to work for the FBI." He yawned. "I was sitting here trying to decide if I'm in deep trouble. What do you think?"

Sara figured Jack expected her to answer when she heard him humming *The Twilight Zone* theme again. "Well, I think it depends if you answer our questions honestly and fully. Jack will read you your rights. Then I'll start with something simple."

"I've memorized those words on the scrap of paper I keep in my wallet. Skip them."

Jack read Hank his rights anyway.

"Why did you bring a gun with you when you went to meet Sheriff Bob?"

Hank bit his lip. "Don't know exactly. Eve handed it to me. Said I might need it." Hank looked at Sara like a dog waiting to be petted.

Sara decided to change her plan. She lifted Bug and put him on the bed next to Hank. "I brought my friend Bug. He likes to visit people in the hospital."

Hank began to stroke Bug's soft hair. "Pretty little thing. His flat face makes him look smart."

"He sure is. He knows when people don't tell the whole truth."

"How?"

Sara ignored Jack's humming. "I'll show you. Hank, why do you think Eve gave you the gun?"

"She was scared. You..." He waved his hand between Jack and Sara. "...and Sheriff Bob would try to arrest her."

"Why would she think that?"

"She was always afraid."

"Why?"

"Don't know."

Sara tugged on Bug's leash, so he moved away from Hank's hand. "Bug is moving away from you. He doesn't believe you."

Hank shrugged his shoulders. "She and Aiden kept a lot of gold around."

"They should have thought the police would protect them and their gold."

"They thought you and for sure the sheriff would talk too much, and people would start trying to find their gold."

"What else?"

"She was afraid." He gulped. "She'd be accused of killing Aiden."

Sara thought she'd finally gotten an honest answer and went on to her next series of questions. "Did you recognize the murder victim when you first entered the Last Chance Bar?"

"No, it was dark. I pulled the curtains open."

"So did you recognize him then?"

"Sure, his blue eyes were staring at me."

Jack stopped humming; Sara managed to not say *gotcha*. "Did you turn him over then or first move him from under the counter?"

"Eve wanted him in a location easier for Etta to find. I moved him."

"I don't understand why you and Eve would visit the Last Chance Bar early in the morning."

"It wasn't in the morning. It was about eight on Sunday night. Eve and I sometimes go there in the evening for…"

"A little excitement?"

"Yeah, that's it. The bar is real cozy."

Sara tried to ignore the mental image growing in her mind. The wood floor of the bar was dirty, splintered, and disgusting. The counter wasn't much better. "Was Eve surprised when she saw Aiden's body?"

Hank leaned back on his pillow. "Don't remember her being surprised. Funny, she pulled plastic gloves out of her jean's pocket and started looking for something."

Jack grabbed Sara's arm. "Let's talk in the hall."

Sara scooped up Bug. "We'll be right back."

As Sara stepped to the door, Hank said, "She was looking for broken glass. After she bagged the big pieces, she told me where to put the body."

Jack stared at Sara. "Why do cases always break on weekends? Are we sure he's not hallucinating from his medications?"

"I'll ask for a psych profile to be done on Hank ASAP. I don't want the comments we got to be stricken from the record because a defense lawyer claims we questioned Hank when he was heavily sedated. You'd better get the doc you talked to in the ICU to reaffirm that Hank is up to being questioned."

"And?"

"I'm too tired to pursue the case this weekend. Sanders needs some company. And I don't think any of the likely suspects are going to disappear."

"We're done for the weekend?"

"Yes. I'll notify the DA's office that this case could turn into a jurisdictional fight. No one wants it."

CHAPTER 24: Angry Blondes

Monday

Aura of the Southwest on Canyon Road in Santa Fe was a chic gallery with walls and display cases in black and light aqua. The two clerks wore black slacks and tops with hand-woven scarves in various shades of aqua. Both ignored Sara and Jack when they entered the shop. Sara figured the clerks assessed them as unable to afford the wares in the gallery. The clerks also resisted "bothering" the manager in the back room until Jack showed his badge and insisted.

The manager—Courtney Howard—made the two clerks seem dowdy and pleasant. Courtney wasn't a natural beauty. She wore her blonde hair pulled back into a severe French twist. Her eyebrows were too prominent and her nose too big, but from her discreetly polished mother-of-pearl fake fingernails to her perfect pearl earrings, she looked expensive.

Sara expected Jack to be bowled over when Courtney fluttered her eyelashes, but he wasn't. He said, "We're investigating a man you know as Aiden or Alex Cortez."

Her perfectly outlined pink lips changed from a pout to a sneer. "I don't know him well."

"Don't diss me. We know your father and Mr. Cortez own this gallery."

"The man is a fake."

"When did you learn he was already married?"

Courtney's voice lost a bit of its haughtiness. "Come to my workroom."

The workroom had a file cabinet, two easels, and a large table with several paintings and photographs in various stages of being framed. "His wife sent a copy of his marriage license and a note to my parents' home several weeks ago. She had the gall to ask my father how much her joint holdings with Alex were worth to him? She didn't even try to contact me. She called me 'a foolish child' and asked if I was pregnant yet."

Sara noted Courtney's voice wavered but there were no tears in her eyes and her fists were clenched. She wondered whether the victim liked tough women or whether their experiences with him made them tough. Probably a little of both. Sara knew her motherly routine wouldn't induce the young woman to talk. So, her comments and questions were direct. "Etta did you a big favor. When was the last time you saw the man you knew as Alex Cortez?"

"Don't know. Several weeks ago."

"I think we'd all better sit down." Jack pulled chairs to the table "We won't leave until we get straight answers. When did you last see Alex—the man you wanted to marry."

"Marry? I wouldn't marry him."

Sara handed her a copy of the letter Etta received. "The lawyer, representing Alex, notified Etta that Alex wanted a divorce because he wanted to marry you."

"Means nothing."

"Your father ran roughshod over a lot of people during the last thirty years. Those people are talking. They think you're spoiled."

Jack snickered. "They say you met your match in Alex Cortez. Do you really want us to keep talking to your father's associates in the oil and gas exploration companies of New Mexico and west Texas?"

Sara thought she saw Courtney blink. "I've found those wildcatters have a colorful way of talking about women, especially if they think they're loose. Save yourself a lot of heartache. When was the last time you saw or talked to Alex Cortez?"

"What if I ask for a lawyer?"

"Fine. A resident FBI agent has an office at the edge of Santa Fe. Your lawyer can meet us there. Until now, we were just asking for simple info."

Jack snickered. "Seems odd you want a lawyer unless you're hiding something. We know Alex Cortez was a jerk. When was the last time you saw or talked to Alex?"

Courtney flipped open her phone. She pointed to the date. "We had lunch on Friday a week ago in Silver City."

Sara noted Etta reported finding the victim's body the following Monday. The medical examiner estimated the victim had been bound for two or three days before he was killed on Sunday afternoon or early evening. Courtney had to be one of the last persons who saw Alex alive besides the murderer. "Why did you meet there? It wasn't convenient for you. Your home in Santa Fe and your parents' home in Carlsbad are both more than five hours away from Silver City."

"I'd taken the day off and drove down from Santa Fe. Alex and I needed to talk."

"About what?"

Courtney stared at Sara. "Things. You're too old to understand."

Jack looked up from scanning something on his phone and laughed. "You' haven't seen her boyfriend."

Courtney squinted.

"I saw *CHEERS* written next to your appointment at eleven with Alex. Is that where you met?

Courtney was silent.

"We've already talked to a waitress and bartender at the place. They said you two had a big row."

"I'm calling my lawyer."

***

Sara talked to a sergeant in the Silver City Police Department as Jack arranged for Courtney's lawyer to meet them in the FBI's satellite office in Santa Fe. As soon as Sara had outlined the situation, the sergeant said, "Heard there was a murder at Golden Gully. We're glad the body was found on federal land, and we didn't have to work with the Catron County Sheriff's Office."

Sara was curious about what he was implying but wanted answers to her basic questions before Courtney's lawyer appeared. So, she sent photos of Courtney and Alex after the sergeant agreed to have an officer stop by the Cheers restaurant and see whether anyone besides the waitress and bartender, whom She and Jack had talked to previously, remembered the couple.

The sergeant called back an hour later. "Your couple made quite a scene. The owner confirmed the stories of his waitress and bartender. He also said that the man was a regular, but the woman didn't look like the woman he usually saw with the man. And she paid with her credit card."

Sara was pleased but couldn't resist asking one more question. "Why don't you like working with the Catron County Sheriff's Office?"

"No one in law enforcement in southwestern New Mexico was surprised when Hank shot Sheriff Bob. The big question in our minds is: why? Never the obvious in Catron County." The sergeant chuckled. "I always deal with Sheridan when Silver City must work with Catron County. He's a junkyard dog with a long memory."

***

Sara thought the interview with Courtney in the FBI satellite office in Santa Fe started well. Courtney quickly conceded that she'd paid for her lunch with Alex at the Cheers restaurant and even added, "Cheap b****** wouldn't pay any of his bills to me."

　　　　　　　　　　　　　　　　　　　　J. L. Greger

Sara immediately asked, "What bills?"

The lawyer nudged Courtney and she said, "I claim my fifth amendment rights."

The rest of the hour-long interview followed the same pattern. Jack or Sara asked a question; Courtney refused to answer.

***

As soon as Jack jumped into the car, he said, "When I was a kid, I loved playing the video game *Angry Birds*. This case reminds me of the game. Only this should be called Angry Blondes. Do you realize all our suspects are blonde or once were? And they're as mean as the birds in *Angry Birds*." Jack shook his head. "Sorry I couldn't get Courtney to slip up and say more."

"I really thought the picture of Etta Cortland when she was dating Alex might snap Courtney out of her standard answers to our questions. But it didn't faze her. Even when I pointed out Etta had once been blonde and pretty." Sara thought for a few seconds. "Can't really blame the women for being angry. Our victim certainly treated all of them unfairly." Sara pursed her lips. "I don't like referring to him as a victim. He may be the only one dead, but there's a lot of victims in this case. Besides Etta, Eve, and Courtney, he hurt his daughter, Jennifer, and his family in Wisconsin."

Jack turned onto the I-25 ramp for Albuquerque. "I know you talked people in Wisconsin while we drove up to Santa Fe, but you didn't give me details."

"The mother is now in a nursing home. The siter-in-law didn't tell me much, but an old cop in Mineral Point, Wisconsin—their hometown—filled in the details. About twenty-one years ago—during deer hunting season in the fall—Aaron, Joseph, and Paul Schultz went hunting. The bullet that killed Paul came from Aaron's rifle. Joseph testified at the coroner's inquest that Aaron and he saw movement in a thicket and thought it was deer. Aaron fired. The jurors declared the shooting was an accident."

"Odd, don't you think?"

"Not really, one or two deer hunters are killed most years during deer hunting season in Wisconsin. The cases are almost always closed as accidents. However, the old cop claimed this case aroused suspicion because Aaron and Paul often argued. Aaron left the state less than six months after the accident, Joseph a year later. The sister-in-law claimed neither of them ever contacted their mother again."

"So, you think Joe Schultz of Golden Gulley is Joseph Schultz from Mineral Point, Wisconsin?"

The Man Who Looked for Death   117

"Yes. And Aaron Schultz became Alexander Cortland who worked at the Chino mines in New Mexico about twenty-one years ago. Alex married Etta twenty years ago and disappeared in Brazil about fifteen years ago."

"How long do you think he stayed in Brazil?"

"Good question. U.S. Passport records indicate Alexander Cortland left the U.S. fifteen years ago. They don't mention an Aiden Cortez. Five mining claims were filed in the names of Aiden Cortez and Joe Schultz between three and fourteen years ago. And the residents of Golden Gully and even Sheridan mentioned a strange trapper with blue eyes at various times. The times of those sitings aren't clear, but several seemed to be almost twenty years ago and some as recent as ten years ago."

"So, he returned to the U.S. fourteen years ago, probably illegally. It wouldn't have been hard through Mexico with the Spanish last name of Cortez."

"But he may have started using the Cortez last name earlier."

"Eve Cooney could clear up the confusion."

"Yes, so could Joe. But they won't if we don't scare them with threats of arrests."

"When did Courtney enter the scene? Didn't you tell me there were two mining claims filed in her and Alex Cortez's name during the last three years?"

"Yes. Means she lied when she claimed she first met Alex Cortez a little over a year ago."

Jack shook his head. "Our victim was reckless. No normal individual changes his name that many times or promises to marry several women apparently simultaneously. You didn't find any indication of illegal activities, did you?"

"I suspect the shooting in Wisconsin wasn't an accident. Both Joe's and the victim's actions suggest guilt. I also suspect he broke multiple laws for poaching and petty theft over the last twenty years."

"Nothing major. That's why Sheridan knew of him but never appeared to try to arrest him."

"Let's go back to the question I asked last week. It's time to give our victim a standardized name in the records. I vote for Alexander Cortland because that the name on the most legal documents—his passport, marriage certificate, and twenty mining claims."

"Doesn't matter to me. Though I can't wait to see Joe Schultz's face when we ask him about Aaron Schultz."

"So, we drive to Golden Gully tomorrow?"

Jack shifted in his seat. "I drove to and from Santa Fe today. I can't say I'm eager to drive five hours tomorrow and do another overnight stay at the Catwalk Resort. What will Sanders say?"

Sara didn't answer for several minutes as she texted a message. "First off, I don't want to stay at the Catwalk Resort ever again. Nothing wrong with the place but I felt like I was in a fishbowl there."

"Agreed."

"Yesterday Sanders requested a month leave of absence from the Senate Intelligence Committee for health reasons. They didn't mind because their August break is approaching. Then he decided to cook gourmet style and invited Carbonne and Barbara for dinner tonight. You're welcome to come and bring a guest along."

"What kind of meal?"

"Sanders started making cassoulet yesterday. We ran all over Albuquerque trying to find the duck and the pork belly he wanted. Today he's also making *Tarte des Alpes*—basically a pie with a jam filling—but he's using fresh raspberries to make the filling."

Sara saw Jack was frowning. "Don't worry Sanders's cassoulet is outstanding. It rivals ones I've eaten in bistros in Provence. He'll serve it with a simple salad and fresh bread."

"Sounds like a lot of work for a Monday night meal."

"Sanders likes to cook and needs to keep busy. The problem is we'll gain weight if he continues to cook like this. He's got to find a new hobby." Her phone pinged and she checked her new text. "He's game for a trip to Golden Gully. He even volunteered to drive. We can take my car instead of an FBI van, so it's legal." She stared at Jack. "Will you come to dinner tonight?"

"No guest. I think a pregnant woman and you would scare any of my casual dates, but I'm willing to try cassoulet. I've heard of it but never tried it."

"Good. That means we'll have fewer leftovers."

CHAPTER 25: Sanders Finds a Hobby?

"Don't feel guilty that you must go to work. Bug and I will be fine." Sanders kissed Sara on the cheek. Then he pulled her closer. "Last night was great."

After Sara drove away, Sanders led Bug back in the house. "We're back where we were several months ago. What am I going to do with the rest of my life?"

Bug cocked his head and licked Sanders's hand.

"You're right. I'll worry about dinner first."

Bug ignored Sanders as he chopped the pork belly into pieces but danced at Sanders feet—almost tripping Sanders twice—as the pork belly began to render its fat and brown in the pan. Once the pieces of pork were browned, Sanders removed them. He repeated the process with the duck, pork sausage and onions and carrots. After an hour. Bug was disgusted by Sanders's slow progress and settled into his bed. Bug didn't even lift his head when Sanders finally assembled the casserole. Sanders guessed Bug was used to Sara's cooking which yielded results faster but perhaps was not as good.

As Sanders cleaned up the kitchen, he knew why Sara never made cassoulet, although she ordered it frequently in restaurants. He also recognized it was time to stop stewing about his problem and think about solutions.

He'd learned a lot in the previous two months. One, he would only stay in his position as a staff member for the Senate Intelligence Committee for six months at most.

Two, situations that seemed obvious in the field were not obvious to senators during a hearing. He was surprised the fault wasn't with the senators as he'd always assumed. He'd found most staff in the State Department, CIA, and FBI filed sketchy reports. He'd read hundreds of these reports during the last month while preparing senators for hearings. Most didn't include all the facts needed to understand the situation. State Department staff seldom—and FBI and CIA agents never—included their emotions or descriptions of their allies' or adversaries' suspected feelings in their reports.

Three, the assistant secretaries, who usually reported on situations to the Senate Intelligence Committee, were too political. They avoided revealing anything that might remotely make them or their boss look bad. Thus, they further sanitized field data into unrecognizable mush.

Four, many of the young staffers who worked for the Senate Intelligence Committee, at least two senators, and his old boss—an Assistant Secretary of State—considered the hearings to be battle zones. He knew he couldn't work for his old boss again. She created confrontations unnecessarily.

He thought teaching at university level might be an option. He doubted his insights were unique but thought his experience could be applied usefully in classrooms. Administrators at Quantico had told him several times they would be pleased if he taught more than one class in every twenty-week training session. Many universities had established criminal justice majors and were looking for instructors. To be honest, he didn't want to leave his condo in Washington, which eliminated many of the better teaching opportunities.

He was preparing the raspberry filling for the *Tarte des Alpes* when Sara called around eleven. She wanted to add Jack to the guest list for tonight and reminded him that his pastry might need more added moisture in New Mexico than in Washington due to difference in humidity.

Her call reminded Sanders that he and Sara had partially solved one aspect of his problem two months ago. They had decided trying to establish a single residence, and living together all the time was a mistake. She wanted to keep a home in Albuquerque and continue to participate in various charitable activities at the hospital. He couldn't imagine selling his condo and losing his housekeeper in Washington.

He knew what Sara would say if she heard his musings. *You're not addressing the real issue. You need more than work in your life.* His daughter, who was clerking for a federal district judge in Manhattan, had said something similar: *Get a life. And not my life.* Last week the psychologist had been more tactful. "You're having a midlife crisis. Perhaps it's more severe because of the stress and violence you experienced in Brazil. The solution is to develop interests outside your work. Then you'll be able to face your biggest fears: growing old and retirement."

He knew he needed a hobby. Although he exercised regularly, it was to stay fit and not because he enjoyed it. He liked being around Bug but didn't want to care for a dog himself. Sara had suggested painting, woodworking, photography, or other crafts as creative hobbies. He hated visiting Sara when she was sewing blankets for patients in the local hospitals. The mess—scraps of fabric and thread—everywhere was annoying. Woodworking, painting, and most crafts would be even messier.

"Come on, Bug. We're going shopping. After I pick up fresh bread for dinner, we'll look at cameras."

***

Sanders hoped Sara would get home at east fifteen minutes before their guests. He wanted to show her his new Cannon. The clerk in the camera shop had advised him to start with a basic starter kit with the camera, including lenses, and memory cards and had given him pointers on which lenses and settings to use when doing portraits of Bug and which to use when shooting landscapes in the Gila National Forest. The clerk advised him to return in two weeks with some of his best and worst photos. Then the clerk would help Sanders decide his true photographic needs.

Sara rushed in at five-thirty. She seemed to relax as she smelled the aromas wafting from the kitchen and saw the table was set and ready for guests. She laughed in delight as she studied the shots Sanders had taken of Bug cuddling a toy. "Golden Gully will give you a chance to check out your new camera and lenses in a variety of ways. I think they're always looking for new photos for their website, but Jack and I may destroy the opportunity for you if we arrest the webmaster."

"Who's the webmaster?"

"One of our chief suspects: Eve Cooney."

"I thought the woman you interviewed today sounded guilty."

Sara sighed. "We have at least three viable suspects—all wives or girlfriends of Alex Cortland." She shrugged. "I'll quote Winslow. 'Alex sure knew how to piss off women.'"

The doorbell rang. All three guests had arrived together.

Barbara looked better than Carbonne. "If the baby comes tomorrow, I'm prepared. My mother has agreed to stay with us during the first two weeks after the baby arrives." She pointed to Carbonne. "Mainly to feed him and help me do laundry."

Carbonne sighed. "Technically I'm eligible for twelve weeks of unpaid leave, but I want to use them after Barbara's maternity leave ends." He rubbed his five-o-clock shadow. "However, I'd almost like to use them this week to avoid having to deal with your case. Do you realize how expensive it is to send a SWAT team by helicopter to the Gila National Forest?"

Sara had hoped to avoid a discussion of their current case and had offered a variety of skewered appetizers—mini cheese balls, pineapple chunks, pickled mushrooms—and beverages to the guests. Her efforts failed.

Jack shook his head. "Man, you don't understand this case. We're stranded miles from other agents with questionable local law enforcement officers. They all seem to have shady backgrounds. Sara likes Sheridan Evers, but I agree with the residents of Golden Gully. The man gives me the willies."

Sara pursed her lips and stared at Carbonne. "Don't blame Jack and me for needing help. I talked to Scott. I think one reason you brought in the SWAT team so quickly was it was a way to train Beau, Mace, and Garth on gender sensitivity."

Carbonne's lip wavered. "You caught me in a way." He paused. "Scott and I knew Beau, Garth, and Mace were good at the physical aspects of being SWAT team members, but they thought like agents from the 1950s. They must change."

Jack had straightened from his relaxed position on the sofa as Carbonne talked. "Are you telling me Scott purposely left the most bigoted agents in Golden Gully?" His voice became louder. "I bet you knew the Catron County Sheriff's Office was close to non-functional." He started to stand.

Sara touched Jack's arm. "Calm down. Carbonne only suspected the problems and knew he could trust us to be sensible. It's not worth getting angry about..." She gave Carbonne a big smile. "...but he's not going to nickel-and-dime us on this case either. I think Beau and Mace show promise. So, he's going to have Beau and Mace help us re-interview all the residents of Golden Gully in light of our new evidence." She stood. "Now let's enjoy this meal."

Sanders lightly tapped Barbara's arm. "Barbara why don't you sit at the head of the table? You've got the most important job ahead of you—by my guess—this coming week."

***

As the guest drove away, Sanders kissed Sara's cheek. "I was worried at first."

"I wasn't once I tasted the cassoulet. No argument is important enough to ruin such a dish. Besides, Barbara knows how to manage Carbonne."

"I felt sorry for Jack. You and Carbonne understood the game you were playing. He did not. You really should be honest with Jack about some of the messy details of law enforcement in New Mexico."

CHAPTER 26: The Haunting Past

Tuesday

Joe looked surprised when Jeanne summoned him to the front door of their home. "Joe, FBI agents are here."

Sara noticed Jeanne didn't return to her previous activities but remained behind Joe. "Perhaps we should talk in private."

Joe shrugged. "We can talk in my workroom out back." He led them to what looked like a ramshackle shed on the outside. The inside was like the house—sturdy, organized, and neat. He pointed at a room filled with a spinning wheel, loom, bags of wool, and shelves full of yarn and knitted items. "That's Jeanne's craft room and storage area." He opened the door to a large room filled with carpentry tools, a sink, a drawing table, a table and chairs, and more cabinetry. "Have a seat."

"Joe, tell me about Aaron and Paul Schultz from Mineral Point, Wisconsin."

Joe stared at Sara for at least thirty seconds. "They were my older brothers in another lifetime."

"What happened about twenty-one years ago?"

"I'd hoped I'd never have to talk about those days again." He closed his eyes. "My older brothers were opposites. Paul, the oldest, was blonde and always pleased my parents. After high school, he took the agriculture short course at the University of Wisconsin in Madison for sixteen weeks. When he returned, he worked with my father on our dairy farm for three years before he asked the daughter of our neighbor to marry him."

Joe stopped talking and stared at the ceiling.

"And what about Aaron?"

"He hated the farm and stormed off to UW-Madison to study engineering. My dad refused to support him. Aaron didn't care. Somehow, he worked enough to support himself while he took courses. He returned home to visit our neighbor's daughter occasionally."

"Oh dear."

"You guessed right. Both of my brothers were courting the same girl. Their teenage bickering turned into real fights. She chose Paul. We didn't see much of Aaron during the following two years, except he returned each year during deer hunting season. The one thing my older brothers liked to do together was to hunt deer. I always tagged along. During the second year, Aaron saw Pauls' wife in a store in Mineral Point before we went hunting. She was seven months pregnant and badly bruised. She'd told my parents she'd fallen down the stairs of the old farmhouse she and Paul rented. I believed her. What would I know? I was a junior in high school."

"What did she tell Aaron?"

"Don't know. All I know is Aaron and Paul argued constantly during our hunting trip but always got quiet if I asked questions. After two days, Aaron stormed out and left Paul and me. We didn't see him again until the following year at hunting season. I knew he was looking for a fight when he walked into our house at the start of hunting season. He asked my mother if she knew her daughter-in-law had fallen again. My mother had replied, 'The poor girl seems to have lost her sense of balance. She's always falling or walking into doors.'"

"Did you know your brother Paul was beating his wife?"

Joe sighed. "By then, everyone did, but we never talked about it. My parents were pleased they had two blonde grandchildren. Paul and my father had doubled the dairy herd."

"What happened next?"

"Paul didn't want to go hunting, but Aaron insisted." Joe stared at Sara. "You know the rest. I thought I saw a deer in a thicket. Aaron shot. We heard a scream. It was Paul. He died on the way to the hospital. I testified at the coroner's inquest and somehow graduated from high school the following May."

"What about Aaron?"

"He went to see Paul's widow after the inquest. I don't know what happened. He never said. He just left town."

"Wait. I thought you two left Wisconsin together." Jack looked as mystified as Sara felt.

"Aaron never gave me details about the next six months of his life. I know he dropped out of UW-Madison a semester short of a degree in engineering. I think he traveled to New Mexico, Colorado, and Arizona. Anyway, he showed up a week after my high school graduation. I still remember how he sauntered into our old dairy barn as I finished milking the cows one evening. 'Are you fool enough to stay around these hypocrites? Or do you want to start a new life? I found a place in New Mexico where we can start over as miners.'"

"What did you say?"

"The truth. I didn't want to be a miner, but I didn't want to be a dairy farmer either. He knew I'd liked my shop classes and internship with a builder while in high school. He said, 'There's always work for a good carpenter. Let's go.'"

Sara could see Jack was as fascinated by the tale as much as she was. "What happened?"

"I said, 'I need a day to think,' but I didn't need to think long. I packed my stuff in two old suitcases and hid them in the hay in the barn that night. The next night when Aaron stopped by, I left with him."

"One question. Was Paul's wife a blonde?"

Joe nodded.

Jack coughed. "Does Jeanne know this story?"

"I never told her."

"Did Aaron as Aiden Cortez tell her?"

"I don't know. I only know she always seemed jumpy when Aiden stopped by."

"Did Aiden ever speak of your time in Wisconsin?"

"Never, but he was always melancholy the week before Thanksgiving. That's deer hunting season in Wisconsin."

***

Sara and Jack retreated to the car to check on Sanders and Bug, who had accompanied them on this trip. They found a note.

Bug and I are going to on a hike. We'll be back by two.

"Good." Sara smiled as she read the note. "We'll have plenty of time to wear Jeanne down. If she's tired, she might slip and give us a clue of what she's hiding."

Jack nodded. "Let me take the lead with Jeanne. I'm going to play the underdog, so be bossy."

***

"Jeanne, it your turn now. We'll interview you in your craft room." Sara left Jack with Jeanne while she asked Joe to manage the two children. When she returned to the craft room, she marched around the room opening drawers and inspecting items in boxes and baskets. However, she listened for her cue from Jack.

"I get so tired of being bossed around." Jack nodded. "Don't you get tired of working so hard here and not really being appreciated?"

Jeanne looked down at her lap. "Not really."

"C'mon. Joe gets out of here when he does projects for the forest service. You're always stuck here."

                                                    J. L. Greger

Jeanne sat like a statue.

"Looks to me like Joe bosses you around the house, and Ramona controls you when you work with tourists. Just like Sara gives me orders."

Jeanne bit her lip.

Sara sat down across a small table from Jeanne "Enough chitchat. What was the first thing you did on the Monday morning a week ago when Etta came running into the saloon screaming about a body at the Last Chance Bar?"

"I told you last week."

"Please answer her questions," Jack whispered. "It will be easier for both of us if you do."

Jeanne shivered and answered the question. A pattern emerged. Sara asked questions and Jack coaxed Jeanne to answer each time. Jeanne's answers differed on minor points from what she and Ramona had said previously.

After twenty minutes, Sara and Jack left Jeanne alone in the craft room with two small cameras and a recorder, which Jack had placed under his chair. Sara and Jack stood outside the room and huddled over his laptop screen.

Jeanne sat quietly for only a minute. Then they heard doors to cabinets being opened and closed. The cameras showed Jeanne's feet moving by cabinets and then standing near her sink. Water was running.

Jack ran into the room. Jeanne was washing a set of four double pointed aluminum knitting needles. "How did the needles get dirty?"

Jeanne turned off the water. "I was trying to teach the girls to knit mittens with these. They ate cookies while they were knitting, and the needles got sticky."

Sara strode over and grabbed the needles with gloved hands. Jeanne didn't resist. "These are small gauge needles. I wouldn't think beginners would use them. I wouldn't. What's your real reason for cleaning the needles?"

Jeanne was trembling now. "You've confused me. These weren't the needles the girls were using."

"Then why did you want to clean them?"

Jeanne's shoulders sagged as she murmured, "I dunno."

Sara decided to take a chance, even though Jack was shaking his head. "Would you be willing to let me take these needles for DNA analysis?" Sara doubted usable DNA would be found on the needles but hoped her comment would make Jeanne admit the truth.

Jeanne shook her head. "No, I don't have to let you take them."

Sara shrugged. "Your choice." Jeanne was agitated enough now to slip and say something useful, especially if she perceived Jack as her ally. "Jack, you're the softie, ask her a few questions."

Jack touched Jeanne's chin and brought her face up. "Are you all right?"

After she nodded, he said, "When did you first see the mountain man around Golden Gully?"

"When he brought meat to Ramona and Ray's trailer. It was before I married Joe."

"When did you realize he was living in a nearby cabin?"

"When I lived with Ramona—before I was married—she used to take me along when she delivered bread and jam to his cabin in exchange for the meat."

Sara wanted to scream. This answer was very different than the one Jeanne gave last week. Jeanne and the rest of the crew in Golden Gully had told a lot of lies. They all knew the blue-eyed mountain man was their neighbor Aiden Cortez.

Jack stayed cool. "I'm curious about the relationship between Eve and Aiden. They lived together for years. What's Eve like?"

Jeanne bit her lip. "My mother said, 'If you can't say something nice about someone, don't say anything.'"

"What makes you say that?"

"Eve wasn't nice to Aiden or Hank. She made Aiden sleep in the shed. Poor Hank was too dumb to know she used him to learn about when Sheridan and the foresters would be looking for poachers, like Aiden. She made Hank think he was protecting the gold she kept around for making jewelry." She took the knitting needles from Sara and walked to the door. "I've got to check on the girls."

***

In the car, Jack said, "That woman is near a breakdown."

"I think Aiden excited her more than scared her. And the woman who answered the last question is not an innocent. I'll bet she and Aiden were lovers."

"Possible. Too bad we couldn't get the knitting needles for analyses. Crazy how protective she was about them."

Sara pulled one needle from her purse. She had eight needles. All the same size but not of the same set. "One of them seems to have rolled into my purse."

                                        J. L. Greger

CHAPTER 27 The Conniving Women of Catron County

"Did you ever feel like the boss hates you?"

Mace shrugged.

"I did when Scott sent us back to Reserve with orders to report to Sara Almquist." Beau tipped his chair back and gazed around the cafe. It was supposedly the best in Reserve. That didn't say much.

"Working with Sara isn't so bad. She does the boring stuff. We don't have to get warrants or talk to shrinks and lab zombies. She gave us reasonable marching orders over lunch."

"Yeah, basically she wants us to clean up the mess in the Catron County Sheriff's Office, so it doesn't gum up the investigation of the murder in Golden Gully." He quickly scanned the psychologist's report on his phone and then studied Sara's note. "He doubts our boy Hank is a pervert. Not schizoid either, but he's a little slow."

Mace had been studying Hank's school and employment records on his phone. "C student but well-liked by teachers. They all said he was polite and tried hard. Nothing new. Miss Murphy said the same last week. He worked in a gas station for two years before going to a police training academy."

"Yeah." Beau didn't bother to scan the analyst's report on his phone but went directly to Sara's summary. "Nothing unusual about Hank's financial records, except on the first Friday of every month he always pulls out five hundred in cash. No pattern to his other cash withdrawals. Sara wondered whether Hank was being bribed. His credit card expenditures occurred mainly in Silver City at Walmart, in restaurants, and at a gun shop." He paused. "Are you sure you didn't see any guns except a service revolver and an old shotgun in his apartment last week?"

Mace had been studying Hank's medical records. "Healthy as a horse."

"Checking out Hank today shouldn't take long. We already talked to everyone in the sheriff's office last week. The gossipy biddy at the front desk and Miss Murphy will know if Hank was being bribed. If so, the most likely candidate is Sheriff Bob or Sheridan Evers. They both knew he was incompetent." Beau smiled. "Got to give Sara credit. She had the psychologist stop by and talk to Sheriff Bob." He scanned this report more slowly. "This report is almost funny. Seems Sheriff Bob admitted he was 'afraid' of guns, disliked getting his hands dirty, but liked running for office."

Mace looked up from his phone. "Sheriff Bob's medical records aren't funny. Severe asthma. The surgeon predicted he'd only regain fifty percent of the usage of his right hand. He's only fifty and has been a sheriff or deputy for twenty years. He needs another five to retire."

Beau stood. "We can't stall any longer. Come hell or high water, we've got to keep Sheridan busy, so he doesn't go down to Golden Gully and scare anyone while Jack and Sara are trying to interview them. I texted him to meet us at Hank's apartment."

***

Sheridan was waiting in his car for Beau and Mace to arrive at Ophelia Murphy's house. Beau noticed Sheridan already had a key to Hank's apartment. *Sheridan could have removed or planted evidence. Nothing to do about it.* Sheridan was now the chief law enforcement officer in Catron County.

They quickly identified how Hank had spent so much in the gun shop in Silver City. His collection of archery equipment in a back closet was impressive. Mace took photos of the apartment again. A quick review suggested changes since he'd taken photos the previous week. All food had been removed from the refrigerator. The kitchen was so clean you could eat off the floor. It appeared the drawers in the kitchen had been lined with fresh paper. Beau hoped he didn't have to explain the situation to a federal prosecutor. The site had not been secured, and Garth and Mace had not checked the back closet last week.

Sheridan recognized the inadequacy of Garth's and Mace's previous work. "Should have put a new lock on the door." He then handed Beau a list of the women in the photos on Hank's wall. Someone had penciled in the birthdates of all the women. All but two were now over eighteen. Those two were both seventeen. Of course, several of them could have been underage when the photos were taken.

Prosecuting the child exploitation charges against Hank would be a nightmare. Beau hoped he wouldn't be summoned to court. The next hour with the Catron County authorities in the Village Hall for Reserve would be bad enough.

***

The mayor was pleasant when Mace, Beau, and Sheridan arrived at the Reserve Village Hall. The county clerk ignored them. A young assistant district attorney for the seventh judicial district in New Mexico, which included Catron County, looked scared as she rushed in from her office in Socorro.

Sheridan was on his best behavior. He spat out his snuff before he entered the building. He'd already apprised the mayor and the county clerk of the situation. The sheriff's office didn't have an internal affairs officer. Sheridan had unofficially served in that role when a clerk in the sheriff's office had come to work drunk. Sheridan had suspended Hank but couldn't fire him without some sort of "official" assessment. He thought the mayor should appoint an acting internal affairs officer from her staff immediately.

Sheridan also wanted the DA to accept Sara's and Jack's reports of the incident where Hank shot Sheriff Bob and accept Garth's and Mace's report on the underage pornography. He emphasized the sheriff's staff was so reduced now that they couldn't complete the investigation themselves. Besides, most of the staff were related to the defendant and the victims.

Beau had carefully considered what he should say. It was not tactful to say: *the Feds won't step in unless you foolishly try to ignore the situation and let Hank remain a sheriff's deputy.* Instead, he said, "Juries in state courts are more apt to understand *special* situations than juries for federal trials, but an FBI agent talked to a lawyer in the U.S. Attorney's Office. He felt Hank could not remain a deputy and must be arraigned for at least two crimes: aggravated assault and sexual exploitation of minors."

The county clerk shrugged. "I have no jurisdiction over the sheriff's office."

The mayor nodded. "The lack of an internal affairs officer in the county sheriff's office is not a concern of the village."

When the assistant DA pulled her long hair back behind her ears, she looked like a teenager. "The easiest solution is to let the FBI and federal courts handle all the investigations on Hank. I understand he's the prime candidate for the murder of Aiden Cortez on *federal* land. You might as well add the two other charges."

While the DA nodded in agreement, the mayor said, "We'd be happy if the FBI and federal courts took jurisdiction of these cases."

Beau was irritated. Sheridan had warned him the three women would be difficut, but he hadn't expected defiance.

He knew the federal prosecutor eventually would probably cut a deal with Hank to get his testimony, but the federal prosecutor expected to drop the likely charge of tampering with evidence. The prosecutor didn't want to mess with the exploitation of minors charges.

As Beau glared at the women's blank faces, he couldn't decide whether they were dumb or great poker players. He decided to try to snow them. "The lack of an internal affairs officer could put the county and town, and all of you personally, in legal jeopardy."

The women whispered back and forth. Finally, the mayor said, "I'll appoint one of my staff to serve as internal affairs officer for the sheriff's office during the next month." She smiled. "That should solve Sheridan's most pressing problem." She turned to Beau. "You don't understand the situation in Catron County. No elected official can afford to insult the Eberles."

The assistant DA grimaced and tossed her long hair back over her shoulder. "My boss will talk to the federal prosecutor. I doubt we can assemble a jury in Catron County if we eliminate all relatives of the defendant and potential witnesses."

Beau managed not to curse. Sheridan didn't try to contain his feelings.

***

After the defeat at the village hall, Beau was determined to learn why Hank withdrew five hundred dollars on the first Friday of each month from his checking account. Sheridan was clueless. The gossipy clerk in the sheriff's office simpered. "His lady friends claim he's generous and buys them lots of flowers."

Beau thought that only explained the odd purchases from the Walmart in Silver City. Most men didn't buy several bouquets of flowers every month.

Sheridan sighed. "Ophelia will know."

The conversation with Ophelia was embarrassing to Sheridan.

"Oh, sweetie, you're so naïve." She pinched his cheek. "That's what makes you so cute."

Sheridan's face turned beet red.

"Hank gives me a bouquet every month when he gives me the rent check. I hoped you'd notice and think I had a secret admirer."

"Ophelia, stop it. How would Hank use that much money?"

"He gives it to his mother. She always brags about her son at church circle meetings and says she couldn't manage on social security without Hank's help."

Beau felt sorry for Sheridan. "How about we clock out for the day and have a beer?"

Sheridan snorted. "Whiskey is in order." As they walked to their cars, he muttered, "I'd rather be in a gun fight than face another day with conniving women."

CHAPTER 28: Which Details Are Important?

"You can't come in," Eve screamed.

"We have a search warrant for where Aiden Cortez, aka Alex Cortland, lived and worked and for the vehicles he drove." Sara pushed a copy of the warrant through the inch of space between the door and the jamb when the chain was fastened to the open front door of Eve's cabin.

Eve screamed obscenities before she said, "I'll open the shed but not the cabin. It's where he lived and worked."

"And the root cellar."

"No."

"The barrels of salt were used to tan the pelts found in another barrel. I believe he—not you—trapped animals for fur."

***

Men's clothes hung at the front of Aiden's bedroom closet—as before. But Jack had studied the photographs Winslow had made last week when the shed was searched. Now, Jack threw the clothes on the bed to reveal a door at the back of the closet. Behind it, were rifles, a rack of knives, and traps. Jack put a padlock on the closet and placed yellow tape across the door. "The lab needs to check the weapons."

"I hate to force Winslow to come here again."

Jack laughed. "It will give him an excuse to visit the new schoolteacher at the Zuni pueblo."

Jack roamed around the shed and root cellar looking for more secret compartments while Sara studied the photos Winslow had taken last week and compared them to the current situation. Winslow had been thorough. Eve appeared not to have worked much in the lab during the last week except to mold a couple of rings and place tiny insets of amethyst and topaz into the setting of one ring.

Jack found only one other hidden stash. It was in Aiden's closet. The concrete floor had been poured to leave a two-foot square hollow. In the hollow were shoe boxes filled with vials containing gold flakes.

Sara had tried to discourage Eve from watching the search but had not insisted Eve leave the premises.

When Eve spotted the shoe boxes, she screamed. "I knew the b****** wasn't telling the truth."

Jack winked at Eve. "When wouldn't Aiden tell you the truth? Was it when you bound him to the chair in the Last Chance Bar?"

Eve's jaw hung slack for a few seconds. "I don't have to answer without my lawyer present." She slammed the front door to the shed as she stomped out.

Sara patted Jack on the back. "I don't think this search is worth any more time."

Jack nodded. "Time for more darn interviews. You should take the lead with Ramona because you connected with her last time. Don't rush it."

Sara thought Jack was no longer the green recruit he'd been three months earlier. She suspected Carbonne would be transferring him to another partner after this case. It was too bad. "I talked to Sanders. He and Bug having been sitting and watching the Schultz and Miller homesteads while we were here. He says Bug is bored, and he's seen no movement outside at either site, except for the two girls jumping rope. Of course, Joe or Jeanne could have called the Millers."

***

The smell of freshly baked bread wafted from the Millers' trailer. "We're baking today. Ray reads the newspaper or a novel to me when I'm baking when he's not slicing and wrapping the baked goods so they're ready to sell." Ramona blushed slightly as she wiped her hands on her apron. "I know it sounds silly, but we still enjoy each other's company."

"Sounds wonderful." Sara smiled. "I suspect we wouldn't be here today if the younger residents of Golden Gully had learned to enjoy their partners' company more."

Ramona's face lost its rosy flush. "The second batch of bread is rising now. How can I help you?" She motioned Jack and Sara to the kitchen table where Ray sat.

Sara and Jack had agreed to interview the couple separately, but Sara thought acting casual might lead to a situation more conducive to conversation. Jack didn't flinch when Sara said, "We'll talk to you together. Please don't be annoyed if our questions are tedious. Federal lawyers insist all details in witnesses' testimonies be verified." Sara proceeded to ask questions about the discovery of the body.

"Did you flip the body over when you and Jeanne went to the Last Chance Bar?"

"No. It was obvious he was dead. I thought the police didn't want you to tamper with a dead body." She looked questioningly at Sara. "Isn't that, right?"

"Yes, but many don't take the advice. What did Etta and Jeanne do?"

"Etta stayed with her group at the saloon. She didn't return to the bar. Jeanne started talking about Aiden Cortez as soon as she saw the body. I couldn't figure out why at first. Then I realized the body might be Aiden. I guess she'd seen him more than I had."

Ray spoke for the first time. "Aiden only delivered two sides of deer or elk to us each year. I'm not that fond of game. I worked on a ranch too long. I like beef better, but Joe prefers game to beef. Aiden delivered deer, elk, or antelope to the Schultz's cabin at least once a month. I sometimes helped Joe process the meat into jerky, which the women sold with Ramona's baked goods at the saloon."

Sara must have looked confused.

Ramona added, "Don't worry. We're approved as food processors by the New Mexico Environment Department. You know that's only been a law the last few years."

"Why didn't you mention earlier that Aiden's contribution to Golden Gully was to provide meat?"

Ramona shrugged. "No need to accuse a neighbor of poaching."

"Okay, but what did Eve contribute to your community?"

Ray leaned back in his chair. "Not much."

Ramona squeezed her husband's hand. "That's not a fair statement. She does all of our publicity. Part of the problem is Jeanne and Eve didn't like each other much. I'm not sure why."

Ray muttered, "Jeanne thought Eve's morals were questionable. Keeping Hank around so she could learn gossip from Reserve and get some action is cheap."

Ramona squeezed her husband's hand again. "You're not being fair."

Jack had listened silently to the discussion. Now he spoke. "I'm a city boy. Aren't you lonely here?"

Ray laughed. "Ramona is all the company I need. And I work for local vets and shoe horses at least three days a month. We caretakers have puzzle and game nights twice a month in Green's and Brown's party room. Ramona and I go to Silver City at least once a month to shop, and she shops in Reserve more often."

Ramona squeezed her husband's shoulder. "But we're not young. Joe reports to the forest rangers' station weekly and usually works another day each week on one of their projects. The Schultzes shop in Silver City at least twice a month as a family. During the last five years or so, Jeanne has attended a biweekly book club in Silver City."

"Does she talk about any particular friend at the book club?"

Ramona frowned. "No. I don't remember her saying much even about the books." She smiled at Ray. "He and I like reading books together. He was reading Green's and Brown's newest book to me when you arrived." She winked at her husband. "Brown and Green like to think we don't know *Mogollon Maiden* is about us."

Ray cleared his throat. "Amazing how they twisted a few facts into a bizarre story, but I liked how they portrayed Ramona as a beautiful frontier woman."

Ramona's and Ray's answers were consistent with their previous comments and those of Etta, except Ramona had now admitted she knew the victim was Aiden Cortez. Sara thought this older couple were amazingly happy and well-adjusted. She decided she'd placed the descriptors in the wrong order. They were well-adjusted, which allowed them to be happy. "Do you have any guesses why Hank shot Sheriff Bob?"

"Hmmf," Ray looked at Ramona. "She won't like me saying this, but it's true. Eve has Hank tied up in knots. Poor sap. If she told him to shoot someone, he would."

"You don't think it ties into some Eberle family spat?"

Ramona shook her head. "All I know is Hank is a gentle soul."

Jack leaned forward. "How did Hank feel about Aiden? Weren't Hank and Aiden vying for Eve's attention?"

Ray rolled his eyes. "Aiden lost interest in Eve as anything, but a business partner many years ago. He extracted gold from certain tailings from the Chino copper mine and prospected for gold. She turned the gold into jewelry. Who knows what the fool kid Hank thought."

Sara had almost run out of questions. "Did you know Joe and Alex were brothers?"

Ramona covered her mouth with her hand. "Know is too strong a word. We guessed it because they looked alike in some ways."

"Joe told his girls to call Aiden *uncle*." Ray scratched his chin. "But the girls call us *grandma* and *grandpa*."

Ramona wiped her eyes. "Poor dears don't have any grandparents. My sister and her husband died in an accident years ago. That's why Jeanne came to live with us. Joe has never mentioned his father or mother to me." She looked at Ray.

He answered the unsaid question. "One time, I asked him why he didn't get a dairy cow or two. He replied, 'Hate cows. They're all my father ever cared about.' That was it."

***

Sanders and Bug were waiting in the car when Sara and Jack emerged from the Miller's' trailer. "Bug and I found a wonderful cafe in Alma and shared a green chili burger." He tousled Bug's ears. "Did you know this scamp likes green chili? I tried to scrape the chilis off the pieces of meat I gave him, but I noticed he gobbled the pieces with a bit of chili faster the ones without green chili."

"Of course, Bug is a New Mexican." She cuddled the little dog who contentedly licked her face. "We've sat in a room that smelled like a bakery for the last hour. I'm famished."

"So am I." Jack shook his head. "I hope we aren't reduced to eating jerky from the saloon. Salted, dried meat isn't my thing."

Sara kissed Sanders's cheek. "Could we induce you into eating another green chili burger before we drive to Silver City?"

"Thought you'd never ask. I never realized before how little meat you ate when you shared a burger with Bug."

CHAPTER 29: Some Memories Are Best Forgotten

Sara was tired of running in circles. Everyone in Catron County knew more about the case than she and Jack. She wondered whether years of living in semi-isolation had made the residents of the county distrustful of outsiders. Or had they stayed here because they were basically loners?

Bug brought Sara back to the present when he tried to climb up her blouse to lick her face.

Sanders was questioning Jack about his classes at Quantico. He kept asking the same questions. "What made that lecturer memorable? How have you used what you learned from that instructor?" *Wait. Sanders had made a decision.*

Quantico was only an hour's drive from Sanders's condo in Washington—at least on a day when traffic was light. She knew Sanders had an open offer to increase his participation in the training of FBI agents and Marines at Quantico. She sighed. He'd tell her when he was ready.

So, she quietly sat on the back seat and petted Bug. After a while, she checked her email.

Hank had resisted talking to anyone since she'd shot him last Friday. Today, he told a nurse he'd like to talk to the "lady agent who shot him." Carbonne had sent an agent to talk to Hank, but Hank had just rolled over and ignored him.

Beau's email was funny in an ironic way:

> *Hell is spending a day in Reserve. Mace and I tried but we couldn't get the locals to take control of the charges against Hank. The DA for the state judicial district plans to call the federal prosecutor. She's going to claim she won't be able to seat an unbiased jury. At least, Sheridan now has a temporary internal affairs officer and can start the paperwork to fire Hank.*
>
> *Hank's monthly payments of $500 weren't bribe payments. Ophelia thinks Hank gave the money to his mother.*

Mace and I would like to return to Albuquerque first thing tomorrow.

Sara laughed to herself as she sent a reply:

You can't go home until you finish questioning those in Reserve. You should confirm with Hank's mother that she received monthly payments from Hank. She might also know whether Hank had a reason not to trust or like Sheriff Bob. Other members of the Eberle clan might know about a feud between Hank and Sheriff Bob. The federal prosecutor will want that info before he accepts the argument of the local DA.

Sorry for the bad news. Golden Gully wasn't a joy either today. Sheridan is a wily fox who knows everyone's business in Catron County. Can you get him relaxed and talking?

Sara suddenly realized Jack had asked her a question. "I'm sorry I didn't hear you clearly."

Jack laughed. "Have you finished making Beau and Mace miserable? I assume they had a bad day because your face was scrunched up as you pounded the keys on your laptop."

***

Sanders pecked her cheek as Sara closed the door to their hotel room. "A boring day was what I needed. I was forced to think. I know two of the jobs I've always wanted will open in the next year, but I can't remain a lap dog for the Senate Intelligence Committee that long. Even Bug has more independence than I do in that position."

Sara pulled him to sit on the bed beside her. "I know it's hard. Did your conversation with Jack help?"

"You've already guessed what I decided." He smiled. "I'm going to see if the offer from Quantico still holds. I think lecturing there part-time would be more pleasant than waiting on the senators. And if the jobs I want don't materialize, I'll have started to build my teaching credentials. Many washed-up bureaucrats and politicians teach."

She leaned over and kissed him slowly. "You're not washed up. Fate has forced you to think about career alternatives. You set your goals more than twenty years ago as a college student and as a green State Department attaché. I certainly wouldn't want your company if you were still that kid. You're a seasoned man-of-the-world."

He pushed her back on the bed. His tongue forced her mouth open as he lifted her hips to pull her slacks off.

***

Wednesday

The four met Jennifer for breakfast. Sara had guessed Jennifer might be more talkative if Jennifer saw her as woman with a personal life—dog and significant other—rather than as a cold professional.

Jack hadn't disagreed. "Can't do any worse than we have so far. I'll start the conversation by pointing out those of us without bonds with pets and sexual partners need to talk to others in a similar situation."

The restaurant—a fast food burrito place—was Jennifer's choice. She seemed to want to be sure the owner wouldn't know her mother. Jack started the conversation by noting he had yearned to meet his father for fifteen years after his father deserted his mother. "When I finally met him, I was disappointed. My mother, sister, and I were better off without him. Is that what you learned, too?"

"What makes you think I ever met my father? Why do you think I was so eager to see his pic last week?"

Sara thought Jennifer had overreacted. Her voice had risen half an octave. She sensed Jack was on target.

Jack gulped. "I apologize but your father was living not far away under the alias of Aiden Cortez. We know from credit card receipts he frequented Silver City. Your mother's restaurant is the best in the Silver City area. Think back. Are you sure you never saw his face before I showed you the picture last week?"

Jennifer looked down at her plate. "I've been thinking. I may have seen someone who looked a lot like him several times."

"And?"

"I must be wrong because it doesn't make sense."

Sara thought the girl looked frightened. "Okay, tell us what you think you saw. Sometimes when I've looked at lots of file photos, I think a face looks familiar. I'm often mistaken."

"I'm not sure." Jennifer took a bite of food. "I saw a man who looked a lot like the pic with my friend Courtney. Only the man had no gray in his hair and looked younger than in the pic. No wrinkles." She took another bite of food. "It bothers me because I told Courtney her friend seemed too old for her. She laughed and said..." Jennifer blushed. "It doesn't matter what she said exactly. She indicated he acted young enough for her."

Sara's curiosity was aroused. "Exactly what did Courtney say?"

"He bucks like a young bronco."

Jack kicked Sara under the table. "What's Courtney's last name? How did you meet her?"

"Howard. I met her at boarding school in Pennsylvania. She was five years older than me." Jennifer looked around the empty restaurant. "Usually, a senior doesn't notice newbies. She looked me up the first year I was in boarding school because we were the only two from New Mexico. Her mother took me to lunch when she visited Courtney at school one time." Courtney wiped tears from her eyes. "I know Mom tried to protect me from the rumors in Hancock and Silver City by sending me to boarding school, but I was lonely. I didn't fit in. And Mom could never visit because of the restaurant." Jennifer sobbed.

Jack looked helplessly at the crying girl. Sara put her arm around Jennifer. "Did you have trouble with your schoolwork?"

"No." Jennifer straightened in her chair but still stared at her plate. "I got mainly As at school."

Sara remembered the pictures of Jennifer in the yearbook suggested she was overweight. "Was the problem you weren't athletic enough?"

"Sorta. I hadn't had dance or gymnastic lessons as a child. Everyone else had, but I could ride horses well." She looked up. "Mom and I used to ride a lot looking at her and Dad's mining claims. Anyway, after the polo coach saw me ride, she convinced me to sign up. I became the youngest member of the polo team when I was a freshman. I was the team captain my last two years at school."

Jack whistled. "That's impressive. Maybe the other girls were jealous."

"No, Courtney explained it to me last summer. It was strange. I hadn't seen her since she graduated four years before. She just appeared at the restaurant one day and suggested I meet her here the next day at noon." Jennifer picked up her fork and stared at her food. "She was sitting in that corner booth." Jennifer pointed the fork at the booth. "All cozy with this man with a black ponytail. He had his arm over her shoulder with his hand cupping her breast. He was nibbling at her ear. Kinda gross. Anyway, she didn't introduce him...or even acknowledge what he was doing. She said, 'Since we're both from New Mexico, I decided to do you a favor. If you want to be popular at school, you need to lose twenty or thirty pounds and not admit you worked in your mother's restaurant this summer. Say you spent the summer working on a dig on the Mayan peninsula and spent some time at a resort in Belize." She flipped me a brochure. "This is the one we stayed at."

"The man stopped nibbling at Courtney's ear. 'Better read up on the Mayans and current digs in Belize.' He studied me. It felt odd. 'Bleach your hair a light blonde and start wearing makeup.' Then he stood up and turned to Courtney. "Let's go Mami. We did our good deed.""

Jack and Sanders gasped. Sara could understand why Jennifer didn't want to think that this man might be her father. She lightly touched Jennifer's arm. "I think Jack gave you good advice earlier. You may not have missed much in not knowing your father—if that man was your father." She reviewed her notes mentally. "Did you ever see him again?"

"Yes, Courtney walked into Mom's restaurant the second day I was back for the summer this year. She took one look at me and said, 'Bet you were more popular at school this year.' Then she invited me to meet her again at this restaurant the next day."

Jack groaned. "It took guts to go. What happened?"

"The man with the black ponytail and Courtney were waiting for me in the same booth. But this time they sat across the table from each other. He called her 'Mami' and she called him 'Papi,' but they didn't touch each other. He asked me about my plans. I told him I'd been accepted into New Mexico State and planned to become a veterinarian."

"How did he react?"

"He shrugged. 'Your mother must be pleased. Las Cruses is only a two-hour drive from Hanover.' He gave me his awful stare and said, 'Were you more popular at school this year?'"

Jack gasped. "What did you say."

"I told him it took me six months to lose the weight. I didn't bleach my hair until after Christmas. By then I'd been accepted at two colleges and being popular with the snobs at school didn't matter anymore. He laughed and said, 'Your mother raised you well.'"

"Then what?"

"Nothing. They left."

Jack looked at his phone. "Thank you for your time." He stood.

Sara didn't move. "Did you ever see or talk to Courtney or the man at any other times during the last two years?"

"Mom had a particularly large group on one of her tours to Golden Gully two weeks ago. While she was regaling the tourists with her stories, I set up the lunch on picnic tables near the Last Chance Bar. I saw three women walking away from the bar along the stream when I first pulled up. They didn't notice me. I'm pretty sure one of them was Courtney. Not many women wear their hair in a French twist anymore."

"Would you recognize the other women?"

Jennifer scrunched her face. "Doubtful. I saw them from the back. The blonde one was several inches shorter than Courtney and wore khaki shorts. The brunette was Courtney's height and wore a blue gingham sundress."

Jack shoved his phone in front of Jennifer. "Was this the short blonde?"

"I don't know." She grabbed Sara's arm. "You took a sample DNA analysis last week. Do you have the results yet?"

Sara saw tears in the girl's eyes. Winslow had used the rapid DNA test to analyze Jennifer's cheek sample. The result indicted Jennifer shared about fifty percent of her DNA with the victim. Sara had originally planned to surprise Jennifer with the news. After listening to Jennifer's stories today, Sara didn't think the news would be pleasant. She didn't lie when she said, "The lab hasn't done the definitive test yet."

CHAPTER 30: Two Fewer Suspects?

"What's next?" Sanders turned to look at Sara in the back seat of the car.

She looked up from her laptop. "Change in plans. The FBI agent in Roswell think it would be a waste of time to go Carlsbad to talk to Courtney's parents unless we have a warrant."

"Good. I'm ready to go home." Jack nodded.

"But I got an interesting letter from Alex's lawyer—well at least the lawyer who sent the request for a divorce to Etta. Seems he appreciated I sent him a notice that we'd tentatively identified Alexander Cortland as a murder victim. He thinks he has several documents we should see—like a new will and letters to be sent to Etta and Jennifer upon Alex Cortland's death."

"We'll need a warrant because the will hasn't been probated yet."

"He says not if Etta gives the okay—which she will if she's not crazy—because he thinks it eliminates her as suspect. So..."

"Why don't you call Etta before we back track to Hanover?" said Jack. "She could be annoyed with us if she knows we met with Jennifer."

"When you talk to her..." said Sanders, "...see whether you can get late luncheon reservations at her place. On the patio. None of us ate much at the burrito joint." Sanders exited U.S.180 to return to Silver City.

***

Etta was a different person than the last time they'd seen her when she greeted Sara and Jack. She appeared to have combed her hair. It was neatly pulled into a bun at the nape of her neck, and she'd removed the gun holster from her hips, but she still wore a shapeless print dress. Jennifer was nowhere in sight. "My lawyer says I should show you the will and the letters." She had a waitress seat Sanders with Bug on the back patio and led Jack and Sara through the kitchen to her makeshift office. She motioned to the letter lying on the card table.

> *To my best pal,*
> *I believe that's what I called you when I left you and Jennifer fifteen*
> *years ago. It's still true. I won't make excuses, but I had to go.*

Here's what's important. Thank you for paying the taxes on our properties and the fees on our mining claims. In my will, I left all but two of the claims to you. Those two go to Courtney. It's part of a deal I struck with her father three years ago. They give him access to large gas rights. You will also get my share of the five claims I made with Joe Schultz.

I've rechecked all our claims. Only six of the old claims and the new claims with Joe are worth retaining. They are the four old claims and the new claims with Joe along the stream by Golden Gully not far from Eve Cooney's cabin and the two next to our property. I've mined the meager gold out of the other fourteen claims and extracted gold from the best tailings from the Chino copper mine during the last fourteen years. Eve and I were partners. I found the gold she used in her jewelry. We split the profits, but she doesn't know the locations of the best sites.

This means I've been nearby for most of the last fourteen years. I was only in Brazil for a year but funneled my annual check to you through a bank in Manaus. Somehow, I think you guessed that. Maybe that's why you sent Jennifer away to boarding school. You didn't want her to learn the crazy mountain man who hunted and prospected around Golden Gully was her father.

You've done a good job of raising her. The gold in our six good claims should be enough to pay her expenses while in college and veterinary school.

I apologized to her in the letter I wrote to her and stated the truth. She was better off without me. I ruined every woman I knew, except you. And I came awful close to ruining you, too.
Alex Cortland, your husband

Etta watched them read the letter. "You've got to understand how it was with Alex and me. He was so exciting, but he was only happy when he was in danger. You wouldn't believe the gullies we trekked while prospecting. But then Jennifer came along. I couldn't take the risks anymore."

As Etta spoke, Sara thought how happy Sanders seemed at times in Brazil. She wondered whether Sanders could also be considered a thriller seeker with a death wish. Of course, Sanders was driven by goals and more ethics than Alex. Still, it bothered her.

"I'd rather you didn't read his letter to Jennifer until she reads it. The problem is I don't know how to tell her about her father. She blames me for chasing him away. Maybe I did after he two-timed me with Eve when Jennifer was a baby."

"You knew?"

"Everyone did. There weren't any other prospectors or trappers with black hair in the area at the time. I suspect he went to Brazil more because of her than because of me. I was no looker even then, but I made few demands on him." She pulled at her dress. "Since then, I never tried."

Sara tapped Jack's arm. "Should I?"

He nodded. "Etta, sit down." He pushed her onto a foldable chair.

Sara leaned across the table and grasped Etta's hands. "Etta, it's our job to figure out who killed Alex, no matter what. We talked to Jennifer without your knowledge. She met Alex twice in the last two years when he was with one of her school friends."

"That b******."

"She didn't at the time know who he was. And she didn't like him much. I think it's why she was so eager to have her DNA tested." Sara shrugged. "I don't know how she guessed. Probably in the same way you knew Alex wasn't still in Brazil."

"Did the b****** touch her? Molest her?"

"No." Sara thought Etta understood Alex well—at least his weaknesses. "Because Jennifer was so upset as she described her interactions with him, we didn't give her the preliminary DNA results. I told her the lab hadn't done the definitive test yet—which is true. But you should know, there's no doubt in my mind that Alexander Cortland, aka Aiden Cortez, is the man in the morgue in Albuquerque. And he is Jennifer's father."

Etta stared at Sara. "You're sure he didn't touch her?"

"She didn't appear to be a rape victim to me, but rather a well-adjusted young woman. You'll have to talk to her...soon. I'll get a warrant within twenty-four hours. The two letters and the will shift you from being one of the prime candidates in Alex's murder, but the will might also provoke the murderer or murderers to do something foolish." Sara knew as she spoke, she hadn't told the whole truth. A prosecutor could argue the will gave Etta and Jennifer a motive—inheritance—for murder. But Sara thought the documents gave those excluded from the will—Eve and Courtney—reason to hate Alex more. The murder had been well planned and violent, suggesting pent up anger that Etta didn't have.

"I don't know."

"My friend and dog are on your patio. Jack and I can eat while you talk to Jennifer."

Etta stood. "No, I'll put you in our special occasion dining room. Jennifer and I will join you after you order."

"We have a dog along. Health officials..."

"Won't be stopping by today. Follow me."

***

"Sanders, do you want me to spell you off and drive for a while?"

"No, I may be tired, but you look exhausted. All the tears and emotion between Etta and Jennifer were overwhelming, and I'm used to the *sturm und drang* of a father-daughter relationship." He turned out of the parking lot at Etta's Place. "In a way, I'm jealous of Etta and her daughter. Their bond is amazing. This brouhaha only made it stronger."

Jack turned to Sara in the back seat. "I'm not sure I understand what happened. Etta really loved Alex twenty years ago even though he was a jerk from the start."

"Perhaps, but she stopped trusting him after they'd been married only six months." Sara grimaced. "Why would she trust him? He lied about everything. He was seldom around. He admitted to her that he'd desired his brother's wife and hinted his hunting accident wasn't an accident." Sara sighed. "I think she wanted a child more than she loved him. And that's why she wasn't unhappy when he disappeared."

Jack whistled. "Wait, are you saying she didn't have enough passion for Alex to kill him?"

Sara shrugged. "We must get all the details on Alex from his lawyer's files, but I think we don't need to interview Etta and Jennifer again. They've told us what they know. Or at least will admit." She paused. "Unless we find evidence that Alex molested Jennifer. Etta would make a mother lion look tame if she found anyone hurt Jennifer."

"Agreed," said Jack quickly. "But...I want to explore Alex's psychological profile a bit. Was he a man who only saw women as mothers or prostitutes with no gray in between?"

"Hmmf." Sanders didn't take his eyes off the road. "You are oversimplifying a complex man who was constantly searching for the impossible. It made him reckless and often cruel. The letters to Etta and her daughter were cries for help when he knew it was too late."

Sara yawned. "I think Etta summed it up well. Alex was a risk taker always 'searching for death because it was the only way to find peace.'"

Sanders smiled into the rear-view mirror. "Why don't you take a nap for an hour? Then you can tell me which woman in Alex's life killed him."

Jack whistled. "I still think at least two of them worked together. Etta's the only one big and strong enough to have hoisted Alex onto the chair and tied him up. And remember Jennifer saw three women together near the Last Chance Bar."

CHAPTER 31: The Wrong Suspect

Sara awoke when she heard Sanders speak, "Yes senator." When she sat up, she realized Jack was driving and Sanders was talking on his phone. She must have slept soundly because she didn't remember Sanders relinquishing the driving to Jack.

"No, I'm not alone. Sara, an FBI agent, and I are driving back from Silver City." After that he said little except an occasional "yes" or "no" while the senator appeared to have a lot to say. Finally, he said, "I don't think I can make the eight o'clock flight but if the pilot can wait for a half-hour I can meet it." He listened for at least five more minutes before he disconnected. He turned to the back seat. "I hate to do this to you, but I must catch an air force cargo flight due to leave Kirtland Air Force Base at eight. They'll hold the flight for up to thirty minutes."

Jack tinkered with his GPS. "It says we can be at Kirtland by ten after eight if we continue at the same speed. I'll speed up a bit. If police stop us, I'll say it's an emergency and show my badge."

Sara leaned forward, "I know you have your laptop, but did you leave important papers at my house?"

"That's what I'm thinking about. There's one file that might be useful. Please take photos of its contents and email them to me. I have two changes of clothes in my case; one's even clean."

"Okay. I assume you won't be staying in Washington. Can you say where you're going after you land at Andrews?"

"No."

"Okay, we'll drop you off at Kirtland. Then I'll drop Jack off at the FBI building where he left his car. After I settle Bug at home, I'll go through the stuff you left at my house and email copies of relevant documents by midnight." She paused. "Or do I have to ask Carbonne to open his special room for transmitting classified documents."

Sanders laughed. "I don't ever bring classified documents to your home."

Sara wasn't sleepy but couldn't think of anything to say. Sanders seemed to be transmitting one email after another. Jack concentrated on

I-25 as he sped along at eighty miles an hour. Bug nestled closer to her in the silent car. She decided to catch up on her email and text messages.

After thirty minutes, Sara said, "Beau just texted me. He, Mace, and Sheridan tied one on last night. Seems they think the 'women in power in Catron County' were out to humiliate them. Beau says he couldn't decide whether the women were angry with Sheridan, distrusted the FBI, disliked outsiders, or all three of the above."

Jack snickered. "I'd bet lots of people in Catron County fear Sheridan."

"Maybe, but something came out of their spree besides hangovers. They finally realized what was bugging them. They'd found no cameras or camera equipment in Hank's' apartment. They rechecked his credit card receipts today. There's no evidence Hank bought cameras or photo equipment in the last year. They asked around the sheriff's office whether anyone was a shutterbug. Everybody in the office said Sheriff Bob took a lot of pictures."

Jack sighed. "Darn. Why did Hank have hundreds of photos on the wall in his locked bedroom?" He paused. "It also suggests Sheridan may not be as good a watchdog as he pretends."

"Oh, one more thing. Ophelia says Hank didn't sleep in the locked bedroom. He slept in the other bedroom."

Jack whistled. "How did she know that?"

Sara laughed. "Beau said neither he nor Sheridan had the guts to ask."

"Did Beau have anything else to report?"

"He and Sheridan had a long talk with Hank's mother. She wanted to know whether the FBI agent who shot her son will get into trouble."

"Don't worry." Jack glanced at Sara. "It was a clean shot."

"Beau said Sheridan read her the riot act, and she apologized for the slur when he was through. She also admitted Hank had said several times over the last six months that Sheriff Bob was not 'nice.' His mother couldn't explain what Hank meant by 'nice.' She also confirmed that Hank gave her money monthly."

"Wasn't Sheriff Bob supposed to be released from the hospital today? Did they talk to him?"

"He wasn't due to get home from the hospital until after six. However, his wife, Alice, was talkative when Beau and Mace stopped by. Seems her nephew and his wife were picking up Sheriff Bob from the hospital because they wanted to do some shopping in Albuquerque. Alice gets car sick and was glad to skip the drive to and from Albuquerque."

"What about Sheridan?"

"They didn't take him along to the sheriff's house because he claimed Alice was a 'nervous ninny' and would say more if he wasn't present. But get this, he advised them to 'tell her she was pretty.'"

Jack chuckled. "Anything useful?"

"There were dozens of pictures of young women on the walls. Alice claimed Bob took 'beautiful pictures of his nieces.' Beau wants me to get a search warrant for Sheriff Bob's house, particularly the studio he has in back. He says he and Mace will stay in Reserve tonight and talk to Sheriff Bob tomorrow morning. They hope my conversation with Hank will give me the evidence I need to get them a warrant. They're also going to talk to several of the girls in the pictures."

"So, what are you going to do?"

"Try to talk to Hank tonight after we drop off Sanders."

Sanders interrupted, "Don't forget I need copies of my papers by the time I land at Andrews Air Force Base. The flight will only take three-and-a-half hours."

Sara sighed. "I didn't forget. If your flight leaves at eight-thirty, you should arrive at Andrews by midnight our time."

"It will be tight."

Jack checked his GPS screen. "I'll have you at Kirtland by eight. Then Sara and I can question Hank at the hospital. I can finish the interview when she leaves to get your stuff."

***

When Jack pulled up to the gate at Kirtland, he mentioned Sanders's name and was immediately waved through. Sanders pulled his case out of the trunk at exactly eight. Sara jumped out and pretended to kiss his cheek as she whispered, "Does the flight to Brazil leave at midnight?"

He nuzzled her ear. "Yes. The info should be transmitted in encrypted form. I contacted Carbonne. He'll be in his office by eleven."

She nibbled his ear. "You lied. Do I destroy the originals or put them in the safe in Carbonne's office?"

"The latter. They weren't classified info when I came, but the chair of the Senate Intelligence Committee added a bit of info that changes everything." He gave her a real kiss and ran inside.

She pulled Bug out of the back seat, and they jumped into the front.

Jack laughed. "Are you sure Sanders doesn't make up these secret missions to get great send-offs. I didn't think you two would ever stop necking."

***

                                    J. L. Greger

Hank stared as Sara strode into his hospital room carrying Bug. Jack—one step behind her—closed the door. "You got it all wrong."

"We've guessed you aren't into child pornography. Do you think Sheriff Bob likes young girls too much?" Sara pulled up a chair next to the bed, situated Bug on it, then helped Hank sit up in bed, and tucked two pillows behind his back.

Hank scratched his head. "I started thinking about that several months ago when Eve showed me pictures that he'd taken of her." He shook his head. "She thought the pictures would turn me on." He blushed. "They did. Then she showed me other pictures. They...made me nervous. I didn't say anything because I didn't want her to think I was country bumpkin. She kept giving me photos every time I visited, but they didn't turn me on anymore. About a month ago, I put a lock on my second bedroom—when Ophelia was out—and put up all the photos. That's when I realized several of girls were still in high school when the photos were taken. That's wrong. I didn't know what to do."

"Is that why you shot Sheriff Bob in the hand?"

"No. Someone called Eve Friday morning. She got all excited and yelled a lot at the person. Then she told me that Sheriff Bob was supposed to deliver a box of photos." He licked his lips. "She said I should shoot him if he didn't give me a box. I didn't want to do it, but she claimed he was threatening to ruin her life. She cried. Kept saying the 'photos were just for me.'"

Sara thought about the situation on Friday. Sheriff Bob had been wired but his voice had not been clear much of the time. Very little of what Hank had said had been audible. "Tell me about what happened as Sheriff Bob pulled up to where you were standing on Friday."

Hank closed his eyes. "I saw a box on the front seat, like Eve said I would. I leaned in to get it. Sheriff Bob said he was delivering it to someone else. Eve warned me he might be tricky. He placed his hand on his chest said something like, 'Don't talk about the photos when they arrest you.' Then he quickly moved his hand down. That's when I yelled and shot him."

Sara was confused. "Okay, I understand you thought Sheriff Bob was behaving strangely, but why did you shoot him?"

"He was pulling a gun from under the box. Eve had warned me he might try to shoot me, and I knew he could be sneaky."

Sara was still confused until Jack said, "Sara, I taped the wire on Sheriff Bob's chest. He may have put his hand on it to muffle the sound when he spoke to Hank about the pictures."

"Okay, but why the sudden movement to the package?"

"I'll bet he had placed a gun under the package." Jack continued, "He told me he thought he needed a gun there. I told him it was unnecessary."

"What happened to the gun?"

Jack began to pace around the room. "In the flurry, I forgot to look for it. I don't even know if Bob hid one under the box."

"What do you know?"

"Neither you nor I took it. Sheridan stayed in the Jeep—I think. The nervous deputy Tim talked to Sheriff Bob and lay in the back seat for a while. He may have taken it. I'll call Beau and Mace now and tell them to talk to Tim."

Sara placed Bug on the bed. Hank rubbed Bug's silky ears. "Sure would like a dog when they lock me up for years."

"Hank, we're going to check your story. You may not have much time in jail if you cooperate. Now think hard. Do you know who called Eve on Friday morning?"

"I think it was a man."

"Why?"

"Eve's voice is different when she talks to men than when she talks to women."

Sara reviewed those near the scene. The manager of the Catwalk Resort and the residents in Golden Gully would not have known about the box. That meant the caller was Sheriff Bob, Tim, or even Sheridan.

She looked at her watch. It was time to go. She squeezed Hank's hand. "I'm going to leave a pencil and paper by your bed. If you remember anything about Friday morning or the photos, write it down. Jack is going to stay with you until another agent can get here to stay with you tonight."

She carried Bug to the door. "Bug and I will be back tomorrow to talk to you. I'm sorry I shot you, but I thought you were going to kill Sheriff Bob for no reason."

"I figured."

CHAPTER 32: The Price of Excitement

Sara calculated her schedule. Normally it would take an hour to drive from the hospital to her home. Maybe less at night, maybe a lot more if there was an accident on I-25. If she took only a half-hour to find Sanders's papers, she should reach the FBI building by eleven-thirty. She tore out of the hospital.

She made good time on the highway going home but had problems as she sorted through Sanders's files. Nothing in the three files she found in the side pocket of his case looked like important information—nothing on Brazil or on drugs. She dug through the clothes in his case. She felt bad about messing up the neatly folded clothes. It reminded her how persnickety Sanders could be. All his shirts were ironed. In an inside pocket of a folded jacket at the bottom of the pile, she found three folded pages. They were a list of Brazilian-sounding names with contact info. Most of the addresses—but not all—were in Brazil. She put the pages in her purse, thought a second, returned to the bedroom and zipped up the case. She rolled it to her car where Bug was waiting. She had left him in his carrier when she entered the house. He had insisted on a pit stop at the hospital. She thought he could wait for another.

She rushed south on I-25 until she saw flashing lights. It looked like an accident. She had passed an exit a mile back. She jumped out of the car and showed an officer her FBI identification and explained she had time-sensitive materials that needed to be delivered to FBI agents immediately.

The state trooper shook his head. "The crashed cars are blocking all three lanes."

"Could I drive on the shoulder? It's an FBI emergency. You can talk to the SAC at the FBI. He's waiting for me."

"Okay, lady. Be careful."

Sara swallowed hard. The shoulder was narrow before it sloped into the median strip between the north and the south lanes of I-25. She checked Bug's carrier was firmly locked in place and slowly pulled her SUV forward. She was lucky. The second car in the crash didn't completely fill the third passing lane. She inched forward carefully to avoid the state police officers and the EMTs moving around the scene.

When she passed the parked ambulance, she sighed. Bug whimpered slightly. He must have sensed her nervousness. They sped down the highway.

Carbonne was pacing by the front door of the building. He let her in and nodded to the security guard who skipped his usual searches. Sara, rolling Sander's case and carrying Bug, raced after Carbonne to his office. He unlocked the door to the encryption room at the back. She raced in.

"Everything is on and ready to go." He closed the door.

Sara encrypted and then transmitted the three pages. She sent a separate email outlining the material in the other files and waited. Less than a minute later. She received an email:

Received what I needed. My plane is approaching Andrews.
Love
Sanders

Sara petted Bug and looked at the clock on the wall. It was ten to twelve. She wondered *when* or *if* she'd hear from Sanders again.

His trip to Brazil was apt to be dangerous. He had almost completed his two assignments while serving as the acting ambassador to Brazil. At least one major Brazilian drug cabal had been partially dismantled when he'd brought its leaders back to the US for trial several months before. But drug cabals were like hydras. They could regenerate quickly and produce new heads. Those new leaders would not want Sanders to return to Brazil. They'd probably shoot him on sight, despite the potential consequences.

She thought of the list she had just sent him. His other assignment in Brazil had been to identify Brazilians—especially in the military and the police—who were sympathetic to the U.S. Those individuals could also be targets of gangs or of certain politicians in Brazil. So, they were in danger, too. She'd looked for two names on the list. Both were there.

She placed all his papers in the safe Carbonne had left open. She locked it. She opened the door and rolled Sanders's suitcase out with Bug trotting behind her.

"Well?" Carbonne was seated at his desk but made no pretense of working. The wrinkles on his forehead were deeper than she'd noticed before. Barbara was due anytime now. It had not been fair to force him to come out late at night.

"It's out of my hands now." She couldn't explain it, but tears were dripping from her eyes. "I...have a bad feeling about this trip. Thanks for opening the encryption room for me."

Carbonne hugged her. "The next SAC is in for a surprise when he learns of your unofficial role."

She pulled back. "Are you leaving? I know being a SAC is a pain."

He laughed. "No way. I guess Sanders inspired me to think about being an undercover agent again. The excitement is contagious, but Barbara wants me to be a stable, safe pencil-pusher. Seeing your face, I realize the price for that excitement is too great."

Sara smiled. "How is Barbara?"

"When I left, she said she hoped the next emergency dash I took would be to take her to the hospital. She's eager to become a mother."

"You'd better get home. Bug and I..."

"No, you're not going to do any work." He grabbed the handle of Sanders's bag. "I'll walk you to your car."

CHAPTER 33: A Murder Weapon

Jack whistled as he paged through the search warrant Sara handed him. "I've already sent it to Beau and Mace. They plan to serve it around nine this morning."

"Did you get any sleep last night after I talked to you?"

"A little. I'll probably go home early after I clear any other materials Beau and Mace need." She tried to smile. "I hated to think my personal problems would necessitate ten extra hours of driving for them this weekend."

Jack had updated Sara on the rest of his conversation with Hank as she drove home the previous night after sending the document to Sanders. She'd prepared a request for a search warrant of Sheriff Bob's home with an emphasis on his studio, cameras, dark room equipment, and computers. She had guessed Bob processed all his photos digitally and had little dark room equipment, but as usual she tried to make the warrant as inclusive as possible.

Sara had called the judge at six to explain how this case had changed from charges against a young deputy to probable charges against the chief elected law enforcement officer in Catron County. There was little doubt the federal prosecutor and state district attorneys would insist the FBI complete the investigation. However, she had not notified any state or Catron County officials because she feared Sheriff Bob might be notified and would destroy key evidence. The judge had quickly agreed.

Jack stared at her but didn't say the obvious. She knew she looked terrible. She had worked most of the night because she couldn't sleep. She was too worried about Sanders.

Jack reached down and petted Bug. "The pup looks more rested than you do, but I'll bet Beau and Mace look worse than you. They went drinking with Sheridan last night again. Beau claims Sheridan is the closest thing to Matt Dillon he's ever seen, except Sheridan has a 'bigger gut.'"

Sara was suddenly concerned. "Please tell me Beau didn't slip and tell Sheridan about their raid on Sheriff Bob's home at nine."

"Cool it." Jack plunked into a chair. "Remember Sheridan and Beau together figured out Hank wasn't a pornographer two nights ago during their first drinking spree. Sheridan's not dumb. He knows Beau and Mace talked to the sheriff's wife and several women in the photographs yesterday. Beau is convinced Sheridan wouldn't tell anyone of his suspicions because Sheridan said last night, 'I'd better go home. Ophelia will ask too many questions if I show up at her house at one in the morning.' Furthermore, Beau said he told Sheridan, 'Getting a warrant is up to Sara. I figure she'll rag on some poor judge until she gets a warrant for us around noon tomorrow.'"

"I'm just edgy, but Beau is a little worried about Sheridan, too, or he wouldn't have mentioned noon, not nine a.m." Sara began scanning her computer screen.

"We all are. None of us ever realized how much we depend on local law enforcement officers in the western counties of New Mexico." He studied his phone. "I guess that's everything I got from my conversation with Beau this morning." He put his phone back in his pocket. "You know, Hank grows on you. I hope he can build a case for self-defense."

"It all depends on finding the gun Hank claims Bob had with him. I doubt Deputy Tim will admit what he did over the phone, but he's apt to be talkative when he realizes Sheriff Bob has no authority over him any longer."

"That's what Beau and Mace figured. They don't plan to question Tim until they've searched Bob's home and have talked to more women today. They and Sheridan guess most of the girls with pompoms in the photos were underage high school cheerleaders when the photos were taken." He turned to leave. "Beau and Mace could use lab help if they find anything at the sheriff's home."

"I realized that at four this morning. Winslow and a lab van departed Albuquerque before six. He should arrive in Reserve by ten. Beau and Mace will want his help sooner, but it's the best I could do."

"I'd better remind Beau and Mace to look for guns as they search Bob's house. The nervous deputy could have given the gun back to the sheriff's wife." He sighed.

"Wait." Sara looked up from her laptop screen. "The autopsy report finally came in with most of the lab data. After you talk to Beau, you may want to see if I have new info."

***

Sara stared at the autopsy report. She was so tired. The words didn't make sense. She called Isaac Newsome. "Isaac, I've had only four or five hours sleep in the last twenty-four hours. Please talk me through your report on Alexander Cortland."

Isaac groaned. "Anything specific?"

"No. Go through everything."

She heard slamming of drawers. "I didn't want to start the next autopsy anyway. First point, Alex had considerable lung scarring of the type seen among miners. His radon levels were not above normal for here in the Southwest. Thus, I concluded, he'd developed the lung problems while mining copper, not uranium. The lung damage was bad enough I'd expect he had a persistent cough but didn't need oxygen therapy."

"That makes sense. He worked for a while at Chino open-pit copper mine and prospected for gold for years."

"Aha. The soil under his fingernails was sandy with low levels of silt and clay but high in metals. Typical of mine tailings in the Southwest."

"Good. We found tons of tailings around his workplace. Winslow thought he smelled almonds when we inspected the area. So, I assumed Alex was using a cyanide method to extract gold from the tailings."

"Sounds logical to me. However, low levels of cyanide are difficult to detect on autopsy. They might have exacerbated his breathing difficulties or chest pains. Might also have induced mental confusion. However, I did have the lab check for mercury toxicity."

Sara knew Isaac appreciated active responses. "I didn't see any evidence he created mercury amalgam of gold in ore at his current workplace, but fifteen years ago, he prospected for gold in the Amazon where it's a common practice."

"His hair samples indicted he hadn't used mercury recently. But the tips of his long hairs had high concentrations of mercury. Moreover, there was necrosis of tubular epithelial cells in his kidneys, loss of Purkinje cells in the cerebellum, and elevated levels of mercury in the brain. He probably hadn't used mercury to extract gold from ore during the last year, but he had used mercury at some time previously. The hair suggests as recent as five years ago."

"I'm guessing the poorly healed second- and third-degree burns on his hand, which you pointed out during the autopsy, could have been due to an accident when vaporizing the mercury during the extraction of gold."

Isaac's voice was raised by a half octave. "Aha. You may be tired, but you're not brain dead like many of your colleagues. Logical, but unprovable. Note the mercury toxicity would also have contributed to his mental and lung deterioration and his apparent clumsiness."

"No one mentioned Alex was clumsy."

"Nevertheless, I found six healed bone fractures. One occurred in the last year. The others showed varying degrees of calcification."

"Any other abnormalities?"

"He was extremely thin. I suspect it wasn't due to intentional dieting, although his clothes suggest he was a dandy. I saw degeneration of the gut mucosa. Both cyanide and mercury could have exacerbated those gut lesions."

"Okay. I get the picture. Alexander Cortland was a sick man. What can you tell me about how he died? We suspect the body was moved several times before the sheriff's deputies saw it."

"The partial healing of several wounds on the wrists and ankles suggests he was bound—perhaps for several days—and the early wounds had a chance to start healing. I found no signs of healing of the wounds on his knees. It suggests he might have fallen onto his knees around the time he was killed, but blood pooling in the buttocks, shoulders, and back of the legs indicates he lay supine for hours after his death."

"Again, this is consistent with the scene. There was a chair and rope near the body. Neither had retrievable fingerprints, but both had specks of Alex's blood. Perhaps he tipped the chair when trying to escape."

"As I told you just before you left the autopsy, he appeared to have been stabbed though the ear canal. I think the murderer would have sat astride him to do it. The angle of the wounds in the brain suggests the body was prone at the time."

"Why didn't it bleed more?"

"The light smears of blood on his right cheek and his neck suggested the killer cleaned him up."

"The murderer was in no hurry. That suggests confidence."

"I don't know if confidence is the right word. Lab results indicate the victim was dehydrated at the time of his death and would not be as strong as usual, but he was a big man. There were no drug residues in his blood. It's likely two people were involved: one sitting on his legs and/or hips; one doing the stabbing. I'd say the murderers were determined."

"You hadn't identified the murder weapon before I left."

"It took a while to categorize the instrument. At first, I thought it might have been a pencil, but there were no paint or wood residues in the wounds. The puncture wound was too deep to be the usual three- or four-inch darning needle. We finally decided it was most likely a size three or four knitting needle. I think metal because bamboo or plastic ones would have snapped. It appears the murderer made several thrusts. At least two penetrated the medulla just above the brain stem."

"Isn't that unusual?"

"Quite so. It certainly wasn't a spontaneous action."

Sara debated how to ask her next question. "I picked up a knitting needle in the home of one witness—I guess suspect now—who seemed obsessed with her knitting. If I dropped it off, could you tell me if it is a possible weapon? I doubt it will have Alex's DNA on it."

Isaac coughed. "I noticed you didn't explain how you got the needle. Are you sure you want me to see it? I can tell you how to size the needle."

CHAPTER 34: Photos Tell Stories

"Sir, we have a federal warrant to search your home, studio, and cars, and to collect all cameras, photographic equipment, computers, and photos of young women." Beau handed the warrant to Sheriff Bob Eberle.

The sheriff awkwardly tried to open the envelope but couldn't because only his fingertips extended beyond the ball of gauze and tape encasing his right hand. "Mother, come help me." He placed his bare foot and leg across the doorway to block Beau's entry.

Beau studied the man. He'd seen pictures of the sheriff around the county offices but hadn't met him before. The sheriff looked shorter and less in condition in in a gray running shorts and T-shirt than he had in his official photos. In most of the shots Beau had seen, the sheriff wore a felt Stratton hat and stood with his shoulders back and arms akimbo. It was obvious why he wore a hat. His thinning gray hair barely covered his scalp.

The man straightened. "You've goofed. I'm the sheriff of Catron County not some lackey deputy."

"Sir, we have statements from several women and your deputy, Hank Eberle, that indicate you took pornographic photos of women under the age of eighteen. We hope we don't find anything to substantiate those claims, but we must search your home and studio."

Bob's wife, Alice, appeared and read the warrant aloud. After few sentences, she began to wail. "What will the neighbors say? Bob, can't you stop this search? There's nothing wrong with your pictures of our nieces." When her husband didn't reply, she stormed toward the stairs to the second floor. "I'll call Sheridan. He'll act."

Mace quickly stepped over the sheriff's outstretch leg and followed the woman. "Ma'am, you can make any calls you wish, but I want you to stay here where I can watch you."

She slumped onto the sofa shrieking. Sheriff Bob seemed to shrink a bit more each time she screamed.

"Where are your cameras and photographic equipment?"

Bob led Beau to the locked *casita* behind the house. After he unlocked the door, Bob sat on a stool in front of a screen that Beau recognized as a backdrop for several of the photos. "I'd rather stay here than listen to Alice."

Beau wished Winslow and the lab crew had arrived, but he'd been afraid to wait any longer to do the search because he feared one of the women or their families might warn Bob that the FBI agents were asking questions.

He and Mace had used the time between seven and nine to interview two women. They'd interviewed four others the day before. All admitted they were under eighteen when the pictures were taken. Four of the women had been embarrassed by the photos. Two had laughed and said the sheriff had given them only fifty dollars for posing for the shots.

As he opened drawers, Beau quickly realized Sheriff Bob was fastidious. There were about a hundred manilla envelopes. Most had a young woman's name on the front. He checked only five of the envelopes. In each, plastic album pages displayed about a dozen photos of the young woman. The first page generally was of the young woman in a cheerleading outfit, prom dress, or bathing suit demurely smiling at the camera. The second and third pages were photos of the young woman in various stages of undress and in provocative poses. Beau thought Sheriff Bob was a talented photographer and knew how to use sophisticated programs to place the girls in a variety of improbable settings. One of Bob's favorite settings appeared to be to place the girls on the fields of various national football teams.

Beau did the math. There were only about fifty students in Reserve High School. There were pictures of dozens of different Reserve Mountaineer cheerleading squads. These photos had to go back years. Bob had been photographing underage women for at least ten, more likely twenty years.

He read Bob his Miranda rights. "How did you talk the girls into posing for you?"

Bob shrugged. "It was easy. I have pictures of all the women in several families for two generations."

Beau hadn't expected such a frank answer. He doubted Bob understood his Miranda rights and explained the case was apt to be tried in a federal court. The charges would probably result in prison time and certainly loss of his job.

Bob shrugged. "I knew I should quit, but I couldn't. And I thought no one, but Ophelia and a few prudes, would care." He began to sniffle.

"What about Sheridan? Did he know?"

"He's one of the prudes." Bob wiped his eyes. "Ever since he shot the rancher twenty years ago, he's been protective of teenage girls. Thinks they're innocent. Boy, he' hasn't seen what I have." Bob smiled. "So much pent-up energy."

Beau heard Winslow's voice in the house, but he couldn't resist asking one more question. "What about your wife?"

"Alice didn't care as long as I left her alone." He paused. "I guess I should say she didn't know." He shook his head. "Maybe it's true. She thought I liked girls in pretty dresses."

***

"Look for handguns as well as pornography."

"Yep." Winslow didn't look up but continued to unpack his gear in the studio. "Sara emailed me that Hank is claiming he thought the sheriff had a gun under the package. I'll look for the gun and physical evidence in the studio while the data analyst..." He pointed to a middle-aged woman. "...checks out the computers."

Beau opened the file drawers with the manilla envelopes. "There are about a hundred cases. Many occurred more than seven years ago, and some of the women may not want to press charges."

Winslow flipped through the pages of photos in one envelope. "I'd like to find some negatives, undeveloped film in a camera, or shots on the computer that were edited later. Otherwise, Bob could claim he received the photos from Hank. I'll also look for evidence that he sold the photos. We'll download everything on or deleted from his computers."

Beau slapped Winslow on the back. "I take it you've handled cases like this before. Mace and I are going to go through the rest of house now. We'll leave the sheriff and his wife with you. I don't think they'll try anything, but you never know. Record anything, they say. Mace and I have explained their rights to them."

***

Sheridan strolled into Bob's home at eleven-fifteen. He winked at Beau. "I didn't rush over so you had time to ask a few questions to prove I wasn't involved in the pornography. I guess I should have guessed Bob was up to mischief." He coughed. "I've been around Ophelia too long. That's what she'd say. God knows Bob didn't spend much time in the office. I always figured he was glad-handing."

A woman's scream echoed through the house.

Sheridan lowered his voice. "Alice is still carrying on. How's Bob holding up? Did you search his person for a gun. He could be suicidal."

Beau knew his face turned white. He hadn't searched Bob nor his wife for a gun. "Let's do the search now. Mace and I have checked out the first floor, partially for guns, and found a rifle and shotgun in a locked case in the front closet and a service revolver in an unlocked drawer in the kitchen."

"Hmmf." Sheridan walked to the purple powder room off the living room and pulled open a drawer. He threw the tubes of lipstick onto the counter and reached into the back of the drawer. He held up a small Glock handgun. "Bob isn't much of a shot, but Alice wins in competitions."

Beau shook his head. "How did you know it was there?"

"After she drank too much at a party, Alice showed Ophelia the secret compartment." He smiled. "Ophelia thought Alice might have used the gun to ward off advances from Bob." He shook his head. "Poor Bob."

***

Mace looked at the four handguns found around the house before he locked them into a case. "Any one of these could have been under the box in the car. There's no way to identify the gun. Sure would help if Hank could describe the gun."

Beau led Bob to the kitchen and tried to question him about how Hank had shot Bob's hand. Although Bob had answered questions about the pornography, he refused to discuss the shooting without a lawyer present.

Beau was unable to reach Sara. Jack explained she was taking a nap. "I think she realized even she couldn't resolve the current mess." He explained the federal prosecutor had talked to the district attorney for the judicial district including Catron County. They'd concluded that any charges against Sheriff Bob should be heard in federal court, but the federal prosecutor was not prepared to arraign him yet. All the lawyers agreed that Sheridan, as acting sheriff, should notify the county board of the situation.

***

Winslow entertained the group at lunch as he described how Bob's organization had made the collection of data easy. "He kept great records on the sale of his photos. The pics of young women in the Denver Broncos Stadium are his best sellers. I wonder if he reported their sales on his income tax."

Beau sent a text to Sara to have FBI analysts check Sheriff Bob's tax returns. *It was the type of detail that would appeal to her.*

Tim remained tense throughout the lunch. He didn't laugh at Winslow's comments on the sales of the pornographic pictures. "The

J. L. Greger

Broncos are popular in Reserve. Bets on the games here in town are always over the point spread, never on whether the Broncos will win."

Winslow and Mace, at Beau's request prior to lunch, tried to engage Tim in a discussion of pornography. The deputy didn't seem to appreciate the concept of statutory rape. He twice said, "I'm sure the girls posed willingly for Sheriff Bob. Besides, those girls weren't children. Several of them were pregnant when they married only a year or two after the photos were taken."

Beau was glad Mace recorded the conversation. The prosecutor might be able to use the recording to extract testimony from Tim later.

However, Beau decided trying to question Tim about a hidden gun today was a mistake. He had other concerns. The search for knitting and darning needles in Golden Gully would take several hours. This meant he and Mace might spend another night in Catron County.

That was a problem. His wife and teenage daughter never stopped arguing. Now his wife was complaining she needed help in monitoring their daughter's activities. His wife suspected their daughter was vaping regularly with friends because her clothes often had a sweet, fruity smell when she arrived home late from school or outings.

His daughter was the age of the girls in the photos. Two of them had admitted they posed because they earned a little money for cigarettes or booze. He feared his daughter would pose if offered enough money. He needed to get home tonight—no matter how late.

***

Joe Schultz turned ashen when he saw the warrant. "Don't you have to explain why you want to look at all Jeanne's knitting supplies?"

Beau didn't feel like being on the defensive. *It was time for the residents of Golden Gully to take responsibility for their actions.* "It's part of our ongoing investigation into the death of *your* brother Alex Cortland."

Joe stepped back. "It's just Jeanne has been so obsessed with her knitting and darning needles. She's been crying that five or six of her needles were missing. I don't see how she'd notice. She has so many."

Beau didn't want to listen to Joe's problems. "Is Jeanne here?"

"No, she's at the saloon selling items to tourists. I'll call her."

"No need. We understand most of her knitting supplies are in her workroom in the shed, but we'll scan your entire home for needles." Beau signaled to Sheridan and Mace to search the house first because the search would become more difficult when Jeanne was tracking their steps.

They weren't lucky. Jeanne ran into the house screeching while Mace and Sheridan were searching her bedroom for knitting supplies.

When Beau stopped her from entering the bedroom, she began to pound on his chest.

Joe immediately tried to divert his wife's wrath. "Dear, don't make things worse by getting charged with assaulting an officer. If you're angry, hit me. Calm down."

His words seemed to enrage her at first, and she pounded repeatedly on Joe's chest as Joe kept saying, "It's all right, baby. Together we can sort this out." Finally, she just sobbed and let him guide her to her workroom in the shed.

Mace and Winslow found not only a basket of knitting supplies in the couple's bedroom but also knitting baskets in the girls' rooms. In the workroom, they found three shelves covered with yarn and a drawer filled with dozens of knitting needles from skinny ones to one as thick as a finger. They found the darning needles and sewing supplies in another drawer.

Sara had sent Beau not only the warrant but also a short essay on knitting. She had explained that small knitting needles—with low numbers, i.e. one through four—were used to make baby clothes and socks. The thicker needles produced bigger stitches. Yarn darning needles—with eyes and sharp or rounded points—probably wouldn't be numbered. Only ones that were more than six inches long were of interest. The needles might be metal, bamboo, plastic, or ivory.

The warrant authorized collection of all knitting needles less than size six—the thinner needles—and any darning needles longer than six inches, regardless of their composition.

Beau tried to explain to Jeanne that he and Mace were not there to arrest anyone but to gather relevant evidence. She was still wailing when they left to talk to the Millers.

***

Ramona was at the tavern, but Ray allowed Beau and his crew to search for knitting needles after Ray explained, "Ramona knits me a sweater most years for Christmas, but she says ' it's not worth her time to make me socks.'"

The agents found only size eight and larger needles at the Millers' home, but they confiscated four large darning needles.

***

Green had giggled. "Search away. We don't knit," when Beau had asked to see all his and Brown's knitting needles. When Winslow found four thin sock knitting needles and a long darning needle stuffed behind a pillow on the sofa in the shed, Green had stopped laughing. "They're not ours. One of the ladies must have left them."

Green and Brown spent thirty minutes searching for proof of who had attended the get-together in their party room on the Saturday night after Alex Cortland's body had been found. The Schultzes, the Millers, Brown, Green, and Eve had signed an amendment to the residents' agreement to share profits from Golden Gully. The amendment removed Aiden Cortez's name from the list of the residents. Green explained. "We didn't want Aiden's relatives to claim his share of our profits." Winslow claimed the needles and all the relevant documents.

***

Eve behaved as expected. She refused to open the door to allow her home or shed to be searched until she saw the new search warrant. They found no knitting or darning needles on her property.

***

Beau was pleased because he thought if he and Mace left immediately, they could get back to Albuquerque by ten, or more realistically ten-thirty. Then disaster hit. Sara called.

She played a recording of Hank's admission to her ten minutes earlier. "Sheriff Bob kept looking at the box on the car seat as he talked to me. After a while, I realized he wasn't looking at the box but a pretty little thing only six inches long by the box. It had a green handle. Not grass green. Not dark green, but I guess a light green. It took me a while to know what it was. When he grabbed for it, I didn't think. I just shot his hand."

Sara sighed. "I believe Hank because he's not smart enough to make up the story." She sighed again. "You didn't happen to see a small revolver today that fits that description?"

Beau didn't know whether to laugh or to cry. "Sheridan found a gun that fits the description in a secret unlocked compartment of a drawer in the sheriff's home. Both the sheriff and his wife had access to the gun. We have it." He held his breath, hoping Sara wouldn't order him to make an arrest tonight.

Sara sighed again. "I doubt Sheriff Bob or his wife are going anywhere. The sheriff's DNA on the gun won't prove much, but I'll tell the judicial officials that lab results won't be available until Monday. Have a great weekend with your family. But remember on Monday, you must figure out who transferred the gun from the sheriff's car to the unlocked drawer in his home. It's either Sheridan or Tim with Alice's help. You also must assess whether Alice should be charged with abetting Bob's crimes."

Beau now realized why Carbonne had liked Sara as his partner when he worked undercover. She knew how to cover for her partners.

Jack would be a good addition to the SWAT team after Sara trained him for a few more months.

CHAPTER 35: Where Do the Clues Lead?

Although Sara was dog-tired, she couldn't fall asleep as she lay on a cot in the FBI *sleep-over* room. She was worried about Sanders, annoyed by the judicial impasse on her current case, and worried she and others would end up wasting a lot of time commuting to Catron County during this week.

She decided she needed to do something easy and returned to her office to review the file Alex's lawyer had provided. His lawyer had emailed her copies of every—he claimed—item in his file for *Client: Alexander Cortland, aka Aiden Cortez*.

The lawyer had only met Alexander Cortland four times. He'd drawn up a will for Alexander Cortland fourteen years before. The will provided that upon his death all mining claims and property Alex owned with his wife Etta Cortland would become entirely hers or if she was deceased, her daughter's. Alex had also arranged for the lawyer to monitor the annual transfer of funds from an account in Manaus, Brazil to Etta and to file a report with him through a post office box in Glenwood, New Mexico.

Sara was surprised that the lawyer had included a handwritten description of Alex in the file.

> *Full beard, long black hair, shabby work clothes, a cast on his left leg, and a bandaged left hand and arm. Client claimed he'd been burned in a smelting accident in Brazil two months before.*
>
> *Questionable use of names. Alexander Cortland in will and documents sent to wife. Aiden Cortez for documents sent to him.*
>
> *The funds in the account in Manaus appear to be legal and derived from gold mining operations in Brazil.*

Sara glanced at the annual reports the lawyer had sent to Alex. There was no evidence that the lawyer had received any other correspondence from Alex until two years ago.

Then the lawyer had helped Alex create a limited business partnership with Leslie (Tex) Howard of Carlsbad. Alex assigned two of his old mining claims to Howard's daughter and invested $100,000 in a gallery called Aura of the Southwest in Santa Fe in return for a fifty percent interest in one of Howard's gas exploration companies. The lawyer had also represented Alex when he purchased a house in Santa Fe.

Again, the lawyer had included a handwritten note in the file:

> *Hair still long but client wore stylish black jeans, shirt, and expensive leather jacket. Wants now to use name of Alex Cortez in all documents.*

The next documents in the file were more interesting. Tex Howard threatened to sue Alex when he learned that Alex only co-owned the two old mining claims assigned to Courtney. The only apparent follow-up in the file was the lawyer's letter sent to Etta requesting a divorce.

That's when the lawyer began to earn his fees. He met with Etta Cortland and Courtney Howard. The copy of his report to Alex was succinct.

> *Etta Cortland hired a private investigator and traced you to your home in Santa Fe. She will give you a divorce and your mining claims in return for $500,000 in cash and full ownership of any property now in both your names.*

> *Courtney Howard wants you to sign a prenup agreement that grants her all your property and mining claims acquired prior to your marriage. Her father, Tex Howard, has acquired a complete list of your assets including those in Brazil.*

> *You cannot satisfy both women.*

The third time he saw Alex was a month before Alex was killed. Alex wanted a new will. In essence, Courtney got Alex's shares in her father's gas exploration company. Eve got all his possessions in the shed on her property, except for the gold in the box in his bedroom closet. That gold went to Hank for "relieving him of Eve." Etta got everything else, including his house in Santa Fe.

A week later Alex signed the new will and gave two sealed letters to be delivered to Etta and Jennifer Cortland upon his death. He also

                                                    J. L. Greger

authorized the lawyer to share all information in his file *if* he died under mysterious circumstances. At the time, Alex said, "I thought Courtney was a sweet girl until I saw her with my daughter. She's meaner than Tex."

Sara closed the file. No wonder the lawyer had been cooperative and not requested a warrant.

***

On the previous Tuesday, Sara had requested the resident agent in Santa Fe to search Alex's house. The agent had been busy and hadn't searched the house until Wednesday and emailed his report on Thursday afternoon.

> *The Cortland, aka Cortez, house was empty, except for two changes of clothes—black jeans, black T-shirts, black dress shoes, a designer leather jacket, and underwear—and a bed in one bedroom, a refrigerator packed with beer, and a small table and chairs in the kitchen. The kitchen cabinets also contained an array of liquors.*
>
> *Found three items on the table. One was a bill from a cleaning woman, dated two weeks ago. Contacted her. She claimed she cleaned the house once a month but there was never much to do. She had emptied wastepaper baskets but left the two envelopes on the table where she found them.*
>
> *The aqua-colored envelopes with Aura of the Southwest letterhead had been opened. Neither were dated. Both looked like they'd been wedged in a door. Both are handwritten. One said:*
> > *Dad knows you saw your lawyer. We know you*
> > *are not trying to get a divorce anymore. You owe*
> > *me. I bet your innocent daughter would be upset if*
> > *she knew your secrets.*
> > *C*
> *The other said:*
> > *I've been patient, but not anymore. You owe me.*
> > *C*
> *Padlocked the house but doubt it's worthwhile for the lab crew to try to collect further evidence. Sent the three items on the table to the lab to check for prints and DNA.*

Sara figured the bill had arrived after Alex had been detained by his killers. Alex hadn't seen it. It also meant the resident agent in Santa Fe was right. It was unlikely any more evidence would be found in a thoroughly cleaned house. However, if the lab found Alex's DNA on the other two envelopes and letters, she could assume he's seen the threats. Sara requested a warrant to search Courtney's condo in Santa Fe, the gallery Aura of the Southwest, and Courtney's room in her parents' home in Carlsbad. She knew neither she nor Jack had the energy to serve the warrant and question Courtney until Monday.

***

She and Bug wandered down to Carbonne's office. His secretary informed Sara that Carbonne had taken Barbara to University Hospital around three when she went into labor. "I guess I should have notified you, but he said Barbara didn't want any visitors, except her mother, until tomorrow afternoon."

Sara checked her email. There was a text message from an unknown number:

Checking on friends in Manaus.
Love,
S

Sara doubted Sanders wanted a response. He appeared to be okay. Or at least there was nothing she could do for him. Suddenly, she felt sleepy. She and Bug went to bed as soon as they got home.

***

Saturday

Sara liked racing with Bug down the dimly lit halls of the FBI building on Saturday morning. Bug was so proud when he reached her office first. He twirled in front of the door in a *Chin spin*—a trick she'd taught him to entertain patients in the hospital.

As she opened the door to her office, she heard Winslow's voice. "Boy, do I have a surprise for you." He waved lab printouts in front of her face. "The little Glock revolver Sheridan found in Sheriff Bob's house was a gold mine. I found tiny bits of dried blood in the crevices. Rapid DNA test indicate it's Bob's blood."

Sara smiled and tried to look enthusiastic. "Great, but we don't know whether the blood was from when Hank shot Bob in the hand."

Winslow was unfazed. "There's a new test that indicates the age of blood spots. And two good prints—the thumb and forefinger—match Tim Eberle's prints in the AFIS database. You'd think he would have been smart enough to wipe the gun."

Sara nodded. "Were the wife's prints on the gun?"

J. L. Greger

"Don't know. She's not in the AFIS database. Bob's prints were on the gun, but that doesn't prove anything."

"I'll notify the federal and state prosecutors. Maybe this will help them settle their jurisdictional debates. Looks like Beau and Mace could make an arrest or two on Monday or at least ask some uncomfortable questions of Deputy Tim, Sheriff Bob, and his wife." She turned on her computer. "Oh, did you think to check if Sheridan's prints were on the gun?"

Winslow straightened. "I'm no beginner. I compared the prints on the gun to those in the AFIS system for every member of the Catron County Sheriff's Department. No other matches. And I checked. The gun is registered to Sheriff Bob."

"Maybe you can perform another miracle for me. Did a courier deliver the envelopes and pages the resident agent in Santa Fe found in Alex Cortland's house in Santa Fe?"

"Yes, the agent requested we check for fingerprints and DNA with an emphasis on matching those of Courtney Howard and Alex Cortland."

"Sounds good to me." She scanned her email. "Looks like the geological report came in at five yesterday. It should keep Bug and me busy until we visit Carbonne's new daughter in the hospital. When he called me at nine this morning, he said Barbara had been in labor for fourteen hours, but Barbara and baby Willow are fine."

"When was the baby born?"

"I think around five this morning."

"Shucks. I didn't win the office pool. I bet the baby would arrive at one this morning."

Sara frowned. "What are you talking about?"

"One of the analysts last Wednesday organized a betting pool on when Carbonne's baby would be born. Most of the staff in the building participated." He shrugged. "Guess you missed the action because you were in Catron County."

Sara suspected she wouldn't have been told about the office pool even if she'd been in the office on Wednesday. She had several friends in the building, but most of the agents and staff viewed her as an outsider. She guessed it was her own fault. She was too goal-oriented and didn't chitchat with others over lunch or during coffee breaks. She'd learned years ago as a young faculty member at Michigan State it was unwise to confide anything important with competitive colleagues. Maybe this was one of her traits that appealed to Sanders.

"Last night I thought of another question I had for you, but I didn't write it down." She shrugged. "I'll email you when I remember. Oh, another point. I'm surprised to see you here today. I thought you'd visit the new schoolteacher at the Zuni pueblo. Jack said..."

Sara was amazed to see Winslow blush. "That big mouth. He knows I don't want to talk about Clara." He rushed out of Sara's office.

Sara wondered whether Winslow's romance had cooled. Too bad. She hated to see such a nice young man so lonely that he enjoyed the company of an old woman like herself.

***

The geological analyses from the New Mexico Bureau of Geology and Mineral Resources in Socorro were complex, and Winslow had been thorough in collecting samples all over Eve's property.

The report noted the ten samples collected from the deep—several feet deep—layer of gray gravel on the quarter acre behind the root cellar contained dangerously high levels of cyanide. The land required remediation. Sara wasn't surprised. Eve had admitted her partner extracted gold from mine tailings, and Winslow had smelled an almond odor—indicative of cyanide—behind the shed. The lab noted the samples had a mineral composition like tailings previously analyzed from the Chino open pit mine but with no gold or copper and more zinc. Sara silently blessed the analysts for pointing out that cyanide extraction of gold from tailings often involved the addition of zinc or activated carbon to precipitate the gold from the cyanide solution. The note saved her hours of searching for information on the source of the tailings and the extraction process.

She sent the Bureau's report to EPA and the New Mexico Environment Department. If she and Jack were unable to build a case against Eve, at least they would have the satisfaction of knowing Eve would be pestered by environmental agencies for the rest of her life and would not be allowed to continue to extract gold from any more tailings in such an environmentally unfriendly way.

The analyses of the pulverized ore in the canisters in the root cellar and in the jars in the shed revealed they were examples of low-quality gold ore. The vials of what looked like gold flakes were what they appeared to be. The Socorro lab noted the gold had a high copper content, consistent with what would be called rose gold. The big surprise was two of the rock and soil samples Winslow had collected along the stream were graded as low-quality gold ore, but four were graded as medium-quality.

Sara guessed Eve and Alex had run a lucrative gold processing business. Albeit the profits might have been swallowed up if they'd met environmental standards. One thing puzzled her. Why had Alex processed the tailings and low-quality gold ore when Eve's cabin was almost sitting on better quality ore?

Bug whimpered, and Sara decided it was time for a walk. As they wandered outside, she remembered what she'd wanted to ask Winslow. It was funny how often it happened. Once she relaxed, she usually remembered important details.

***

"Winslow, think about when you were collecting samples at the Last Chance Bar. You said Eve wandered by. Can you remember what she said?"

Winslow stopped staring at his computer screen and saw Sara holding Bug. "You know he shouldn't be in the lab. But I guess he's safe when you're holding him." He puckered his lips. "I was finishing up my work at the Last Chance Bar. She wanted to take pictures of the scene. Seemed to think they would add excitement to the Golden Gully Facebook page and website." He shook his head. "Strange."

"Didn't you tell me you recorded the conversation?"

"Yep." He moved from the lab bench to his desk and opened a drawer. "I thought I sent it to you." He pulled out his phone and fiddled with it.

The recording was poor quality and hard to hear at points, but Sara was impressed with how Winslow had engaged Eve in conversation. "Play the last sentences again."

Eve's cooing voice came from the phone. "He's also a prospector...and a lousy partner and lover. He's talked to me less during the last month than you just did."

Sara winked at Winslow. "She was making a pass at you. Maybe Hank wasn't satisfying her either."

Winslow reddened slightly.

"You got her to lower her guard and reveal a bit of her real self. Good job."

As she carried Bug toward the door, she noticed a young woman with a cute bob hairdo at the desk on the other side of the lab bench. Sara was trying to grow her hair out into a bob but knew her thin, fine hair would never have the body of the woman's thick, black locks. Sara had never seen her in the lab before. "Are you new to the lab?"

Winslow rushed to Sara's side. "This is Clara, my friend from the Rez. I picked her up on my way back from Golden Gully last night. She wanted to do some shopping in Albuquerque this weekend."

Jack had been right. Winslow was enjoying the trips to Catron County because they gave him a chance to court the young schoolteacher.

"Clara, I'm glad to meet you. I suspect Winslow isn't much of a shopper. Make sure he takes you to the shops at Uptown."

CHAPTER 36: Jack Gets a New View of Art

Monday

Sara looked tired on Monday morning. Her eyelids were droopy, and the corners of her mouth sagged When Jack asked whether she'd heard from Sanders, she said, "He reached his destination."

Last week, Jack thought Sara had seemed to enjoy the excitement of Sanders's secretive world. Now as he studied her face, he remembered a comment Carbonne had made. "Sanders is the type of man you want heading security operations for the U.S.—brilliant, dedicated, and capable of molding almost any group of individuals into a unified team, but he's hell to live with. He's a user."

He guessed they'd both had a bad weekend. He'd gone to a party and come home alone Saturday night. Most of the women he was attracted to were smart enough to know that police—even FBI agents—often had irregular work hours and jobs that shouldn't be discussed.

Jack realized Sara had changed the subject when she pointed to photos of needles on her computer screen. It was amazing how easy it was to tune out soprano voices. Two of the women he'd dated had claimed he didn't listen to them. It had been true. They had chirped constantly but said little. That couldn't be said for Sara. She was an alto, and what she was saying was important.

Winslow had accomplished a lot on Saturday despite his girlfriend's presence. He'd visually checked for blood on all the confiscated knitting needles and yarn darning needles. Typical of Sara, she explained Winslow could have speeded his search for blood on the needles with luminol, but that chemical could destroy DNA evidence. She thought there were new blood-detection chemicals, which weren't supposed to be destroy DNA, but Winslow apparently didn't trust them. Winslow found nothing of interest on the knitting needles but found blood or human debris stuck in the eye of one darning needle.

Jack stared at the needle. He'd never seen anything like the one Sara pointed to on the screen. It was almost as thick as a small knitting needle with a half-inch long eye in its eight-inch stem with both ends rounded. Winslow's attached note indicated this was one of five items—

a set of four small-gauge sock knitting needles and the darning needle—found behind cushions in Green's and Brown's party room. Winslow had done rapid DNA tests on them. He found Alex's DNA in the eye of the needle but no detectable DNA or fingerprints elsewhere on the other needles. Winslow thought they had been washed and/or wiped, but he noted regular DNA tests sometimes detected DNA in washed samples that were missed by the rapid DNA tests.

"We've made progress. This darning needle meets the size specifications the medical examiner provided. It could be the murder weapon."

"Yeah, but I think Beau mentioned all the adults of Golden Gully had met in the party room the Saturday after Alex's murder to sign a new community agreement. I guess it suggests the murderer is less likely to be Courtney."

"Speaking of Courtney, I've got a search warrant for her condo in Santa Fe, the Aura of the Southwest Gallery, her car, and her room in her parents' home in Carlsbad."

***

Courtney was as snooty as the last time. It was obvious Sara wasn't in the mood to humor her. In front of the clerk in the gallery, Sara said, "Courtney, it's time to think about your options. We know you had a motive for killing Alex Cortland. I guess you knew him as Alex Cortez. We found threatening notes from you to Alex in his house."

Courtney puckered her pink frosted lips. "Lots of women hated Alex's guts."

Sara smirked. "Here's how it is going to work. We think at least two of you worked together to kill Alex. The first one of you who talks can probably strike a deal with the prosecutor. And don't think your father can hire a crackerjack lawyer to get you off in a state trial This will be prosecuted in federal court. So, are you ready to talk? We'll be here for a while because we have a search warrant for this shop, your condo, and your car."

Courtney's eyes flashed defiance. "I won't talk until I speak to my father and my lawyer."

"Fine." Sara checked her phone. "You should know two FBI agents are now at your parents' home in Carlsbad with search warrants."

Jack was impressed at Sara's thoroughness. She had arranged for a resident FBI agent in Santa Fe to meet Sara, Jack, and a crime lab tech at the shop and had the resident agents from Roswell go to the Howards' home in Carlsbad at the same time. Although Sara was always thorough, she was especially meticulous when she disliked a suspect.

He studied Courtney. Her lacquered veneer was perfect but somehow grating. He didn't have time to analyze his response to the woman. He was in Santa Fe to collect evidence to force her to talk later. There was a lot to do.

While the resident FBI agent checked the numbers on the speed dial on Courtney's cell phone before he monitored Courtney's call to her father and lawyer, Jack arranged for the records on usage of the land-line phone in the gallery and Courtney's phone to be sent to the FBI. Sara called the agents in Carlsbad. Tex Howard was not at home, but Courtney's mother was talkative.

The clerk in the gallery was helpful. When Jack showed her a picture of Alex, she said, "That man occasionally picks Courtney up for lunch or dinner, but Courtney never introduced him. I don't know his name."

Jack then showed the clerk a picture of Eve Cooney. The clerk recognized her immediately. "She sells jewelry on consignment in our gallery and brings in new pieces at least once a month." She pulled a dozen pieces of rose gold jewelry from two display cases. "I can pull her file. We have records on the sales of her work."

The file was interesting. The gallery had sold dozens of Eve's pieces since it had opened eighteen months earlier. The pieces sold ranged from two-hundred dollars for simple rose gold earrings to four-thousand dollars for a turquoise and pearl encrusted rose gold necklace. Both Eve and Courtney had signed the payment slips. It appeared Eve received fifty percent of the sales price for her items that sold.

Sara then asked to see files for other items sold on consignment. Other artists got twenty to forty percent of the sale price of their work. Courtney had signed all consignment and payment slips. The clerk couldn't explain the basis on which artists were remunerated, except the artist got less if Courtney had to "fix" their work. Courtney refused to even acknowledge she knew Eve or had signed the consignment and payment slips.

Meanwhile, the resident agent and crime lab tech had inspected Courtney's red Mazda Miata and collected samples. Their most interesting finds were wadded up credit slips from gas stations in Silver City and Reserve.

***

The investigators and Courtney moved to her condo. A large provocative photo of Courteney's bare torso from the back in sepia tones hung over the fireplace. Jack wasn't sure why Sara spent so long studying the right corner of the photo as everyone else looked for real evidence. He didn't ask. She'd tell him when she was ready.

There was no evidence of Alex's—or for that matter any other man's—presence in Courtney's packed clothes closets. The small safe in the bedroom contained a few expensive pieces of jewelry. The refrigerator contained only diet beverages, frozen diet dinners, and fruit.

The office in the condo was equipped with a computer, a large-scale, high-density printer, and a smaller printer. Stacks of photographic paper were on built-in shelves on one wall.

The second side room was a sewing room and lined with shelves and drawers. Scarves like those worn by the clerk and Courtney were piled on the shelves. Jack and the other agent began to open drawers. He cringed when he found a drawer full of large needles like the potential murder weapon. The crime tech collected everything in that drawer for later analysis but only photographed the rest, including the frilly long dresses hanging in the closet.

Finally, Sara called everyone to the living room. On her laptop were photos of items in the gallery. She pointed to the right corner of several seemingly old photographs of women in western gear or dresses reminiscent of the 1880s and 1890s. Then she tinkered with her laptop and brought up several odd photos of hands and feet. "Do you see the small silver stamp in the right corner of all of these photos?"

The resident agent, who Sara had worked with before, winked. "I've got a feeling it's going to be important."

Sara pointed to the right corner of the photograph over the fireplace. There was a small silver shield with B on it. "They're all done by the same artist. Does a badge and a B remind you of anyone?"

All Jack could do was gasp.

Sara gave one of her evil broad grins. "I think Sheriff Bob sold his work on consignment at the gallery." She turned to Courtney. "Do you know Sheriff Bob Eberle of Catron County?"

Courtney cleared her throat. "Who's he? You know you can't ask me questions until my lawyer arrives."

Sara closed her laptop. "Call him and tell him to meet you back at the gallery."

***

Jack showed the clerk a photo of Bob in his uniform. "No, I've never seen him." He showed her a picture of Bob that Mace had taken when Bob had on shorts and a T-shirt. The woman studied the picture and shrugged. "Maybe once."

J. L. Greger

Sara pointed to several of the sepia-toned photos. "Do you have a file for this artist's work?"

The clerk contorted her face. "I'm not sure how his work is filed."

"Okay. Who delivered them?"

"That's my problem. Usually, the first I saw them was when Courtney was framing them in the back room." The clerk led Sara and Jack to the back room and pulled open a drawer. She pulled out a box of stickers—silver shields with a B in the middle. "Courtney labeled them with these."

"Okay, see if they're filed under Sheriff Bob or Bob Eberle."

The clerk pulled a file. "Yes, it's labeled as Sheriff Bob."

Sara studied the pages in the file. "Seems like this artist's work is not sold on consignment. The artist receives a flat fee for his negatives or the computerized original photo. Two hundred dollars each."

The clerk looked surprised. "That low? His prints are some of our best sellers. The small prints, depending on the frame, sell for about a hundred dollars. The large ones sell for as much as six-hundred dollars. We also allow clients to select a print to be made even larger or framed in special ways." The clerk blinked. "Of course, Courtney does all the matting and framing. That take time."

A grunting noise came from the door to the showroom. Courtney, under the supervision of the resident agent, had entered the workroom.

The clerk looked down. "And Courtney is very good at framing photos to show them to their best advantage. She makes the prints of the women in cowboy gear or old dresses look like antiques with distressed wooden frames. She uses modern, sleek frames for the studies of hands and feet. They're so avant-garde." She pointed to a framed photo on the worktable. A woman's manicured foot was next to the hairy legs of a man. The artist had hand-painted the woman's toenails purple, and the mat was a sickening, grayed purple shade.

Jack had stared in disbelief at the six-hundred-dollar price tag on the piece. He thought the photo was disgusting and guessed "avant-garde" was a nice way to describe it. He felt sorry for the clerk. She wasn't apt to have a job by the end of the week. He spoke loudly so Courtney could hear him. "You certainly are a good salesperson. I hope the owner appreciates you."

The resident agent took the hint and guided Courtney back into the showroom.

Jack looked around the workroom. In a far corner, Sara seemed absorbed in examining several unframed photos of women in corsets and pantaloons. Jack thought those shots were more consistent with the works of Sheriff Bob's he'd seen in Reserve. Sara flashed an excessively broad grin. "Look closely at these pics. Does anything look familiar?"

Jack glanced where Sara was pointing. He studied the woman's face. "Darn. That's Jeanne Schultz. With her hair all fancy."

"Notice anything else?"

"No."

"I think the photo was shot in the bedroom of Eve Cooney's cabin. I noticed a rustic four poster bed in the cabin. It struck me as odd because the room was devoid of much else." She shoved her laptop toward him with several photos of the room.

Sara was right. He pointed to a large photo on the wall. A naked woman with a bun at the nape of her neck sat with her back to the camera and her arms akimbo. "That's Courtney. The shot is like the one in her condo where her head is turned to show her face in profile."

Sara shrugged. "Doubt Courtney will talk to avoid us showing these pictures to people in Catron County or Silver City. Bet Jeanne will talk even though the pictures of her are only slightly racy." She pulled on Jack's sleeve. "There's more."

He followed her into the showroom where the crime lab person and resident agent were busy cataloguing framed photos and consulting with the clerk. He saw Courtney standing in front of the gallery pacing. Jack guessed she was eager for her lawyer to appear.

Sara pointed to a stack of aqua and purple placemats and table runners. "I think I saw woven pieces in Jeanne's workroom in those colors."

"And?"

"The shop must be a major source of income for the Schultzes."

CHAPTER 37: Gotcha!

A lawyer greeted Beau and Mace at the door of Sheriff Bob's home. He sat at the kitchen table with the SWAT team members as they questioned Alice, Bob's wife. They showed her copies of several of the photos, which Sara had emailed from the Aura of the Southwest Gallery.

Alice immediately said, "I told you Bob liked to take pictures of women in pretty dresses. I made those dresses when Ms. Howard commissioned Bob to create the vintage photographs."

"Do you have the dresses?"

"Of course not. Ms. Howard gave me the fabric and patterns and kept the dresses afterwards." She smiled. "She paid me more for the sewing than she paid Bob for the photos. Of course, his work took only a few hours. I spent days making all the ruffles on those dresses."

"Had you seen the photos previously?"

"Of course. Bob printed one of each of the vintage shots for me. I put them in a collage in our bedroom. Do you want to see it?"

The lawyer whispered into her ear. She pushed him away. "But I did nothing wrong."

"How did you meet Ms. Howard?"

"She came to the house about three years ago and said she was starting a gallery in Santa Fe. She was looking for artists and said she'd gotten our names from Eve Cooney."

The rest of the conversation with the Alice yielded nothing, except an understanding of why Bob had spent so much time on his hobby. It was a way to escape Alice's constant chatter.

***

The interview with Bob and the lawyer was more intense. Bob was ready to negotiate. Beau and Mace couldn't make promises but were eager to listen. Bob wanted all charges against him regarding child pornography dropped in return for his cooperation in explaining Eve Cooney's role in the shooting. The lawyer explained any mention of the child pornography would embarrass his family and endanger him when in prison.

"Eve called me on Friday morning a week ago. She said, 'Hank is upset over your photos of the cheerleaders. He must be stopped, or we all will go to jail over your *dirty* photos.'" Tears rolled down his cheeks. "'It was the first time I'd thought about my happy photos in that way." He hunched over the table more. "Eve kept screaming about what happened to child pornographers and sheriffs in jail." Bob sobbed.

His lawyer shook his head. "He called me. He was out of his mind with worry and fear."

Beau wondered whether Bob had any experience in theater. He was putting on a real show, and the lines seemed rehearsed. "What happened when Sheridan and Sarah asked for your help?"

"I called Eve back. She thought if I did it right, it would look like I killed Hank in self-defense. She promised she'd have Hank hyped up and with a gun when he met me. All I had to do was bring a gun with me and tell him he was dumb. It would make him mad. When he started to pull his gun, I could shoot first."

"How would she 'hype up' Hank?"

Bob lowered his head. "Hank would do anything to please Eve. She's something special in bed. I know from experience."

Mace shook his head. "What made you think you could shoot faster than Hank?"

Bob's head nearly touched the table. "I knew Hank would hesitate and probably wouldn't shoot me, but I was scared. Ask anyone. I was nervous that day."

Beau thought Bob had finally said a verifiable sentence. The whole SWAT team had heard the tremor in Bob's voice as Sara and Jack tried to prep him to pick up Hank. "I don't understand how she knew about the box."

"I called and told her. She was the one who thought I should hide the gun under the box."

"After you were hurt, how did you get the gun back to your house?"

"Told Tim to put the gun in the box and take it to my wife."

Beau realized in all the excitement, no one on the SWAT team or the agents at the site had noticed the box was missing. Sara usually specialized in arcane details like that. He was glad she'd goofed.

The lawyer leaned forward. "We also expect Bob's wife will not be charged with abetting the crime."

"She hid it, and in doing so, abetted a crime." Beau said.

The lawyer smiled. "Think of the big picture. You want Eve in jail and Tim removed from the sheriff's office. Bob's given you that."

"I need more on Eve."

The lawyer whispered in Bob's ear then turned to Beau. "We need assurances he'll only be charged with assault on a peace officer in the state system. That's one year's jail time."

Bob shook violently. "Eve will kill me like she did Alex."

"Can you prove that statement?"

"No, but Jeanne and Courtney can. They all hated Alex."

"Why?"

"He cheated them of money...and was stupid enough to have promised to marry each of them at some time."

Beau sighed. Sara had made it clear that Courtney wouldn't crack without damning evidence. Eve was even tougher.

"What do you know that would make Jeanne talk?"

"Alex had been humping Jeanne for the last five years. She told everyone she was going to book club meetings in Silver City. Check the motel in Alma."

***

Mace sighed. "My back hurts from sitting in this car so much."

Beau agreed, but they drove to Alma anyway.

The owner of the Alma Inn refused to answer Beau's questions, and his registration records weren't particularly helpful. Someone, who signed in as AC and paid in cash, appeared on the register twice a month. Beau tried one more bluff. "Has the IRS ever audited you?"

The owner finally admitted he'd seen a woman, who looked like the pictures of Jeanne Schultz. She had entered a room rented by a man he knew as Aiden Cortez on several occasions. "She always arrived around one and left by four."

On a whim, Beau showed the owner a photo of Eve. The owner looked at the photo. "She never stopped by. No need. She and Aiden lived together." When Beau flashed a picture of Courtney, the man turned red. "She often showed up around six and spent the night."

Beau coughed. "On the same day? Same room?"

"Yep. Aiden lived dangerously. Not too surprising they killed him."

"What do you mean?"

"We folks here don't need fancy FBI agents to tell us the obvious. Aiden Cortez—or whatever he called himself—got himself killed because he asked for it. It's easy to see why our federal taxes are so high. You agents aren't very smart if you don't know it has to be one of his women."

***

Beau and Mace agreed to start the discussion with Jeanne gently and ask about the photos first.

"We're investigating Courtney Howard for irregular business practices. We know you posed for some photos she was selling in her gallery, Aura of the Southwest."

Jeanne stared at them. "The FBI doesn't investigate honest businesses."

"They do when child pornography is involved."

Jeanne looked at the floor but didn't appear to blush. "I don't want to answer questions on that topic when my girls are here." She called the girls and told them to spend the next hour with Ramona at the saloon.

Beau thought she'd be more talkative if he set the stage right. He popped onto his laptop screen a photo of her in a corset and pantaloons and then one of the juicier shots of a cheerleader. "We don't think you were involved in the pornography, but you must know about the business practices of Courtney Howard and the photographer, Sheriff Bob. How did you meet Courtney Howard and Sheriff Bob?"

"It's a long story."

"We like long stories." Beau moved her from the door to her kitchen. She sat stiffly in a chair after Beau sat down at the table. Mace stayed in the kitchen for a while and then wandered through the house.

"Eve Cooney and I have driven together to market our crafts at fairs for years. My earnings were pitiful. Maybe, an extra thousand dollars a year for all my work. Then about five years ago, Eve started talking about how we needed a shop where we could sell our goods all the time. During the next year, she had me pose in old cowboy gear for Sheriff Bob. We sold the pictures at a fair." She shook her head. "Those stupid pictures sold better than my sweaters and were cheap to make."

"What happened next?"

"After the first fair, Eve suggested Sheriff Bob make the photos look old. Eve helped him print them in sepia tones and framed them in old frames she got at garage sales. Then he shot lots of pictures of me, Hank, Alex, and Eve in cowboy gear and with horses."

"The pictures at the gallery in Santa Fe were mainly in old fancy clothes."

Jeanne nodded. "Three years or so ago, Eve announced she'd found a potential gallery for our work. That's when I met Courtney, who had all sorts of dresses made. Sheriff Bob took hundreds of pictures but kept complaining that he wanted to do artistic shots. He started making the weird photos of hands and feet."

"Why were they weird?"

Jeanne stared at Beau. "Did you ever try to wrap your legs around someone else's legs to show off the pedicure on your toenails? Hank was nice because he was embarrassed, too. Alex liked creating the scenes and made ugly comments. I didn't want to do those shots."

"Why did you?"

"Courtney paid more for them."

"What did you tell Joe when you made all the money?'

Jeanne sniffled. "I couldn't tell him. I put the money I earned in an account in the girls' names in a bank in Silver City." She smiled. "They now have almost ten thousand to help them escape Golden Gully."

Mace had returned to the kitchen. "No one else is here. Hit it."

"We know you were meeting Alex at Alma Inn at least once a month for the last five years."

"I thought you were investigating Courtney's business and Bob's pictures. I don't want to answer questions about Alex."

Beau reread her Miranda rights. With her straight brown hair pulled back in a ponytail and no makeup, it was hard to believe she was a murderer. "I don't think you meant to kill Alex, but you were dragged into the mess by Courtney and Eve. The first one who admits the truth will be given a deal. Sara and Jack are talking to Courtney now."

"I want a lawyer, and I don't want Joe to hear my comments. He's a good man who works hard."

Beau called Sara and was shocked by her advice. "Sara says if you prefer to be questioned by a woman, we can transport you to Reserve. She can be there in five hours. Your lawyer can meet you there. But she thinks you should know one thing first. Joe is Alex's younger brother."

Jeanne's eyes widened and her jaw dropped. She gasped. "Can't be." She began to hyperventilate.

Sara had guessed right. Both Joe and Jeanne had hidden secrets from each other.

CHAPTER 38: Is the Confession True?

Sheridan greeted Sara at the front door of the Catron County Sheriff's Office. "Bob has made it easy for me. He resigned. Have the d*** prosecutors got their guts up and made up their minds?"

Sara kept walking. "The federal prosecutor will arraign Bob on Wednesday morning on the charge of assault on a police officer. If he pleads guilty, child pornography will not be mentioned, and his wife will not be charged with serving as an accessory after the crime. There are no federal prisons in New Mexico, so he will probably serve three years in the low-security federal institutional facility in Englewood, Colorado."

"You got him a good deal." Sheridan pointed to the door of the conference room.

Sara stopped walking. "He cooperated, but the deal will fall apart if Tim doesn't cooperate. The federal prosecutor will agree to the plea of an accessory after the crime if Tim resigns from the Catron County Sheriff's Office. In return, the prosecutor will require Tim to accept six months of probation and to complete three hundred hours of community service, probably for the U.S. Forest Service."

"Don't worry the d*** sucker will cooperate."

"Don't tell me what you'll do." Sara winked at Sheridan. "The lawyers are offering good deals because Jack, Beau, Mace, and I appreciate your help. We all think the Catron County Sheriff's Office should not make national headlines for crime in its ranks. Beau and Mace will meet with Tim and his lawyer tomorrow to get a signed plea agreement, but he'll have to be arraigned in Albuquerque later in the week." She knocked on the conference room door.

Beau emerged. "You made good time."

Sara laughed. "Jack broke every speed limit. He really wants this to be our last trip to Catron County."

"Where is Jack?"

"He's rounding up food for all of us. Did you clarify the details with Green and Brown?"

"Yep. The only event in their party room since Alex died was the meeting to amend the bylaws of the residents of Golden Gully. The room

                                          J. L. Greger

is always locked, except during meetings, because Green and Brown want to keep the bathroom private. I believe them because they both gave the same answers when Mace and I talked to them separately."

"Good. How did they explain the inconsistency in their earlier interviews?"

"They didn't really check the Last Chance Bar on the night before Alex was found. They said the curtains at the window were open and they shone a flashlight in and saw nothing."

Sara snorted. "Probably not true. However, we think the body was under the shelf because of stains there. The answer is plausible, and they know it. I guess it's the least of our problems now. Do you think Jeanne will talk?"

"She's moaned a lot, cried a bit, but said nothing after I called you. Her lawyer has been here for an hour. He called me in about five minutes before you arrived to ask if you and Jack would arrive soon. Otherwise, he and Jeanne wanted a dinner break."

Sara saw Jack coming down the hall with boxes of food. She opened the door to the conference room and tried to look compassionate with a slight smile. "Jeanne, we came as fast as we could. We've brought food." She stepped aside for Jack and Beau to enter.

As Jack called out the choices listed on each box, Sheridan muttered, "I guess Mace and I aren't needed. Looks too d***crowded in there."

"Agreed, but there's enough food for everyone. Take two of the boxes."

***

Jeanne bit her lip and trembled slightly. "My lawyer said I should tell you the truth, but there's a lot I don't understand about the days before Alex was killed. Eve called on a Friday afternoon. I remember because it's a big day with tourists. Eve insisted I meet her at her cabin and bring the key to the Last Chance Bar. I did." Jeanne frowned. "Courtney was there. She was crying."

After thirty seconds of silence, Sara said," Do you know why Courtney was upset?"

"Alex had dumped her." Jeanne twisted a tissue in her hands. "That's when it gets strange. Eve told me to call Alex and invite him to the Last Chance Bar." She twisted the tissue more. "Told me to tell him— This is hard to say—I wanted to meet him at six in the Last Chance Bar because Joe and I had a fight." She wiped her eyes and sat motionless.

Sara handed Jeanne a pack of tissue. "What happened?"

"He was pleased."

"What did Eve do?"

"Told me to be there by six-thirty and pushed me out the door because she said she had work to do."

"What happened when you got to the bar?"

"She and Courtney were already there. Eve told me to sit on the chair and pull off my top, while she and Courtney crawled under the shelf and pulled the curtain to hide themselves." Jeanne pulled out another tissue and wiped her eyes. "I can't believe I did it."

"And?"

"Alex whistled when he saw me. He pulled me off the chair, kissed me, and unzipped his pants. Suddenly I saw a lasso slung over Alex's head and felt another rope hit me as it was looped around Alex's waist. He pushed me away and tore at the rope at his neck. He gasped, 'What?' as the ropes tightened." Jeanne sat with her eyes wide open as if in a daze.

"What happened next?"

"I'm still not sure. Courtney and Eve moved rapidly. Alex was twisting and kicking as he pulled at the rope around his neck. His gasps were horrible. I think Courtney kicked him in the groin. The next thing I knew, I was lying on the floor and Alex was sitting in the chair. The bar was quiet except for Courtney's and Eve's panting. I thought Alex was dead because his head drooped forward as he sat bound in the chair. Courtney said, "Jeanne, you're such a baby. You fainted.""

"And what did you do?"

"I asked, 'Why did you kill Alex?' Eve laughed. 'He's not dead, just softened up so he'll talk.' Then she complained that Alex was cheating her and hiding gold from her. She wanted to know where he hid the gold. Courtney complained he had threatened to tell her father about—I'm not sure—her sexual preferences. He also seemed to have taken something from her condo."

"What did you do?"

"I asked if I could leave. They said I could, but said I had to return around six the next morning with food."

"Anything else?"

"Eve warned me. 'If you do as I say, your family won't be hurt.'"

"What did you do or say?"

"Nothing. I was scared." She paused for thirty seconds. "I packed up a basket with a loaf of bread, a jar of mayonnaise, lunch meats, a couple of apples, and lemonade mix and returned early on Saturday."

"When you returned, was anything different in the bar?"

"Courtney was gone. Alex had a black eye and a rag stuffed in his mouth." Jeanne shivered. "Eve told me I was as responsible as she and

                                          J. L. Greger

Courtney if anything happened to Alex. Now, my job was to keep everyone away from the bar. She suggested I say that Brown and Green missed a tourist at closing. The tourist had made a mess of the bar, and I didn't have time to clean it until Sunday afternoon. She'd even posted a new sign on the front door—*CLOSED FOR REPAIRS*."

"Weren't you worried about Alex?"

Jeanne stared at the table. "I was more worried about Joe and the girls. By Sunday afternoon, I'd decided things had to change in the bar. I packed up a bunch of placemats, which needed to be fixed with a darning needle, in my knitting basket and told Joe I was going to see Eve about a new design idea for the placemats." She stared at the table.

"What did you find?"

"The curtains to the bar were closed. Courtney was sitting on Alex's hips pulling at ropes around his legs. Eve sat on his shoulders and kept repeating, 'Bad boys must pay for their mistakes.'"

"Wasn't he screaming?"

"He couldn't. He had a rag in his mouth, and his face was red. It became redder when Courtney pulled the ropes, so his legs were forced back. I begged them to stop. I know it was silly, but I told them about my ideas for a new way to finish off woven placemats or scarves with silver thread using a darning needle. Eve seemed interested. She pulled the eight-inch needle from my hand. This would work." Jeanne closed her eyes.

"Be strong, Jeanne. You're almost at the end of your story. What happened next?"

"Courtney told me to be useful and sit on Alex's legs when she slid up a bit on his hips. Eve scooched forward and placed his head between her knees and turned it to the side." Jeanne grabbed Sara's hand. "Alex just lay there panting."

Sara squeezed Jeanne's hand.

"Eve lifted her hand with the needle slightly and pushed the needle down into his ear. She did it again and again. On the second or third time, Alex relaxed. He was no longer trying to move under me. Eve said, 'Alex won't lie again.' They crawled away and rolled him on his back."

Sara rubbed Jeanne's hand.

"Alex's blue eyes were staring at me. Blood ran from his ear, his nose, his mouth. I screamed and screamed. Then I ran as fast as I could run. No one followed me. I ran and ran and eventually found Green and Brown. They came to the bar with me."

"What did they see?"

"The sign was gone. Alex was gone. My knitting and weaving were gone. The whole floor was wet, and the place stunk of bleach. Brown and Green guided me home and told Joe I'd been sleepwalking."

"What did you do when you got home?"

"Went to bed and went to work at the saloon the next morning. I'd almost convinced myself it was bad dream when Etta came running into the saloon and said she'd found a body in the Last Chance Bar."

"Have you talked to Eve or Courtney since then?"

"I saw Eve at the residents' meeting in Brown's and Green's playroom. She pulled me aside and said if I didn't want to be executed for murder, I'd keep my mouth shut. She reminded me my needle was the murder weapon."

***

Throughout the interview, Jack had focused a camera on Jeanne. Two lawyers in the federal prosecutor's office had watched the proceedings. They now had questions, and Jack took over the interview. After an hour, Jeanne's lawyer said his client couldn't withstand any more and wanted to take her home.

Jack turned to the camera. "What do you what us to arrest her for?"

"Murder one," said one lawyer.

"With a chance for a plea bargain," said the second. "Get her to Albuquerque right away. We'll meet with her at eight tomorrow. I've already notified your SAC, Carbonne, to set her up in a safe house with a suicide watch for the night."

The first lawyer said, "And I've sent agents to arrest Courtney Howard in Santa Fe. Beau and Mace should arrest Eve Cooney immediately. Both Ms. Howard and Ms. Cooney are wealthy and are flight risks."

Beau's phone beeped. "I received the arrest warrant for Eve and will utilize the help of Acting Sheriff Sheridan Evers. Do you want to act against Green and Brown? They lied to us several times."

Both lawyers laughed. "Sorry guys. Someone will have to return to Catron County again to clean up the details."

J. L. Greger

CHAPTER 39: The End?

Saturday

Sara awoke when her phone rang at five in the morning. Sanders was jubilant. Brazilian officials wanted him to help them complete their investigation of police corruption in the Amazonas State. They had already fired almost one-quarter of the police in the state for being drug gang members. They thought his testimony and records would aid in the prosecution of more high-level officers. They also wanted him to arrange the extradition of all U.S. citizens involved in the Brazilian drug trade back to the U.S.

Sanders doubted he'd be able to return to Albuquerque for two weeks. Sara didn't care as long as he was happy and safe.

She planned to spend time with Willow, Barbara, and Carbonne this weekend after she watched federal prosecutors negotiate with Jeanne, Eve, Courtney, and their lawyers this morning. The negotiations were always like sausage making. Usually the final product was acceptable, but the process was ugly. Even so, she was eager to get to work. Today should conclude the main action in this case, and this should be the last Saturday she had to work for a while.

***

The day proceeded as expected. Courtney and Eve refused to answer most questions. The federal prosecutors decided the two women should be held in custody without bond until their arraignment for first-degree murder on Tuesday.

Sara suspected Joe's appearance at the negotiations influenced the lawyers. They agreed to charge Jeanne with third degree murder with parole possible after three years if she testified against Courtney and Eve. Jeanne was allowed to go home with her husband on the condition she be present for arraignment on Monday and sentencing on Tuesday.

The bad news was the prosecutors deemed Green's and Brown's testimonies crucial to their cases. The "inconsistencies" in their statements had to be cleared up by Tuesday. They were also curious about why the deputies in the Catron County Sheriff's Office were so slow to share information with FBI agents but decided not to make any further charges against those in the sheriff's office.

***

Thirteen days later

"How about you and Jack joining Mace and me for coffee? We want an update on Catron County. We've heard a rumor that Ophelia Murphy has been appointed Sheriff of Catron County."

This was the first time any agent, except Jack or Carbonne, had invited her to coffee. Being a skeptic, Sara wondered whether Beau knew Scott had asked her to evaluate Beau's and Mace's progress in learning to accept minorities and women as equal partners or even bosses. "Why don't you bring your coffee to my office in twenty minutes? Jack will have finished talking to Etta Cortland by then. I even have homemade brownies and oatmeal cookies."

After the group had assembled around Sara's plate of treats, Jack shook his head. "There was no way to clear Hank of all criminal charges."

Mace shrugged. "He's not a pornographer. He was building the case against Sheriff Bob. And he shot Bob in self-defense. So, what's left?"

"He placed the bomb in our federally-owned vehicle and fired shots at us. Our psychologist rejected my idea that Hank was not psychologically responsible for his actions."

Beau chewed on his second brownie. "What does Sheridan say?"

"He liked Ophelia's and Sara's solution." Jack patted Sara on the back. "Funny, I thought Sheridan would be upset when the Catron County Commissioners appointed Ophelia as his boss after he turned the job down as being too political. However, he claims Ophelia has already gotten the support of the Eberles, has begun needed reforms in the records system of the sheriff's office, and plans to run for the permanent position."

Sara cleared her throat. "There was a price for the Eberles' support. I had to convince the prosecutors to reduce the federal charge of destruction of federal property against Hank to a state charge for a petty misdemeanor because no property was destroyed, thanks to Sheridan's actions. Hank was sentenced to a year's probation and ordered to do three hundred hours of public service, but Ophelia wasn't satisfied."

Beau eyed the plate of brownies but didn't take a third one. "Why does she care?"

Jack coughed. "What Sara can't seem to spit out is simple. Hank is popular among the Eberles. They don't want him. punished. They—really all the citizens of Catron County—don't care about the murder of an outsider like Alex Cortland, but they are upset about becoming a

                                                J. L. Greger

laughingstock nationally. Sheriff Bob's photos—at least those that aren't child porn—are selling like hotcakes on Amazon. Sheridan and Ophelia..."

Sara interrupted. "Actually, everyone suspects the porn photos are even bigger sellers on the black market. Ophelia recognized the mood of potential voters in Catron County and wanted to appoint Hank as a school liaison officer for the sheriff's office after Hank got training on how to spot and handle cases of child abuse and child pornography. However, the federal prosecutors on this case thought Hank shouldn't be employed in law enforcement or a school system. So, Ophelia convinced the mayor of Reserve to hire Hank as a maintenance worker."

Jack laughed. "That's not all Ophelia has done. She thought Green and Brown should be punished because they had delayed the case with all their lies, but the federal prosecutors didn't want to waste time on them. So, Ophelia is forcing them to teach a Creative Writing class in the Reserve High School the next two years for free."

Mace shook his head. "What about Sheridan? He hid the truth from us on several occasions."

Sara laughed. "Everyone thinks having Ophelia as a boss is punishment enough."

"What the heck?" Beau took his third brownie. "Guess this case proves it's hard to guess what's important to locals."

Sara had been tinkering with her laptop during much of the conversation. "Beau, I think you're going to have a chance to learn more about what *locals* want. Officials in Washington are creating a national task force to investigate ways the FBI can work with local governments to reduce child porn, especially in rural areas where residents mistakenly assume they're immune to the problem." She hesitated. "I'm pretty sure you and Winslow will be assigned to the task force."

Beau sneered. "I'm a SWAT member. What a waste of my skills."

Sara tried not to smile. "Generally, membership on a task force leads to a promotion." She noticed Beau lost his look of disdain. She and Carbonne had guessed right. Beau could develop a boarder view of social issues in law enforcement if given the right incentive.

Jack shook his head. "The residents of Catron County have taught all of us a lot. Etta summed it up best: 'Alex looked for death and finally got it.' Brown and Green agreed and plan to title their next novel as *The Man Who Looked for Death* or something like that."

Sara picked Bug up and cuddled him. This case was over, and Sanders was due to arrive in Albuquerque in two hours.

THE END

THE SCIENCE AND HISTORY BEHIND THE STORY

This brief review of mining may help readers of this novel appreciate this complex industry and how it shaped characters and situations in this novel.

History of Gold Mining in New Mexico

There is a long history of mining in New Mexico. The Spaniards' search for the fabled "seven cities of gold" drove much of the exploration of New Mexico in the 1500s. Some claim the first gold rush in the American West occurred in 1820s after gold was discovered in the Ortiz Mountains in northern New Mexico (1).

Today, four hundred ghost towns in New Mexico are remnants of New Mexico's mining history. The most famous ghost town in the state is probably Mogollon (2). Sergeant James Cooney found gold and silver in the Mogollon Mountains in the Gila Wilderness in the 1870s. A miner named John Eberle built the first cabin in Mogollon in 1889. The town of Mogollon became the one of wildest and richest mining towns in the Southwest in the 1890s with a population of at least three thousand. Today, it is a ghost town with a handful of caretakers.

The ghost town of Golden Gully in the novel is fictional but resembles and is located near the ghost town of Mogollon. To honor the early gold miners in New Mexico, the residents of Catron County in this novel include several fictional descendants of Eberle and Cooney.

Mining in New Mexico Today

Traditionally, agriculture and mining were the major sources of revenue in the state of New Mexico. Now the chief drivers of the economy in the state are oil and gas production, tourism, and federal government spending. However, mining is still important. New Mexico is the source of more potash and perlite—both used in fertilizers—than any other state. In 2022, mines in the state produced: over 9 million tons of coal, about 94,5000 tons of copper, and about 229 tons of gold (3). Although New Mexico has a large reserve of uranium, none has been mined since 1998 (4).

J. L. Greger

The largest open-pit copper mine in the state is the Chino Mine, which was first opened in 1910. It is about fifteen miles east of Silver City and is owned by Freeport-McMoRan, Inc., and its subsidiaries (5). The fictional Alex Cortland worked in the Chino Mine.

Generally, gold and silver are found with copper. However, the tailings from copper mines generally are not rich enough in gold and silver to make it economically viable to extract the gold, especially if environmental remediation is necessary. Today the most used methods for extraction of gold from mine tailings and ore involves cyanide (6).

In the past, gold was removed from ore by creating amalgams of gold with mercury. This dangerous process is still used by small-scale miners and in underdeveloped areas (7).

Toxicities Caused by Mining

Miners are at risk of developing pneumoconiosis—commonly called black lung disease—because of inhalation of airborne dust and particles, which cause inflammation and fibrosis in the lung. The disease cannot be cured. Thus, controlling respirable dust is important (8). Although black lung disease is most often associated with underground mining of coal, miners of uranium and copper, even from open pits, do develop the disease, especially if safety procedures are inadequate.

Miners, especially uranium miners, have an increased risk of renal disease and lung cancer (9). Compromised immune function and increased incidence of lung cancer, renal, and liver disease, skin irritations, and gastrointestinal distress have been reported among copper miners (10, 11).

Removing metal from ore is associated with a variety of health problems. The most notorious is the permanent effect of mercury vapors in gold purification on the brain, lungs, and kidneys (7).

Forensic Laboratory Techniques

Several forensic laboratory techniques mentioned in this novel may surprise readers.

Laboratory tests to be admitted in court must be accurate, replicable, reproducible in a variety of laboratories, and explainable to juries. Published standardized DNA collection procedures and tests are now accepted in our judicial system (12). The actual tests can be accomplished in a couple of days, but backlogs and procedural details often delay law enforcement officers from receiving the data in less than two months.

Thus, law enforcement officers often use rapid DNA tests in the field to screen potential suspects (13). These rapid tests are less sensitive than the standardized tests and less repeatable. Thus, DNA collection and analyses must be repeated with standardized procedures in the lab if the data are to be used in courts in most states.

All current DNA tests have three weaknesses: They cannot determine when a suspect was at the crime scene. They cannot differentiate between identical twins, although this is subject to change as technologies improve. They are all subject to contamination if samples are collected improperly.

No one measurement is reliable for estimating the time of death, but potassium concentrations in the vitreous humor of the eye is often combined with other data to estimate the postmortem interval. It is based on the concept that potassium levels in the fluids of the eye rise after death because cell membranes allow the leakage of potassium until the levels reach the concentration of potassium in blood plasma (14).

Scientists can now estimate the age of bloodstains within a two-to-four-week window for blood stains less than six months old. They are quantifying the degradation of mRNA in the dried samples (15).

The murder weapon in this novel is unusual. However, at least six cases of murder or attempted murder have been reported using a needle inserted through the ear into the brain (16).

References

1 Economy of New Mexico.
https://en.wikipedia.org/wiki/Economy_of_New_Mexico#Agriculture_and_mining).

2. Mogollon. https://www.newmexico.org/places-to-visit/ghost-towns/mogollon/

3. Economic impact of the mineral industry in New Mexico. 2024. https://geoinfo.nmt.edu/resources/minerals/impact.html.

4. Uranium mining.
https://en.wikipedia.org/wiki/Uranium_mining_in_New_Mexico.

5. Chino mine. https://en.wikipedia.org/wiki/Chino_mine.

6. The safe and effective use of cyanide.
https://www.smenet.org/What-We-Do/Technical-Briefings/The-Safe-and-Effective-Use-of-Cyanide-in-the-Minin.

                                                J. L. Greger

7. Fact sheet: Mercury, gold mining, and health. https://health.alaska.gov/dph/Epi/eph/Documents/MercuryGoldMiningFactsheet.pdf

8. Black lung disease. https://en.wikipedia.org/wiki/Black_lung_disease

9. Uranium mining and health. Can Fam Physician [2013 May] 59:469-71 PMCID: PMC3653646.

10. Mortality from lung cancer among copper miners. *Occup & Environ Med* [1993] 50:505-9. PMCID: PMC1035476.

11. Risk assessment in mining-based industrial workers by immunological parameters as copper toxicity markers. Indian J Occup Environ Med [2019] 23:21-7 PMCID: PMC6477944

12. DNA profiling. https://en.wikipedia.org/wiki/DNA_profiling

13. Rapid DNA. https://le.fbi.gov/science-and-lab/biometrics-and-fingerprints/codis/rapid-dna#:

14. Review of postmortem interval estimation using vitreous humor: Past, present, and future. *Forensic Pathol* [2016 Mar] 6:12-18. PMCID: 31239869

15. A method to estimate the age of bloodstains using quantitative PCR. *FSI: Genetics* [2019 Mar] 39:103-8. PMID: 30639909

16. Attempting homicide by inserting sewing needle into the brain: Report of 6 cases and review of literature. *Surg Neurol* [2009 Dec] 72: 635-41 https://doi.org/10.1016/j.surneu.2009.02.029

ACKNOWLEDGMENTS

I appreciate the efforts of Lorna Collins for carefully editing this manuscript and of Barbara Hodges for creatively designing the cover. Thank you.

None of my books would be possible without the patience and love of my dogs: Bug, Elf, and Star.

ABOUT THE AUTHOR

J. L. Greger is a biology professor and research administrator from the University of Wisconsin-Madison turned novelist. The pet therapy dog, Bug, in her mysteries and thrillers is based on her own Japanese Chin. She includes tidbits about science, the American Southwest, and her international travel experiences in her **Science Traveler Series**.

The Flu Is Coming. In the first book in the series, a woman scientist traces the spread of a deadly new flu virus among the frantic residents of a quarantined New Mexico community. (New Mexico/ Arizona Book Award Finalist.

Murder…A Way to Lose Weight. A dean in a medical school helps police discover whether an ambitious young "diet doctor," disgruntled patients, or old-timers with buried secrets are killers. (Winner of the 2016 Public Safety Writers Association contest and New Mexico/Arizona Book Award Finalist)

Ignore the Pain. A woman scientist learns too much about the coca trade and too little about a sexy new colleague while on a public health assignment in Bolivia.

Malignancy. A woman tries to escape the clutches of a drug lord and accepts a risky assignment as a science consultant in Cuba. (Winner of the 2015 Public Safety Writers Association contest)

I Saw You in Beirut. A woman's past provides clues for the extraction of a nuclear scientist from Iran. The author's experiences as a science and education consultant in the United Arab Emirates and Lebanon are featured.

Riddled with Clues. A homeless man and a woman scientist are targeted by drug gangs after she listens to the strange tale of an undercover drug agent about his war experiences. The memories of an actual CIA agent in Laos during the Vietnam War are featured. (New Mexico/Arizona Book Award Finalist)

A Pound of Flesh, Sorta. The police and a woman scientist can't decide whether a package contaminated with the bacteria that causes the bubonic plague is a plea for help by a whistleblower or a threat from gang leaders awaiting trial. (New Mexico/Arizona Book Award Finalist)

Dirty Holy Water. A woman who usually serves as a science consultant for the FBI learns there is a thin line between being a victim and being a villain when she becomes the chief suspect in a bizarre murder case. (New Mexico/Arizona Book Award Finalist)

Games for Couples. Did lethal compounds in a cultured meat product—meat made in a test tube—kill a man in a clinical trial? Or did the toxic competition between biotechnology companies and spite of battling couples cause his death? (New Mexico/Arizona Book Award Finalist)

Fair Compromises. Sara Almquist and her FBI colleagues rush to find the culprits who endangered the lives of a hundred attendees at a political rally by poisoning the food with botulism toxin. Their target was a woman candidate for the U.S. Senate. (New Mexico/Arizona Book Award Finalist)

Bungle in the Jungle. The U.S. consular office in Manaus, Brazil, is a "Bungle in the Jungle." Can Sara Almquist and the new Acting Ambassador to Brazil figure out how the staff became enmeshed in the illegal international trade of drugs and cultural artifacts? (New Mexico/Arizona Book Award Finalist

Escape from a Dark Cave. Sara Almquist, an FBI scientific consultant, investigates the murder of a young man near a historic cave in New Mexico. As she reconstructs the victim's final days, she learns the autistic victim found the cave to be soothing. She finds the cave to be depressing.

The Man Who Looked for Death. Who can an FBI agent and a scientist trust as they investigate a murder in the ghost town of Golden Gully? The medical examiner thinks the victim was tortured for several days before he was killed. However, the ten residents in this remote town in the Gila National Forest deny knowing the man. The local sheriff's office is less than cooperative.

J. L. Greger also wrote ***Come Fly with Elf.*** In this picture book for children, a tiny Papillon dog called Elf dreams of flying in a hot air balloon. She has written two collections of short stories: ***The Good Old Days?*** and **Other People's Mothers.**

See more at: http://www.jlgreger.com.